FABLED LANDS

THE WAR-TORN KINGDOM

Dave Morris and Jamie Thomson

Illustrated by Russ Nicholson
Cover painting by Kevin Jenkins

Fabled Lands Publishing

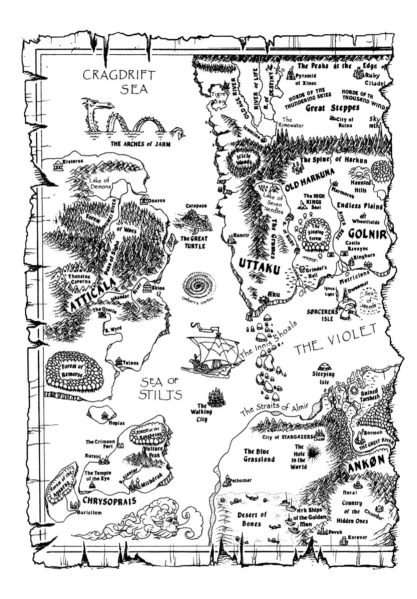

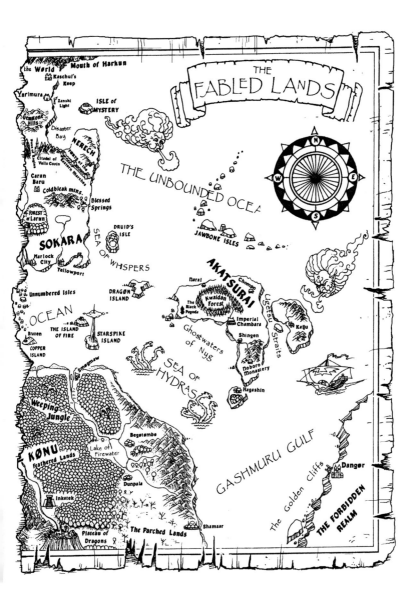

THE FABLED LANDS

the World   Mouth of Harkun

Kaschul's Keep

Yarimura

Zenshi Light

ISLE of MYSTERY

Gemstone Hills

Disaster Bay

NERECH

THE UNBOUNDED OCEAN

Citadel of Velis Corin

Caran Baru

Coldbleak mtns.

Blessed Springs

FOREST of Larun

DRUID'S ISLE

SOKARA

SEA OF WHISPERS

JAWBONE ISLES

Marlock City

Yellowport

Unnumbered Isles

DRAGON ISLAND

AKATSURAI

Naral

Champ

OCEAN

THE ISLAND OF FIRE

STARSPIKE ISLAND

The Black Pagoda

Kwaidan Forest

Imperial Chambara

UGETSU Straits

Kaiju

Ghostwaters of Nyg

Brazen

COPPER ISLAND

Snagmaw

SEA OF HYDRAS

Shingen

Noboro Monastery

Nagashin

WEEPING JUNGLE

Begatomba

KØNU

Feathered Lands

Lake of Firewater

GASHMURU GULF

Dangør

Dunpala

The Golden Cliffs

THE FORBIDDEN REALM

Inkatek

Plateau of Dragons

The Parched Lands

Shamsar

First published 1996 by Macmillan Publishers Ltd

This edition published 2010 by Fabled Lands Publishing,
an imprint of Fabled Lands LLP

ISBN 13: 978-0-9567372-0-5

Adventuring in the
Fabled Lands

Fabled Lands is unlike any other solo role-playing game. The reason is that you can play the books in any order, coming back to earlier books whenever you wish. You need only one book to start, but by collecting other books in the series you can explore more of this rich fantasy world. Instead of just one single storyline, there are virtually unlimited adventures to be had in the Fabled Lands. All you need is two dice, an eraser and a pencil.

If you have already adventured using other books in the series, you will know your entry point into this book. Turn to that section now.

If this is your first Fabled Lands book, read the rest of the rules before starting at section 1. You will keep the same adventuring persona throughout the books – starting out as just a 1st Rank wanderer in *The War-Torn Kingdom*, but gradually gaining in power, wealth and experience throughout the series.

ABILITIES

You have six abilities. Your initial score in each ability ranges from 1 (low ability) to 6 (a high level of ability). Ability scores will change during your adventure but can never be lower than 1 or higher than 12.

CHARISMA	the knack of befriending people
COMBAT	the skill of fighting
MAGIC	the art of casting spells
SANCTITY	the gift of divine power and wisdom
SCOUTING	the techniques of tracking and wilderness lore
THIEVERY	the talent for stealth and lock picking

PROFESSIONS

Not all adventurers are good at everything. Everyone has some strengths and some weaknesses. Your choice of profession determines your initial scores in the six abilities.

- **Priest:**
  CHARISMA 4, COMBAT 2, MAGIC 3,
  SANCTITY 6, SCOUTING 4, THIEVERY 2
- **Mage:**
  CHARISMA 2, COMBAT 2, MAGIC 6,
  SANCTITY 1, SCOUTING 5, THIEVERY 3
- **Rogue:**
  CHARISMA 5, COMBAT 4, MAGIC 4,
  SANCTITY 1, SCOUTING 2, THIEVERY 6
- **Troubadour:**
  CHARISMA 6, COMBAT 3, MAGIC 4,
  SANCTITY 3, SCOUTING 2, THIEVERY 4
- **Warrior:**
  CHARISMA 3, COMBAT 6, MAGIC 2,
  SANCTITY 4, SCOUTING 3, THIEVERY 2
- **Wayfarer:**
  CHARISMA 2, COMBAT 5, MAGIC 2,
  SANCTITY 3, SCOUTING 6, THIEVERY 4

Fill in the Adventure Sheet at the back of the book with your choice of profession and the ability scores given for that profession.

STAMINA

Stamina is lost when you get hurt. Keep track of your Stamina score throughout your travels and adventures. You must guard against your Stamina score dropping to zero, because if it does you are dead.

Lost Stamina can be recovered by various means, but your Stamina cannot go above its initial score until you advance in Rank.

You start with 9 Stamina points. Record your Stamina in pencil on the Adventure Sheet.

RANK

You start at 1st Rank, so note this on the Adventure Sheet now. By completing quests and overcoming enemies, you will have the chance to go up in Rank.

You will be told during the course of your adventures when you are entitled to advance in Rank. Characters of higher Rank are tougher, luckier and generally better able to deal with trouble.

Rank	Title
1st	Outcast
2nd	Commoner
3rd	Guildmember
4th	Master/Mistress
5th	Gentleman/Lady
6th	Baron/Baroness
7th	Count/Countess
8th	Earl/Viscountess
9th	Marquis/Marchioness
10th	Duke/Duchess

POSSESSIONS

You can carry up to 12 possessions on your person. All characters begin with 16 Shards in cash and the following possessions, which you can record on your Adventure Sheet: **sword, leather jerkin (Defence +1), map.**

Possessions are always marked in bold text, like this: **gold compass**. Anything marked in this way is an item which can be picked up and added to your list of possessions.

Remember that you are limited to carrying a total of 12 items, so if you get more than this you'll have to cross something off your Adventure Sheet or find somewhere to store extra items. You can carry unlimited sums of money.

DEFENCE

Your Defence score is equal to:
    your COMBAT score
    plus your Rank
    plus the bonus for the armour you're wearing (if any).

Every suit of armour you find will have a Defence bonus listed for it. The higher the bonus, the better the armour. You can carry several suits of armour if you wish – but because you can wear only one at a time, you only get the Defence bonus of the best armour you are carrying.

Write your Defence score on the Adventure Sheet now. To start with it is just your COMBAT score plus 2 (because you are 1st Rank and have +1 armour). Remember to update it if you get better armour or increase in Rank or COMBAT ability.

FIGHTING

When fighting an enemy, roll two dice and add your COMBAT score. You need to roll higher than the enemy's Defence. The amount you roll above the enemy's Defence is the number of Stamina he loses.

If the enemy is now down to zero Stamina then he is defeated. Otherwise he will strike back at you, using the same procedure. If you survive, you then get a chance to attack again, and the battle goes on until one of you is victorious.

Example:
You are a 3rd Rank character with a COMBAT score of 4, and you have to fight a goblin (COMBAT 5, Defence 7, Stamina 6). The fight begins with your attack (you always get first blow unless told otherwise). Suppose you roll 8 on two dice. Adding your COMBAT score gives a total of 12. This is 5 more than the goblin's Defence, so it loses 5 Stamina.

The goblin still has 1 Stamina point left, so it gets to strike back. It rolls 6 on the dice which, added to its COMBAT of 5, gives a total attack score of 11. Suppose you have a chain mail tabard (Defence +2). Your Defence is therefore 9 (=4+3+2), so you lose 2 Stamina and can then attack again.

USING ABILITIES

Fighting is often not the easiest or safest way to tackle a situation. When you get a chance to use one of your other abilities, you will be told the Difficulty of the task. You roll two dice and add your score in the ability, and to succeed in the task you must get higher than the Difficulty.

Example:
You are at the bottom of a cliff. You can use THIEVERY to climb it, and the climb is Difficulty 9. Suppose your THIEVERY score is 4. This means you must roll at least 6 on the dice to make the climb.

CODEWORDS

There is a list of codewords included at the back of the book. Sometimes you will be told you have acquired a codeword. When this happens, put a tick in the box next to that codeword. If you later lose the codeword, erase the tick.

The codewords are arranged alphabetically for each book in the series. In this book, for example, all codewords begin with A. This makes it easy to check if you picked up a codeword from a book you played previously. For instance, you might be asked if you have picked up a codeword in a book you have already adventured in. The letter of that codeword will tell you which book to check (e.g. if it begins with C, it is from Book 3: *Over the Blood-Dark Sea*).

SOME QUESTIONS ANSWERED

How long will my adventures last?

As long as you like! There are many plot strands to follow in the Fabled Lands. Explore wherever you want. Gain wealth, power and prestige. Make friends and foes. Just think of it as real life in a fantasy world. When you need to stop playing, make a note of the entry you are at and later you can just resume at that point.

What happens if I'm killed?
If you had the foresight to arrange a resurrection deal (you'll learn about them later), death might not be the end of your career. Otherwise, you can always start adventuring again with a new persona. If you do, you'll first have to erase all codewords, ticks and money recorded in the book.

What do the maps show?
The map at the back of the book shows the land of Sokara which is covered by this adventure: *The War-Torn Kingdom*. The map at the front shows the whole extent of the known Fabled Lands.

Are some regions of the world more dangerous than others?
Yes. Generally, the closer you are to civilization (the area of Sokara and Golnir covered in the first two books) the easier your adventures will be.

Where can I travel in the Fabled Lands?
Anywhere. If you journey to the edge of the map in this book, you will be guided to another book in the series. (*The War-Torn Kingdom* deals with Sokara, *Cities of Gold and Glory* deals with Golnir, *Over the Blood-Dark Sea* deals with the southern seas and so on.) For example, if you are enslaved by the Uttakin, you will be guided to *The Court of Hidden Faces* **321**, which refers to entry **321** in Book Five.

What if I don't have the next book?
Just turn back. When you do get that book, you can always return and venture onwards.

What should I do when travelling on from one book to the next?
It's very simple. Make a note of the entry you'll be turning to in the new book. Then copy all the information from your Adventure Sheet and Ship's Manifest into the new book. Lastly, erase the Adventure Sheet and Ship's Manifest data in the old book so they will be blank when you return there.

What about codewords?
Codewords report important events in your adventuring life. They

'remember' the places you've been and the people you've met. Do NOT erase codewords when you are passing from one book to another.

Are there any limits on abilities?

Your abilities (COMBAT, etc) can increase up to a maximum of 12. They can never go lower than 1. If you are told to lose a point off an ability which is already at 1, it stays as it is.

Are there any limits on Stamina?

There is no upper limit. Stamina increases each time you go up in Rank. Wounds will reduce your current Stamina, but not your potential (unwounded) score. If Stamina ever goes to zero, you are killed.

Does it matter what type of weapon I have?

When you buy a weapon in a market, you can choose what type of weapon it is (i.e. a sword, spear, etc). The type of weapon is up to you. Price is not affected by the weapon's type, but only by whether it has a COMBAT bonus or not.

Some items give ability bonuses. Are these cumulative?

No. If you already have a set of **lockpicks (THIEVERY +1)** and then acquire **magic lockpicks (THIEVERY +2)**, you don't get a +3 bonus, only +2. Count only the bonus given by your best item for each ability.

Why do I keep going back to entries I've been to?

Many entries describe locations such as a city or castle, so whenever you go back there, you go to the paragraph that corresponds to that place.

How many blessings can I have?

As many as you can get, but never more than one of the same type. You can't have several COMBAT blessings, for instance, but you could have one COMBAT, one THIEVERY and one CHARISMA blessing.

QUICK RULES

To use an ability (COMBAT, THIEVERY, etc), roll two dice and add your score in the ability. To succeed you must roll higher than the Difficulty of the task.

Example: You want to calm down an angry innkeeper. This requires a CHARISMA roll at a Difficulty of 10. Say you have a CHARISMA score of 6. This means that you would have to roll 5 or more on two dice to succeed.

Fighting involves a series of COMBAT rolls. The Difficulty of the roll is equal to the opponent's Defence score. (Your Defence score is equal to your **Rank** + your **armour bonus** + your **COMBAT score**.) The amount you beat the Difficulty by is the number of Stamina points that your opponent loses.

That's pretty much all you need to know. If you have any detailed queries, consult the detailed rules in the preceding pages.

A selection of pre-generated characters, colour maps of the Fabled Lands world and other bonus material are available on the website:

www.fabledlands.com

1

The approach of dawn has turned the sky a milky grey-green, like jade. The sea is a luminous pane of silver. Holding the tiller of your sailing boat, you keep your gaze fixed on the glittering constellation known as the Spider. It marks the north, and by keeping it to port you know you are still on course.

The sun appears in a trembling burst of red fire at the rim of the world. Slowly the chill of night gives way to brazen warmth. You lick your parched lips. There is a little water sloshing in the bottom of the barrel by your feet, but not enough to see you through another day.

Sealed in a scroll case tucked into your jerkin is the parchment map your grandfather gave you on his death-bed. You remember his stirring tales of far sea voyages, of kingdoms beyond the western horizon, of sorcerous islands and ruined palaces filled with treasure. As a child you dreamed of nothing else but the magical quests that were in store if you too became an adventurer.

You never expected to die in an open boat before your adventures even began.

Securing the tiller, you unroll the map and study it again. You hardly need to. Every detail is etched into your memory by now. According to your reckoning, you should have reached the east coast of Harkuna days ago.

A pasty grey blob splatters on to the map. After a moment of stunned surprise, you look up and curse the seagull circling directly overhead. Then it strikes you: where there's a seagull, there may be land.

You leap to your feet and scan the horizon. Sure enough, a line of white cliffs lies a league to the north. Have you been sailing along the coast all this time without realizing the mainland was so close?

Steering towards the cliffs, you feel the boat shudder against rough waves. A howling wind whips plumes of spindrift across the sea. Breakers pound the high cliffs. The tiller is yanked out of your hands. The little boat is spun around, out of control, and goes plunging in towards the coast.

You leap clear at the last second. There is the snap of timber, the roaring crescendo of the waves — and then silence as you go under. Striking out wildly, you try to swim clear of the razor-sharp rocks. For a while the undertow threatens to drag you down, then suddenly a wave catches you and flings you contemptuously up on to the beach.

Battered and bedraggled you lie gasping for breath until you hear someone walking along the shore towards you. Wary of danger, you lose no time in getting to your feet. Confronting you is an old man clad in a dirty loin-cloth. His eyes have a feverishly bright look that is suggestive of either a mystic or a madman.

Get the codeword *Auric* and then turn to **20**.

2

If you have a **coded missive**, turn to **676** immediately. If not, but you have the codeword *Deliver*, turn to **98** immediately. If you have neither, read on.

The soldier recognizes you. He bows and says, 'Welcome, my lord. I will take you see King Nergan.'

He leads you to Nergan's mountain stockade, where the king greets you warmly.

'Ah, my loyal champion! It is always a pleasure to see you. However, I was hoping you had spoken with General Beladai of the allied army – we need that citadel. Now go. That is a royal command!'

You leave, climbing down to the foothills of the mountains.

Turn to **474**.

3

You have come to the foothills of the Spine of Harkun, in the north west of Sokara. The view is impressive: a massive wall of forested mountains,

whose rocky, white-flanked peaks soar skywards into the clouds. These parts of the mountains are unclimbable but you notice a large cave at the bottom of a mountain.

Investigate the cave	turn to **665**
Go east to the Citadel of Velis Corin	turn to **271**
South into the wilderness	turn to **276**

4

The priests of Alvir and Valmir are overjoyed that you have returned the **golden net**. The high priest rewards you with 100 Shards and a magic weapon, a rune-engraved trident. Note the weapon, a **trident (COMBAT +1)**, on your Adventure Sheet, and turn to **220**.

5

It is a tough climb upwards but not impossible. If you have **climbing gear**, turn to **652**. If not, make a SCOUTING roll at Difficulty 10.

Successful SCOUTING roll	turn to **652**
Failed SCOUTING roll	turn to **529**

6

The chest springs open with a click. Inside you find 60 Shards, a **mandolin (CHARISMA +1)**, and a **potion of healing**. The potion can be used once, at any time (even in combat) to restore 5 Stamina points. There is also an ancient religious text about the gods of Uttaku, called the **scroll of Ebron**, which reveals that one of the gods of the Uttakin is called Ebron, and that he has fourteen angles. Note whatever you are taking on your Adventure Sheet, and then turn to **10**.

7

Much to your embarrassment, you get lost in the vast forest. You wander around for days until you finally emerge at the Bronze Hills. Turn to **110**.

8

You step through the archway. Immediately the symbols on the stone begin to glow with red-hot energy; your hair stands on end and your body tingles. A crackling nimbus of blue-white force engulfs you, the sky darkens and thunder and lightning crash and leap across the heavens.

Suddenly, your vision fades, and everything goes black.

When your sight returns, you find yourself at the gates of a large city, set on an ochre-coloured river. A vile stink of brimstone permeates the air. You wrinkle your face up in disgust and gag involuntarily.

'Welcome to Yellowport!' says a passing merchant.

Turn to **10**.

9

If you have the codeword *Altitude*, turn to **272** immediately. If not, read on.

A notice has been pinned up in the foyer: 'Adventurer priest wanted. See the chief administrator.'

Naturally, you present yourself, and the chief administrator, a grey-whiskered priest of Elnir, takes you into his office. He shows you a special crystal ball that displays an aerial view of Marlock City. You notice several strange-looking clouds hanging over the city. They are shaped like gigantic demons, reaching down to claw at the city laid out below them.

'The crystal ball shows things as they are in the spirit world,' explains the priest. 'These storm demons cannot be seen under normal circumstances, but they are there, almost ready to destroy the city.'

He goes on to tell you that Sul Veneris, the divine Lord of Thunder is one of the sons of Elnir, the Sky God, chief among the gods. He is responsible for keeping the storm demons under control, and thunder is thought to be the sound of Sul Veneris smiting the demons in his wrath.

'Unfortunately, the storm demons have found a way to put Sul Veneris into an enchanted sleep. He lies at the very top of Devil's Peak, a single spire of volcanic rock, reaching up into the clouds. The peak lies north of Marlock City, and west of Curstmoor. We need an enterprising priest to get to the top of the peak and free Sul Veneris from his sleep. But I must warn you that several priests have already tried, and we never saw them again.'

If you take up the quest, record the codeword *Altitude*. Turn to **100**.

10 ☐☐☐☐

If you have the codeword *Assassin*, turn to **50** immediately. If not, read on.

If you have just arrived in Yellowport, tick the first empty box above (use a pencil). The boxes are a record of the number of times you have visited the city. If this is your fourth visit, turn to **273**. If you have visited the city fewer than or more than four times, read on.

Yellowport is the second largest city in Sokara. It is mainly a trading town, and is known for its exotic goods from distant Ankon-Konu.

The Stinking River brings rich deposits of sulphur from the Lake of the Sea Dragon down to the town, where it is extracted and stored in the large waterfront warehouses run by the merchants' guild. From here, the mineral is exported all over Harkuna. Unfortunately, all that sulphur has its drawbacks. The stink is abominable, and much of the city has a yellowish hue. The river is so full of sulphur that it is virtually useless as a source of food or of drinking water. However, the demand for sulphur, especially from the sorcerous guilds, is great.

Politically, much has changed in the past few years. The old and corrupt king of Sokara, Corin VII, has been deposed and executed in a military coup. General Grieve Marlock and the army now control Sokara. The old Council of Yellowport has been 'indefinitely dissolved' and a provost marshal, Marloes Marlock, the general's brother, appointed as military governor of the town.

You can buy a town house in Yellowport for 200 Shards. Owning a

house gives you a place to rest, and to store equipment. If you buy one, tick the box by the town house option and cross off 200 Shards from your Adventure Sheet.

To leave Yellowport by sea, buy or sell ships and cargo, go to the harbourmaster.

If you have the codeword *Artefact* and the **Book of the Seven Sages**, you can turn to **40**. Otherwise, choose from the following options:

Seek an audience with the provost marshal	turn to **523**
Visit the market	turn to **30**
Visit the harbourmaster	turn to **555**
Go to the merchants' guild	turn to **405**
Explore the city by day	turn to **302**
Explore the city by night	turn to **442**
Visit your town house ☐ (if box ticked)	turn to **300**
Visit the Gold Dust Tavern	turn to **506**
Visit the temple of Maka	turn to **141**
Visit the temple of Elnir	turn to **316**
Visit the temple of Alvir and Valmir	turn to **220**
Visit the temple of Tyrnai	turn to **526**
Travel north-east toward Venefax	turn to **621**
Head north-west to Trefoille	turn to **233**
Follow the Stinking River north	turn to **82**
Strike out north-west, across country	turn to **558**

11

A narrow path leads up the hill, the top of which is crowned with a circle of large obsidian standing stones, hewn from solid rock. Despite the bitter wind that blows across these hills, the stones are unweathered and seem but newly lain. They form three archways, each carved with mystic symbols and runes of power.

Turn to **65**.

12

You tell them a story of tragic love between a merman and a human princess. The mer-folk are moved to shed briny tears, and one of them plants a languorous kiss on your lips.

You find you can indeed breathe underwater now. The mer-folk lead you into the depths, where they swim playfully around you.

Suddenly, a hideous form looms out of the murk. It is like a giant squid, but it carries a spear in one of its many tentacles and wears rudimentary armour. Great black eyes shine with an implacable alien intelligence. The mer-folk dart away in fright, leaving you alone with the creature.

If you have the codeword *Anchor*, turn to **116**. Otherwise, turn to **238**.

13

'The Violet Ocean's a dangerous place, Cap'n,' says the first mate. 'The crew probably won't follow you there if they don't think you're good enough!'

If your Rank is 4 or more, turn to paragraph 55 in *Over the Blood-Dark Sea*. If your Rank is less than 4, the first mate advises you against the ocean journey. If you take his advice, turn back to **507**.

If you insist on making the trip, you need to make a CHARISMA roll at Difficulty 12 to convince the crew to follow you. If you succeed, turn to paragraph 55 in *Over the Blood-Dark Sea*. Otherwise, turn back to **507**.

14

Someone stabs you in the back. Lose 5 Stamina points. If you still live, you spin around just as a beefy, disreputable-looking thug comes for you again with a long dagger.

'Get the snooping swine!' yells the man with the eyepatch.

You must fight.

Thug, COMBAT 3, Defence 6, Stamina 13

If you lose, you are dead, unless you have a resurrection deal. If you win, turn to **476**.

15

Three drunken army officers accost you on the street. If you have the title Protector of Sokara, turn to **542** immediately. If not, read on.

'Sho, what have we… hic… Here?' sneers one of them drunkenly.

'Out of the way, you stinking dog!' says another, shoving you in the chest.

Step out of the way	turn to **44**
Return the insult	turn to **266**

16 ☐

If there is a tick in the box, turn to **251** immediately. If not, put a tick there now, and read on.

If you have the codeword *Avenge*, turn to **648** immediately. Otherwise read on.

You remain as quiet as a mouse, behind a pile of coins. After a long wait, the sea dragon slithers into the water, and swims out on some errand. You have some time to loot the hoard. You may choose up to three of the following treasures:

Enchanted sword (COMBAT +3)
Plate armour (Defence +5)
Ebony wand (MAGIC +2)
500 Shards
Magic mandolin (CHARISMA +2)
Gold compass (SCOUTING +2)
Magic lockpicks (THIEVERY +2)
Silver holy symbol (SANCTITY +2)

After you have taken the third treasure, you hear the sea dragon returning. Quickly you climb up through the hole in the roof on to an island in the middle of the lake. From there you manage to get a lift on a passing boat, and make it safely to Cadmium village. Turn to **135**.

17

The horse and you hit the wall. There is a bright flash, and you find that you have passed straight through into the hill. It must be a faery mound!

The horse you are riding abruptly changes shape in a puff of smoke. You find yourself on the back of a little, knobbly limbed, white-faced goblin, who promptly collapses under your weight.

You are in a cavern, lit by mouse-sized faery folk, who flit about in the air blazing like fireflies. The other horses have also turned into goblins, elves and faeries of all shapes and sizes.

'What have we here?' whispers a pale, dark-eyed elf woman, dressed in silvery cobwebs and wearing a gold crown.

'An overweight mortal sitting on poor old Gobrash, your majesty!' groans the goblin you are sitting on.

You realize you are in great danger here. There's no telling what the faery folk will do to you. The queen signals to her people and they close in around you ominously. Make a SANCTITY roll at Difficulty 9.

Successful SANCTITY roll	turn to **626**
Failed SANCTITY roll	turn to **268**

18

You spin them a tale about how your poor brother, a mercenary in Grieve Marlock's personal guard, lost his legs in the fight to overthrow the old king, and that you have spent all your money on looking after him.

Several of the militia are brought to tears by your eloquent speech. They end up having a whip-round among themselves for your brother, and they give you 15 Shards! Chuckling to yourself, you return to the city centre. Turn to **10**.

19 ☐☐☐

Put a tick in an empty box. If all three boxes are now ticked, gain the codeword *Anvil*.

The Dragon Knights are impressed with your combat skills. Your opponent comes round, ruefully rubbing his neck. Grudgingly, he admits to your superior skill and hands you his weapon and armour. You get an ordinary **sword** and a suit of **heavy plate (Defence +6)**. You take your leave, turn to **276**.

'Well, well, well, what have we here, friends?' asks the old man. He seems to be talking to someone next to him, although you are certain he is alone. 'Looks like a washed-up adventurer to me,' he says in answer to his own question. 'All wet and out of luck!'

He carries on having a conversation with himself, a conversation that quickly turns into a heated debate. He is clearly quite mad.

'Excuse me, umm, EXCUSE ME!' you shout above the hubbub in an attempt to grab the old man's attention. He stops and stares at you.

'Is this the Isle of the Druids?' you ask impatiently.

'Indeed it is,' says the old man, 'I see that you are from a far land, so it is up to me to welcome you to Harkuna. But I think you may have much to do here for it is written in the stars that someone like you would come. Your destiny awaits you! Follow me, young adventurer.'

The old man turns smartly about and begins walking up a path toward some hills. You can just see some sort of monolithic stone structure atop one of them.

'Come on, come on, I'll show you the Gates of the World,' the old man babbles.

Follow him	turn to **192**
Explore the coast	turn to **128**
Head into the nearby forest	turn to **257**

While making your way through the back streets of the poor quarter you are set upon by a knife-wielding thug, who is intent on relieving you of your purse.

If you don't want to fight him, you can try a CHARISMA roll at a Difficulty of 8 to try to talk your way out of this unpleasant situation. If you succeed, the thug leaves, confused by your rhetoric (turn to **10** and choose again). Otherwise, you must fight him.

Thug, COMBAT 4, Defence 7, Stamina 6

If you defeat him, you find 15 Shards on his body. If you are defeated, you are stunned into unconsciousness. You come round with 1 Stamina point, and he has robbed you of 50 Shards (or all of your money if you have less than 50 Shards). Turn to **10**.

22

You reach down and deftly pull out the ceramic plug. A gush of foul-smelling emerald green liquid spills on to the floor, and the golem twitches once before collapsing. The other golem is coming to life, however. You'll have to be quick to get it in time!

Make a COMBAT roll at Difficulty 9.

Successful COMBAT roll	turn to **539**
Failed COMBAT roll	turn to **647**

23

As you stride forward, they look up with expressions of luminous rage.

'Get you back, mortal,' warns one, 'or I'll touch you with my grave-cold hands and then it'll be your dying day!'

Attack them	turn to **479**
Call on your god to banish them	turn to **520**

24

You will need to subdue the king and his henchmen with a spell. Make a MAGIC roll at Difficulty 12.

Successful MAGIC roll	turn to **644**
Failed MAGIC roll	turn to **208**

25

Captain Vorkung is impressed with your claims of loyalty to the rightful king. He decides you might be useful to their cause, and you are led , blindfolded, through a secret pass to a mountain stockade.

King Nergan gives you an audience in a makeshift throne room. He is a young, and handsome man, who seems committed to his country. He leads you aside, into a private chamber.

'I have need of one such as you,' he says. 'Yellowport groans under the yoke of Governor Marloes Marlock, the brother of General Grieve Marlock. If you can get into the palace at Yellowport and assassinate Marloes, I will be eternally grateful.'

If you have the codeword *Artery*, turn to **399** immediately. Otherwise, if you wish to accept the mission to kill the Governor of Yellowport, record the codeword *Ambuscade*.

When you are ready, the King wishes you well, and you are led out of the stockade, and back down to the foothills of the Coldbleak Mountains. Turn to **474**.

26

You set sail for Dweomer. The journey takes a few days but, amazingly, it is uneventful. The captain can't believe his luck. You disembark at Dweomer harbour, on the Sorcerers' Isle. Turn to paragraph **100** in *Over the Blood-Dark Sea*.

27

Either you are recklessly brave or very foolish to visit the palace where you assassinated the governor. Provost Marshal Royzer has established new security procedures, and it is impossible for you to see him. Return to **10**.

28

You jump into the air, and hit the ground rolling. You come up, bruised but alive, in time to see the horses ride straight into the rocky wall of a low hill! To your amazement, they pass straight through the rock and disappear. Silence falls across the land like a blanket. There is no sign of them, not even tracks. You camp for the night and the next day set off once more.

North across country	turn to **560**
East to the road	turn to **558**
To Trefoille	turn to **250**
To Marlock City	turn to **100**
West towards the River Grimm	turn to **99**

29

Your ship is sailing in the coastal waters beside Yellowport. There are a number of other ships, mostly merchantmen, but there are also a few warships of the Sokaran Imperial Navy. 'At least we won't be plagued by pirates with the navy around,' says the first mate. Roll two dice:

Score 2-4	Storm	turn to **613**
Score 5-9	An uneventful voyage	turn to **439**
Score 10-12	Sokaran war galley	turn to **165**

30

The market is large and busy. At the corners of Brimstone Plaza, gigantic braziers burn sweet-smelling incense in an attempt to overpower the rotten-egg smell that permeates the whole city. There are many stalls and goods to choose from. You may buy any of the items listed, as long as you have the money and the space to carry it. You may also sell any items you own that are listed below, for the price stated. If you do, don't forget to cross them off your Adventure Sheet.

Items with no purchase price listed are not available locally.

Armour	*To buy*	*To sell*
Leather (Defence +1)	50 Shards	45 Shards
Ring mail (Defence +2)	100 Shards	90 Shards
Chain mail (Defence +3)	200 Shards	180 Shards
Splint armour (Defence +4)	–	360 Shards
Plate armour (Defence +5)	–	720 Shards
Heavy plate (Defence +6)	–	1440 Shards

Weapons (sword, axe, etc)	*To buy*	*To sell*
Without COMBAT bonus	50 Shards	40 Shards
COMBAT bonus +1	250 Shards	200 Shards
COMBAT bonus +2	–	400 Shards
COMBAT bonus +3	–	800 Shards

Magical equipment	*To buy*	*To sell*
Amber wand (MAGIC +1)	500 Shards	400 Shards
Ebony wand (MAGIC +2)	–	800 Shards
Cobalt wand (MAGIC +3)	–	1600 Shards

Other items	To buy	To sell
Mandolin (CHARISMA +1)	300 Shards	270 Shards
Lockpicks (THIEVERY +1)	–	270 Shards
Holy symbol (SANCTITY +1)	200 Shards	100 Shards
Compass (SCOUTING +1)	500 Shards	450 Shards
Rope	50 Shards	45 Shards
Lantern	100 Shards	90 Shards
Climbing gear	100 Shards	90 Shards
Bag of pearls	–	100 Shards
Rat poison	60 Shards	50 Shards
Silver nugget	–	200 Shards

One trader is offering a t**reasure map** for sale at 200 Shards. He will also buy any old **treasure map** for 150 Shards. If you buy the map, note this paragraph number (**30**) for reference, and turn to **200**.

If you wish to buy cargo for a ship, you need to visit the warehouses at the harbourmaster. When you are ready to return to the city centre, turn to **10**.

YELLOWPORT MARKETPLACE

31

A dark emptiness surrounds you. Then, as if in your sleep, you see a tiny glimmer of light off in the distance. Suddenly you wake up, and find yourself coughing and spluttering, up to your neck in water. You look around – you are floundering in the holy waters of Blessed Springs.

Standing at the side of the pool is a tall, slim, moustached man who says, 'I am Aklar the Bold. I found you as bottled dust in the lair of Vayss the Sea Dragon. By sprinkling your ashes into the holy waters, I have brought you back to life. I think a reward is in order, don't you?'

You explain that you have nothing to give. Aklar frowns in annoyance: 'Blast, I knew I should have taken one of the other bottles! Well, you'll just have to owe me a favour. A big favour.'

You can hardly refuse. Record the codeword *Aklar*.

'Well, I must be about my business. We shall meet again, count on it.' With that he leaves.

You stagger out of the pool. Turn to **510**.

32

You head across the hot, dusty and sparsely vegetated land. Vultures circle overhead – presumably they think you're going to die. You wander on, until you come to a ridge. Down below, in a shallow valley, is a great mound of earth. Scorpion men crawl in and out of the many burrows that riddle the earth. The number of scorpion men in the valley makes your heart quail; unless you have the codeword *Artefact*, the place is too deadly to enter. If you have the codeword *Artefact*, turn to **406**. Otherwise, turn to **492**.

33

Resurrection costs 200 Shards if you are an initiate, and 800 Shards if not. It is the last word in insurance. Once you have arranged for resurrection you need not fear death, as you will be magically restored to life here at the temple. To arrange resurrection, pay the fee and write 'Temple of Tyrnai, *The War-Torn Kingdom*, **640**' in the Resurrection box on your Adventure Sheet. If you are later killed, turn to **640** in *The War-Torn Kingdom*.

You can have only one resurrection arranged at any one time. If you arrange another resurrection later at a different temple, the original one is cancelled. Cross it off your Adventure Sheet. You do not get a refund.

When you are finished here, turn to **282**.

34

You make it only fifty feet up the sheer rock face before you lose your footing and fall to the ground. Lose 4 Stamina points. If you still live, turn to **658** where you can try again, if you like.

35

You come to the top of a windswept cliff. An ancient pillar of jumbled rock, pitted and weatherbeaten, stands at the cliff's edge, like a broken finger pointing at the sky. Seagulls sing their song of desolation in the air.

Judging by the runes etched into the rock, the tor dates back to the time of the Shadar, a race that ruled Harkuna so long ago, they are lost in myth and legend.

Examine the runes	turn to **515**
Go down to the beach	turn to **97**
Take the road to Trefoille	turn to **602**
Take the road to Marlock City	turn to **166**

36

Soon you realize you are completely lost in this strange, magical forest. You wander around for days, barely able to find enough food and water. Lose 4 Stamina points. If you still live, you eventually stagger out of the forest to the coast. Turn to **128**.

37

Your men have been fishing with a net. This time, however, they have caught a large shark. Afterwards, when it has been cut open, you find the remains of some poor sailor. Inside his leather pouch, you find a **bag of pearls**, which you can take if you wish. Turn to **507**.

38

Heavy black clouds race towards you across the sky, whipping the waves into a frenzy. The crew mutter among themselves fearfully. If you have the blessing of Alvir and Valmir that confers Safety from Storms, you can ignore it. Cross off the blessing and turn to **209**.

Otherwise the storm hits with full fury. Roll one die if your ship is a barque, two dice if it is a brigantine, or three dice if a galleon. Add 1 to the roll if the crew's quality is good; add 2 if it is excellent.

Score 1-3	Ship sinks	turn to **325**
Score 4-5	The mast splits	turn to **397**
Score 6-20	You weather the storm	turn to **209**

39

You and some of your crew clamber aboard the wreck. You find some dead sailors amid the wreckage. Their bodies are curiously bloated. Make a SCOUTING roll at Difficulty 9.

| Successful SCOUTING roll | turn to **194** |
| Failed SCOUTING roll | turn to **465** |

40

You take the **Book of the Seven Sages** to Pyletes the Sage at the Gold Dust Tavern. He thanks you effusively for bringing it to him. Your reward is secret learning from the temple of Molhern, god of knowledge. Add 1 to the ability of your choice (COMBAT, etc). Also gain the title Illuminate of Molhern – write this in the Titles and

Honours box on your Adventure Sheet. Lose the codeword *Artefact* and cross off the **Book of the Seven Sages**. Turn to **10**.

41

The inside of the dome is lit with an eerie yellowish glow that comes from the sea-moss that carpets the ceiling. At the far end, a grotto in the wall contains an idol made from sea shells and coral, presumably of Oannes, the god of the repulsive ones. At its feet lies the **golden net** of Alvir and Valmir, the object of your quest. Between you and it swim several of the giant squid-creatures, carrying out various undersea chores.

Swim back to Shadar Tor	turn to **35**
Fight your way to the **golden net**	turn to **121**
Trust to your magical prowess	turn to **592**
Rack your memory for a solution	turn to **487**

42

Two hulking shapes appear out of the shadows as if from nowhere. They are hideous creatures: manlike, standing on two legs, but with the tail and hairy features of a gigantic rat. Their yellowing teeth snap at you as they lunge for you; the ratmen also wield wicked-looking shortswords in their hands.

'Gut the human!' yells one of them in a bestial voice.

You must fight them, both at once, as if they were one opponent. If you have some **rat poison**, you can add 3 to your dice rolls. Cross the **rat poison** off the Adventure Sheet if you use it.

Two Ratmen, COMBAT 6, Defence 9, Stamina 9

If you win, turn to **423**. If you lose, turn to **308**.

43

You must fight. Luckily, your magic weapon will be effective.

Tomb Guardian, COMBAT 6, Defence 8, Stamina 12

If you win, turn to **490**. If you lose, you are dead, unless you have a resurrection deal.

44

You decide that discretion would be the better part of valour in this case, and step aside. The officers laugh contemptuously, and swagger past. Nothing else happens tonight. Turn to **100**.

45

The little girl runs off before you can talk to her. You thread your way through the pitted tombstones and brooding crypts of the cemetery, under a pale moon that bathes the graveyard in a sickly, pallid light.

Suddenly, a foul stench fills your nostrils, and a figure rises up out of the shadows! Yellow eyes glow with feral blood-lust, and the creature sinks its black teeth into your arm before you can react. Lose 4 Stamina.

If you still live, you have been infected. Note that you have a Disease (Ghoulbite). Until you can find a cure, you must subtract one from your SANCTITY, COMBAT and CHARISMA (no ability score can drop below 1). The ghoul, a rotting, walking corpse, lunges for you again.

Fight it	turn to **617**
Invoke the power of the gods	turn to **144**
Use **salt and iron filings**, if you have any	turn to **303**

46

Lose the codewords *Almanac*, *Brush* and *Eldritch* if you have them.

You can invest money in multiples of 100 Shards. The guild will buy and sell commodities on your behalf using this money until you return to collect it. 'Don't forget that you can lose money as well,' mutters a sullen merchant.

Write the sum you are investing in the box here, or withdraw a sum invested previously. Then turn to **405**.

MONEY INVESTED

47

The Forest of Larun is a mighty swathe of densely packed trees, a slice of primordial nature in the middle of busy, industrious Sokara.

Venture deeper into the forest	turn to **596**
North to the Bronze Hills	turn to **110**
West to the River Grimm	turn to **333**
South into the countryside	turn to **560**
East to the road	turn to **387**

48

The warden is in charge of security. 'We have had an unfortunate, umm... accident,' he says worriedly. 'In the crypt below the temple we sometimes experiment with the corpses of the dead – you know, the occasional zombie, part of the rituals in honour of the particular aspect of Nagil we revere here. It seems a ghoul has escaped from the pits, and is terrorizing the city at night. We'd rather someone like you sorted the problem out before the city militia got to hear of it. Destroy it and bring me the ghoul's head.'

If you want to take up the mission, record the codeword *Ague*. 'Search for it at night!' says the warden as you leave. Turn to **100**.

49

Not taking any chances, you charge the soldier, yelling a warcry. He starts back in astonishment. Just then, several archers pop up from behind the rocks above, and let loose a volley of arrows. One takes you in the leg. Lose 3 Stamina points.

If you still live, you fall to one knee, and the soldier melts away into the rocks. Alone, and wounded in the leg, you cannot climb upwards. You have to go back down though the descent will be difficult with a dodgy leg. Roll a die, adding one if you have some **climbing gear**.

Score 1-3	turn to **529**
Score 4-6	turn to **474**

50

The new provost marshal of Yellowport is Royzer. He used to be Marloes Marlock's second in command. Since the assassination of the old provost, Royzer has ruled the city with an iron hand: patrols are frequent and spies are everywhere. You will have to be careful not to get yourself recognized. Turn back to **10** and choose an option from the list there.

51

The war galley pulls alongside, and grappling hooks fly through the air, fastening your ships together. The captain leaps across and his men swarm on to your ship. A battle ensues. Roll three dice if you are a Warrior, or two dice if you belong to any other profession. Add your Rank to this roll. Then, if your crew is poor quality, subtract 2 from the total. If the crew is good, add 2. If the crew is excellent add 3.

Score 0-4	Calamity; you are killed	
Score 5-9	Crushing defeat; lose 1-6 Stamina	turn to **153**
Score 10-13	A draw	turn to **242**
Score 14+	Outright victory	turn to **62**

52

If you are an initiate it costs only 10 Shards to purchase Lacuna's blessing. A non-initiate must pay 25 Shards. Cross off the money and mark 'SCOUTING' in the Blessings box on your Adventure Sheet.

The blessing works by allowing you to try again when you fail a SCOUTING roll. It is good for only one reroll. When you use the blessing, cross it off your Adventure Sheet. You can have only one SCOUTING blessing at any one time. Once it is used up, you can return to any branch of the temple of Lacuna to buy a new one.

When you are finished here, turn to **544**.

53

The creature bursts open in death, spilling a black inky cloud into the water. The sac in which this ink is kept falls free from its body. You can take the **ink sac** if you wish – note it on your Adventure Sheet. You also find coral jewellery worth about 15 Shards. Nothing else occurs during your foray into the depths, so you return to land. You climb back up the path that leads to the clifftop tor without incident.

| Take the road to Trefoille | turn to **602** |
| Take the road to Marlock City | turn to **166** |

54

You drive back the storm demons long enough for you to work free one of the stakes that is holding Sul Veneris down. Turn to **365**.

55

You remember that this is a trap set up by the cannibal cultists of Badogor. While one pretends to be hurt, two others skulk in the shadows, waiting to ambush the curious. Forewarned you are able to take them by surprise. You cut one down in seconds and the figure on the ground runs off with a shriek of terror. The third cultist, however, turns to fight you.

Cultist, COMBAT 3, Defence 5, Stamina 7

If you win, you find a **bag of pearls** on his body. Turn to **10**.

56

A strange-looking craft is bobbing in the water. It is shaped like a cone, floating on its base, and as you draw nearer, you realize it is made entirely of metal! Its sail, a huge piece of cloth, seems to have collapsed and is spread out around it, on the surface of the sea. Great blue and white letters, in some foreign script, are painted on its side. You notice an opening on one side.

Enter the strange craft	turn to **496**
Leave it and sail on	turn to **85**

57

You manage to lose them amid the back streets of Yellowport. Once the heat is off, you return to the city centre. Turn to **10**.

58

He doesn't notice you hiding in the shadowy doorway of a nearby derelict house. As he passes, you step out and attack, taking him completely by surprise. He goes down with your first blow. Searching him, you find 25 Shards, which you can take if you wish. Then you flip up his eyepatch. Nestling in the eyesocket is a sparkling gem, a flame opal. You pluck it free. Note the **flame opal eye** on your Adventure Sheet and delete the codeword *Barnacle*. Quickly, you haul the body into the shadows and head for the city centre. Turn to **400**.

59

Your deft fingers find a false spine of carved wood among the titles in the bookcase. Pressing it, you hear a click and the bookcase swings out from the wall. Beyond lies a hidden room where you find a **verdigris key**. Note this on your Adventure Sheet if you decide to take it.

Leave at once	turn to **10**
Go upstairs to find Lauria	turn to **386**
Wait for her to return	turn to **534**

60

You are crossing the wild country of north-east Sokara. Roll one die.

Score 1 or 2	Caught in an animal trap! Lose 2 Stamina
Score 3 or 4	Nothing happens
Score 5 or 6	Attacked by a wolf, and must fight.

Wolf, COMBAT 3, Defence 5, Stamina 7.

If you win, you get a **wolf pelt**.

When you are ready you can go:

North	turn to **518**
South	turn to **458**
West	turn to **201**

61

'Wait,' you cry, 'I have seen the light! I wish to join your cult!'

'What!' yells the chef. Then his shoulders sag in resignation.

'We cannot refuse a new member,' says the leader with obvious disappointment. 'And we cannot eat our own people,' he adds sadly.

A short ceremony later – fortunately, the initiation does not involve any cannibalistic rites – and you are a full member of the Cult of Badogor. Write 'Unspeakable Cultist' in the Titles and Honours box on your Adventure Sheet. You lose 1 point of SANCTITY for joining such a vile cult.

You take your leave, and they wish you well, all smiles and friendship.

'Remember, never say his name! And don't forget to bring us new recruits,' says the leader. 'And some people for dinner!' adds the chef.

Hastily, you head for the city centre. Turn to **10**.

62

The Sokarans surrender. Their captain has been killed in the battle, and his marines have had the fight knocked out of them. The war galley isn't carrying any cargo, but you find an **officer's pass** on the body of the captain, and a chest in his cabin, which contains 150 Shards. You have to hand out 50 Shards to your crew, but you can add 100 Shards to your Adventure Sheet. You leave the galley to limp back to Yellowport while you sail on. Turn to **439**.

63

If you have the codeword *Attar*, turn to **578** immediately. If not, read on.

A small boy runs up to you, saying, 'Help us, help us! The Man-eating Blood-Thursday Gob-gobbler has got my little sister!'

His mother, a flaxen-haired beauty, comes up behind him.

'Surely you mean blood-thirsty, not Thursday?' you ask.

'Oh no,' replies the young mother, 'the Man-eating, Blood-Thursday Gob-gobbler is so named because it hunts only on Thursdays!'

The boy's name is Mikail, and his mother is Lynn. Her husband is away in the army, and her young daughter, Haylie, was taken by the beast last Thursday. Apparently, several people have disappeared, never to be seen again.

'Please, help us!' plead the villagers.

Help them	turn to **600**
Refuse to help	turn to **427**

64

Your amateurish tinkering sets the trap off, and the chest explodes! You take the full force of the blast: lose 5 Stamina points. If you are still alive, you also find that the contents of the chest have been vaporized, except for a sturdy metal scroll case, containing a piece of ancient religious text about the gods of Uttaku.

You discover from the scroll that one of the gods of the Uttakin is called Ebron, and that he has fourteen angles. Note the **scroll of Ebron** on your Adventure Sheet if you wish to take it.

Turn to **10**.

There are three stone gates engraved with ancient runes. Each gate is marked with a name: Yellowport, Marlock City and Wishport. From here, you can see the coast and the whole of the island, which is heavily forested.

Explore the coastline	turn to **128**
Head into the forest	turn to **257**
Step through the Yellowport arch	turn to **8**
Step through the Marlock City arch	turn to **180**
Step through the Wishport arch	turn to **330**

THE GATES OF THE WORLD

66

You stand your ground. The ghostly horses stream past you on either side, neighing wildly at the sky. Nimbly, you leap at one, and manage to wrap your arms around its neck, and swing on to its back. The horse feels quite solid, but appears to be a luminous, pale-green colour. You look up through a cloud of sparks emanating from the horse's mane just in time to see a rocky wall of a low hill looming up out of the evening mist. Your horse is galloping full tilt right into it!

Hold on	turn to **17**
Leap off	turn to **28**

67

Your ship is thrown about like flotsam and jetsam. When the storm subsides, you take stock. Much has been swept overboard: you lose 1 Cargo Unit, if you had any, of your choice. Also, the ship has been swept way off course and the mate has no idea where you are. 'We're lost at sea, Cap'n!' he moans.

Turn to **90**.

68

To renounce the worship of Alvir and Valmir, you must pay 30 Shards in compensation to the priesthood.

The priest simply points to a ship limping into harbour – its shattered masts, torn sails and battered hull mute testimony to its storm-tossed voyage.

'The captain did not revere the Twin Gods,' whispers the coral-jewelled priest darkly.

Do you want to change your mind? If you are determined to re-nounce your faith, pay the 30 Shards and delete Alvir and Valmir from the God box on your Adventure Sheet.

Turn to **154**.

69

To renounce the worship of Tyrnai, you must pay 50 Shards to the warrior priests, and suffer the Ceremony of the Wrathful Blow. A priest will strike you once; it is better to be struck by a priest than by Tyrnai himself!

If you are determined to renounce your initiate status, pay the 50 Shards, delete Tyrnai'from the God box on your Adventure Sheet. The High Priest smashes you across the jaw, saying, `I'm doing you a favour – believe me!' Lose 1 Stamina point. If you earlier arranged a resurrection here, it is cancelled with no refund.

When you have finished, turn to **526**.

70

Your ship is thrown about like flotsam and jetsam. When the storm subsides, you take stock. Much has been swept overboard; you lose 1 Cargo Unit, if you had any, of your choice. The ship has been blown way off course and the mate has no idea where you are. `We're lost at sea, Cap'n!' he moans.

Turn to **90**.

71

If you have the codeword *Ague*, turn to **517** immediately. If not, read on.

Nagil is the Lord of the Lands of the Dead, and his temple in Marlock City is covered in friezes and gargoyles of ornate design, depicting the souls of the dead on their journey to the underworld. Inside, it is cool and dark, hung with black velvet drapes.

A poster on the wall reads: `Wanted: person of unusual resourcefulness. See temple warden.'

Become an initiate	turn to **409**
Renounce worship	turn to **187**
Make resurrection arrangements	turn to **478**
Visit the warden	turn to **48**
Leave the temple	turn to **100**

72

You manage to shrug off the effects of the gas.

Attack the beast	turn to **371**
Run off	turn to **527**

73

If you are an initiate it costs only 10 Shards to purchase Elnir's blessing. A non-initiate must pay 25 Shards. Cross off the money and mark `CHARISMA' in the Blessings box on your Adventure Sheet.

The blessing works by allowing you to try again when you make a failed CHARISMA roll. It is only good for one reroll. When you use the blessing, cross it off your Adventure Sheet. You can have only one CHARISMA blessing at any one time. Once it is used up, you can return to any branch of the temple of Elnir to buy a new one.

When you are finished here, turn to **568**.

74

A fisherman will take you all the way to Yellowport for 15 Shards. Cross the money off your Adventure Sheet. Amazingly, despite the apparent fragility of the small vessel, you arrive without incident. Turn to **10**.

75

The high priest takes you to a private chamber.

`You may be just what the temple needs,' he says, `a good, old-fashioned thief! There is a suit of armour made entirely from gold – ceremonial only of course. Nevertheless, we would like to, er, have it donated to us.'

`I see,' you reply, `and where is the armour?'

`Well, that's the tricky part – it's in the Temple of Tyrnai, in Caran Baru. In fact, it's worn by the idol of Tyrnai himself in the temple! Can you bring us the gold chain mail of Tyrnai? In return, we will instruct you in the roguish arts.'

If you want to take up the mission for the temple of Sig, record the codeword *Armour*.

Turn to **235**.

76

You are an accomplished street brawler, and after only a few minutes' furious fighting, the three officers are laid out unconscious in the street. Several people gathered to watch the brawl – most of them give a cheer at your performance. General Marlock's troops have not endeared themselves to the population.

You find about 25 Shards on them along with an **officer's pass**. Take whatever you require and turn to **100**.

77

`It is fortunate that we have a Chosen One of Maka at this temple,' says the high priestess. `Only the Chosen Ones have the goddess-given powers to cure the afflicted!'

It costs 75 Shards (only 30 if you are an initiate of Maka) to be cured of a poison or a disease. Make any necessary payment and remove the poison's or disease's effects, then turn to **141**.

78

Make a SCOUTING roll at Difficulty 10.

Successful SCOUTING roll	turn to **524**
Failed SCOUTING roll	turn to **415**

79

Make a SCOUTING roll at Difficulty 14, as you try to lose them in the tunnels. It is hard because they know the layout better than you do.

Successful roll	turn to **224**
Failed roll	turn to **381**

80

You grab the woman's wrist a split-second before she can cut the strings of your money pouch. You drag her around to face you, but she meets your outraged scowl with a swashbuckling grin.

`You've got good reflexes,' she says. `Most of the street scum around here are too drink-sodden or dimwitted to notice the loss of a few Shards. Want to earn some real money?'

Accept her offer	turn to **425**
Refuse and leave	turn to **10**

81

This could be a tough fight.

Golem, COMBAT 5, Defence 10, Stamina 10

If you win, turn to **94**. If you lose, turn to **488**.

82

You are following the course of the Stinking River – and it certainly does stink, laden with sulphur as it is. Roll a die.

Score 1 or 2	Stung by a large golden insect. You are poisoned (COMBAT -1 until you find a cure)
Score 3 or 4	Nothing happens
Score 5 or 6	Catch a **smoulder fish**. Note it on your Adventure Sheet.

When you are ready, you can:

Follow the river north	turn to **310**
Follow the river south to Yellowport	turn to **10**
Go west to the road	turn to **558**
Go east into the countryside	turn to **278**

83

Your ship is thrown about like flotsam and jetsam. When the storm subsides, you take stock. Much has been swept overboard; you lose 1 Cargo Unit, if you had any, of your choice. Also, the ship has been blown way off course, and the mate has no idea where you are. `We're lost at sea, Cap'n!' he moans.

Turn to **90**.

84

Your ship awaits you in the harbour. The crew are in good spirits, as ever when a new voyage is about to begin.

Go ashore	turn to **142**
Set sail	turn to **222**

85

You are sailing around Scorpion Bight.

Sail north along the coast	turn to **190**
Sail west towards Yellowport	turn to **29**
Sail east into the Sea of Whispers	turn to **136**
Sail south into the Violet Ocean	turn to **416**
Go ashore at Scorpion Bight	turn to **176**

86

The temple of the Three Fortunes is a squat, square building. A frieze above the door depicts three women weaving a tapestry. 'That's the Tapestry of Fate, where our destiny is woven,' comments a priest.

Become an initiate	turn to **258**
Renounce worship	turn to **573**
Seek a blessing	turn to **603**
Leave the temple	turn to **400**

87

You are on the road between Blessed Springs and Venefax. Pilgrims, the sick and the injured travel this route to the holy waters of Blessed Springs to find salvation. Roll a die.

Score 1 or 2	Attacked by a mad pilgrim. You must fight.
	Pilgrim, COMBAT 3, Defence 5, Stamina 6
	If you win, you get his **staff**.
Score 3 or 4	Nothing happens
Score 5 or 6	Blessed by a priest. Write 'Safety from Storms'
	in the Blessings box on your Adventure Sheet

When you are ready, you can:

Go to Blessed Springs	turn to **510**
Go to Venefax	turn to **427**
Go north into the countryside	turn to **548**

To find out how well your investments have done, roll two dice. You can add 1 to the dice roll if you are an initiate of the Three Fortunes. Also add 1 if you have the codeword *Almanac*, add 2 if you have the codeword *Brush*, and add 3 if you have the codeword *Eldritch*.

Score 2-4	Lose entire sum invested
Score 5-6	Loss of 50%
Score 7-8	Loss of 10%
Score 9-10	Investment remains unchanged
Score 11-12	Profit of 10%
Score 13-14	Profit of 50%
Score 15+	Double initial investment

Now turn to **104**, where you can withdraw or leave the sum written in the box there after adjusting it according to the result rolled.

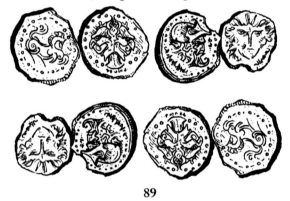

89

The undead pirate reaches for you, but it is too slow. Then it speaks, its voice seeming to sound inside your head.

'Damn you, and your kind, thieving sea centaur! I curse you forever: may you never swim again in the seas you love. You will walk for the rest of your life as a human, doomed to wander the surface world, unable to find the peace of coral caves!'

Quickly, you swim away, unable to believe your luck! What a convenient curse. You find yourself already changing back to a human, and you make it to your ship, coughing and spluttering. Your crew haul you aboard. The gems are worth 300 Shards – add that much to your money. You sail on, lucky to be still human. Turn to **507**.

90

Your ship is limping through unknown waters. The sun beats down, and the wind drops to a whisper.

'What direction, Cap'n?' asks the bosun.

Make a SCOUTING roll at Difficulty 10.

Successful SCOUTING roll	turn to **633**
Failed SCOUTING roll	turn to **484**

91 ☐

He smiles and takes you into the Gambler's Den. It is a smoke-filled casino, full of all kinds of dubious-looking characters, playing cards and dice. If you want to gamble, decide how much you want to bet, to a maximum of 20 Shards, and roll two dice.

Score 2	win five times your bet
Score 3-4	win twice your bet
Score 5-9	lose your bet
Score 10-11	win twice your bet
Score 12	win five times your bet.

When you are ready to leave, put a tick in the box and turn to **109**, unless the box is already ticked, in which case turn to **100**.

92

He falls dead at your feet. Searching him, you find 25 Shards you can take if you wish. Then you flip up his eyepatch. Nestling in the eye-socket is a sparkling gem, a flame opal. You pluck it free. Note the **flame opal eye** on your Adventure Sheet and lose the codeword *Barnacle*. You hurry off before a patrol arrives. Turn to **400**.

93

If you have the codeword *Azure*, turn to **359** immediately. If not, read on. A mad beggar, covered in sores and grime, accosts you in the street. 'O noble one, aid me for the love of the gods!' he rants, frothing at the mouth and gesticulating wildly. 'I need coins to eat, food to spend, and blessings to wear!'

Ignore him and return to city centre	turn to **10**
Give him 5 Shards	turn to **227**
Bless him	turn to **632**

94

At last, the golem is defeated. You manage to get into the temple without being noticed by anyone else. Inside, it is cool and dark, filled with an unearthly stillness. You reach forward to strip the armour off the idol of Tyrnai.

Make a THIEVERY roll at Difficulty 12.

Successful THIEVERY roll	turn to **509**
Failed THIEVERY roll	turn to **228**

95

You are greeted warmly and politely by the provost marshal who treats you as one of his own. However, there are no more missions, and after thanking you once again, he politely sends you on your way.

Return to **10**.

96

One of the militiamen kicks over a table, blocking your escape. You set your back to a corner of the room and grimly prepare to fight for your life. Fight them one at a time:

First Militiaman, COMBAT 4, Defence 7, Stamina 5

Second Militiaman, COMBAT 4, Defence 7, Stamina 4

Third Militiaman, COMBAT 4, Defence 7, Stamina 5

If you win, turn to **432**. If you surrender, turn to **218**.

97

You climb down a narrow track to the beach. The sea pounds the rocky shore, and the spray lashes your face. A mournful, yet utterly captivating singing suddenly fills your ears. You look out to sea, and spot several mermaids and mermen, cavorting in the surf.

'Come, come to us...' one of them calls in a lilting voice that fills you with a yearning desire to plunge into the sea and swim out to them.

Make a SANCTITY roll at Difficulty 10.

Successful SANCTITY roll	turn to **584**
Failed SANCTITY roll	turn to **159**

98

The soldier recognizes you and bows.

'My lord,' he says, 'We are a small group now, left here to act as raiders behind enemy lines. Thanks to your heroic actions, the Citadel of Velis Corin is now ours – the king has moved his court there. Go to the citadel if you would speak with the king.'

There is nothing else of interest in the mountains, so you return to the foothills. Turn to **474**.

99

You are on the east bank of the River Grimm, a great, powerful river, which rushes past towards the sea. You can travel to Golnir from here.

Cross the bridge to Conflass	*Cities of Gold and Glory* **168**
Ford the river to the south	*Cities of Gold and Glory* **306**
Follow the river north	turn to **333**
Head for the Curstmoor	turn to **175**
Head towards Devil's Peak	turn to **560**
Go south to the mouth of the river	turn to **579**
Go to Marlock City	turn to **100**

100

Marlock City is a huge sprawling metropolis, enclosed in a fortified wall said to have been built one thousand years ago by the ancient Shadar empire. It is the capital city of Sokara. Marlock City was once known as Sokar, until General Grieve Marlock led the army in bloody revolt against the old king, Corin VII, and had him executed. The

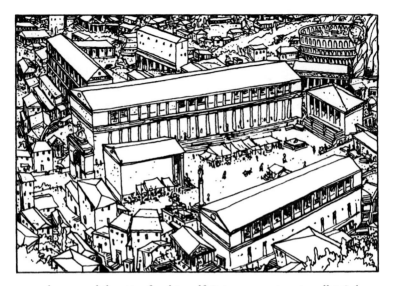

general renamed the city after himself. It is now a crime to call it Sokar.

The general lives in the old king's palace, and calls himself the Protector-General of all Sokara. Whereas the old king was corrupt, the general rules with a fist of iron. Some people like the new regime; others are royalists, still loyal to Nergan, the heir to the throne, who has gone into hiding somewhere.

Outside the city gates hang the bodies of many dead people. Labels around their necks read: 'Rebels, executed by the state for the good of the people'.

'You'd best behave yourself if you don't want to end up like one of them,' grates a guardsman, nodding toward the swinging corpses, as you pass through the great eagle-headed gates of Marlock City.

You can buy a town house in Marlock City for 200 Shards. Owning a house gives you a place to rest, and to store equipment. If you buy one, cross off 200 Shards and tick the box next to the town house option.

To leave Marlock City by sea, or to buy or sell ships and cargo, go to the harbourmaster.

Visit the Three Rings Tavern	turn to **158**
Visit the temple of Alvir and Valmir	turn to **154**
Visit the temple of Nagil	turn to **71**
Visit the temple of Sig	turn to **235**

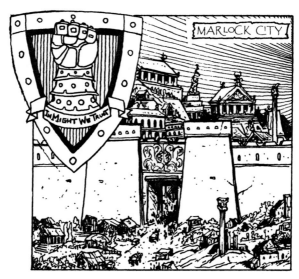

Visit the temple of Elnir	turn to **568**
Visit the market	turn to **396**
Visit the harbourmaster	turn to **142**
Go to the merchants' guild	turn to **571**
Explore the city	turn to **138**
Visit your town house ☐ (if box ticked)	turn to **434**
Visit the House of Priests	turn to **535**
Visit the general's palace	turn to **601**
Travel east towards Trefoille	turn to **377**
Head south-east towards the Shadar Tor	turn to **166**
Follow the River Grimm north	turn to **99**
Journey north into the Curstmoor	turn to **175**
Head west to the River Grimm delta	turn to **579**

101

You yell the name of their god again and again. The cultists clap their hands over their ears, hopping about in horror.

'Aargh!' howls the leader. 'Stop your blaspheming, you heathen devil!'

In their confusion, you make it to your equipment. Now you can fight your way out. Make a COMBAT roll at Difficulty 13. If you fail, turn to **204**. If you succeed, you manage to fight your way to freedom with the loss of 4 Stamina points and head back to town, turn to **10.**

102

If you have the codeword *Defend*, turn to **655** immediately. If not, read on.

`What are you doing back here,' asks Grieve Marlock, angrily. `You should be defending the citadel! You know, that castle in the Pass of Eagles, up north! Get back there and talk to Orin Telana!'

If you have a **coded missive**, turn to **677**. Otherwise, you are shown out in short order. Turn to **100.**

103

You set sail for Copper Island. The uneventful journey takes only a few days. The captain cannot believe how smooth the voyage has been. You disembark at the harbour of Copper Island. Turn to paragraph **99** in *Over the Blood-Dark Sea*.

104

Lose the codewords *Almanac*, *Brush* and *Eldritch* if you have them. You can invest money in multiples of 100 Shards. The guild will buy and sell commodities on your behalf using this money until you return to collect it.

`Don't forget that you can lose money as well,' mutters a sullen merchant who leaves the guild penniless.

Write the sum you are investing in the box here – or withdraw a sum invested previously. Then turn back to **571.**

MONEY INVESTED

105

You will have to fight it.

Scorpion Shaman, COMBAT 5, Defence 8, Stamina 9

If you win, turn to **532**. If you lose, your adventures are over unless you have a resurrection deal.

106

Cross off the money. The young man smiles ingratiatingly, and hands you the pearls. Make a MAGIC roll at a Difficulty of 10.

Successful MAGIC roll	turn to **306**
Failed MAGIC roll	turn to **489**

107

If you are an initiate it costs only 10 Shards to purchase Tyrnai's blessing. A non-initiate must pay 25 Shards. Cross off the money and mark `COMBAT' in the Blessings box on your Adventure Sheet.

The blessing works by allowing you to try again when fail a COMBAT roll. It is good for only one reroll. When you use the blessing, cross it off your Adventure Sheet. You can only have one COMBAT blessing at any one time. Once it is used up, you can return to any branch of the temple of Tyrnai to buy a new one.

When you are finished, turn to **282**.

108

That night, your sleep is restless. You dream a most vivid dream. You are attacked by a gigantic sea monster, a mighty octopoid thing that encircles the ship with tree-like tentacles and pulls it under the waves. You sink into the bottle-green depths until you are caught in a glowing golden net.

You wake in an undersea palace of multi-coloured coral, with mermaids to attend you. They lead you past trident-armed merman guards into a great hall. Seated upon two giant shells, like thrones, are the king and queen of the deep, with green hair, sea-grey eyes, and crowns of pale gold. Shoals of iridescent angel fish dart about in an intricate flashing dance of colour, dancing for the rulers of the land beneath the waves. In awe, you bow before them.

The queen indicates that you should entertain them, for they are bored! A silver flute appears in your hands. Make a CHARISMA roll at Difficulty 11.

Successful CHARISMA roll   turn to **132**

Failed CHARISMA roll   turn to **457**

109

You are about to leave when you see a crowd gathered around a slim, pasty-faced scholar at a card table.

'By the Three Fortunes, but I'm hot tonight!' he cries. It seems he is on a winning streak. You notice a couple of dodgy-looking ruffians watching the scholar carefully.

Wait and follow the scholar   turn to **540**
Return to the city centre   turn to **100**

110

You are walking through the Bronze Hills. Virtually the whole area has been given over to mining. Everywhere, quarries and mine shafts abound. It is a horrible expanse of torn-up earth – hardly any areas of green are left. Great heaps of excavated rock, leeched of their useful minerals, mar the landscape. You find a quarry that is open to the public. That is to say, if you pay 50 Shards, you can dig for an hour in a silver mine.

Pay 50 Shards and mine for silver   turn to **668**
Go to Caran Baru   turn to **400**
South into the Forest of Larun   turn to **47**
West to the River Grimm   turn to **333**
North west into the Western Wilderness   turn to **276**

111

Your knowledge of the arcane arts is too limited to help you here.
Fight your way to the **golden net**   turn to **121**
Swim back to Shadar Tor   turn to **35**

112

The merchants' guild is comparatively small here. Most of its work involves financial services for the army. Here you can bank your money for safe-keeping, but there are no facilities for investment. You can deposit or withdraw money – note that you are in Caran Baru and turn to **605** – or return to the town centre, turn to **400**.

113

If you have the codeword *Armour*, turn to **550** immediately. If not, but you are a Rogue, turn to **75**. Otherwise, the high priest has little to say; your audience is cut short. Turn to **235**.

114

You are known as the priest who outwitted the storm demons to save Sul Veneris. You are shown in to see the chief administrator, who welcomes you freely. He can heal you of all lost Stamina points, and cure you of a disease or of poison free of charge. He cannot, however, lift a curse. 'Whenever you need help, come to me!' he says.

When you are ready, turn to **100**.

115

If you are on a quest for the temple of Nagil, to bring it the head of the escaped ghoul, turn to **446**. If you do not want to look for the ghoul yet, or have already done so, turn to **226**.

116 □

If there is a tick in the box, turn to **322** immediately. Otherwise, put a tick in it now and then read on.

You realize the creature is one of the legendary repulsive ones. It is swimming past you, intent on its own business, so you follow it, in the hope it will lead you to the sunken city of Ziusudra. Turn to **547**.

117

There are several people with eyepatches but none with a velvet one. You ask around among the taverns and bars of the rougher areas in Caran Baru. Make a CHARISMA roll at Difficulty 11.

Successful CHARISMA roll   turn to **149**
Failed CHARISMA roll   turn to **468**

118

The overseer of the mines is a fat, cruel-looking man. He welcomes you with a promise, 'In one month, you'll be dead, slave.'

You spend the next few weeks in chains, working 15 hours a day, deep underground, digging at a rock face in the tunnels of the mines in the Bronze Hills. You are fed on gruel and black bread. You realize you will not live long down here and that you must escape if you are to survive.

If you have the codeword *Ashen*, turn to **351**. Otherwise, turn to **565**.

119

Gain the codeword *Ashen*.

You hear shouts from outside, muffled by the swirling sulphurous fog.

A stab of icy panic pulses at your heart, and an instant later the door bursts open. Three militiamen armed with maces burst through the doorway. Behind them, a tall cadaverous gentleman wrapped in a cape is stamping in fury.

`A thief in my house!' he rages. `Do your duty!'

You realize the truth: Lauria has used you as a decoy to cover her escape. You'll get even later – if you survive.

The militiamen race forward to seize you. Make a COMBAT roll at a Difficulty of 12.

Successful COMBAT roll	turn to **588**
Failed COMBAT roll	turn to **96**

120

Your ship is sailing in the coastal waters off the Shadar Tor. You can just see the tor, a jumbled mass of rocks, sitting on the clifftops as it has done for a thousand years. Roll two dice:

Score 2-4	Storm	turn to **324**
Score 5-9	An uneventful voyage	turn to **559**
Score 10-12	A merchant ship	turn to **207**

121

You wait outside, hoping to take the repulsive ones singly as they emerge. You will have to fight three of them, but you may do so one at a time.

First Repulsive One, COMBAT 4 Defence 6 Stamina 10

Second Repulsive One, COMBAT 3, Defence 5, Stamina 10

Third Repulsive One, COMBAT 4, Defence 6, Stamina 10

Subtract 1 from your dice rolls for every fight because you are unused to underwater combat.

If you beat all three, turn to **213**. If you lose, your adventuring days are over, unless you have a resurrection deal.

122

If you have the codeword *Acid*, turn to **543** immediately. If not, but you have a **copper amulet**, turn to **384** immediately. Otherwise, read on.

Guildmaster Vernon of Yellowport is surprisingly eager to see you. He is a hugely fat and bejewelled merchant, and he tells you that a group of ratmen have made a base in the sewers beneath the city. They come out at night to raid the warehouses and homes of the merchants of Yellowport.

'We need an adventurer like yourself to destroy their king,' explains the guildmaster. 'Without him, the ratmen wouldn't be able to organize a feast in a larder. We will pay you 450 Shards if you succeed.'

Vernon tells you that the sewers can be entered via an old disused well in the poor quarter.

Whenever you are ready to enter the sewers, and you are in Yellowport, turn to **460**. Note this option on your Adventure Sheet. Now you can return to the city centre (turn to **10**) or go down the sewers straight away.

123

This is the east bank of the River Grimm, near its source in the Spine of Harkun, far to the north.

You reach a ford where you can travel to the west bank for 1 Shard. You could try swimming across instead, but the current is strong: you need to succeed at a SCOUTING roll at a Difficulty of 10 to do so.

Swim or pay to cross	*Cities of Gold and Glory* **53**
Failed attempt to swim	*Cities of Gold and Glory* **76**
East to the wilderness	turn to **276**
North to the mountains	turn to **3**
Follow the riverbank south	turn to **333**

124

Heavy black clouds race towards you across the sky, whipping the waves into a frenzy. The crew mutter among themselves fearfully. If you have the blessing of Alvir and Valmir, which confers Safety from Storms, you can ignore the storm: cross off your blessing and turn to **420**.

Otherwise the storm hits with full fury. Roll one die if your ship is a barque, two dice if it is a brigantine, or three dice if a galleon. Add 1 to the roll if you have a good crew; add 2 if you have an excellent crew.

Score 1-3	Ship sinks	turn to **346**
Score 4-5	The mast splits	turn to **583**
Score 6-20	You weather the storm	turn to **420**

125

You mumble a prayer to the gods, but you're not sure if you got the ritual right.

The beggar thanks you and babbles, `Yes, yes, a new doublet for an old beggar. I shall wear it with pride!' He wanders off, stopping passersby to show off what he thinks are his new clothes. Poor old fool.

You return to the city centre. Turn to **10**.

126

If you have the codeword *Aloft*, turn to **199** immediately. If not, read on.

You come across a strange sight. A man lies staked out on the ground, asleep. Blue energy crackles up and down his body, and a hefty-looking hammer, glowing red, is still attached to his belt. It is Sul Veneris, the one you have come to free.

As you are about to lift out the stakes, a whistling, keening blast of ferocious wind engulfs you. You are surrounded by whirling storm demons – vaguely man-shaped creatures of thunderous energy which try to sweep you into the air and off the edge of the peak.

You try to recite the rituals of dismissal associated with such demons. Make a SANCTITY roll at Difficulty 12.

Successful SANCTITY roll	turn to **421**
Failed SANCTITY roll	turn to **210**

127

Make a THIEVERY roll at Difficulty 9.

Successful THIEVERY roll	turn to **269**
Failed THIEVERY roll	turn to **183**

128

You make your way around the coast. The interior of the island appears to be heavily forested. After a while, however, you come to a bay in which a couple of ships are anchored. A small settlement nestles on the beach, and you make your way towards it. Turn to **195**.

129

`Pssst, come here, friend!' someone whispers from the shadows.

Go over to him	turn to **641**
Ignore him and leave	turn to **100**

130

You are greeted by several of the knights.

`We'll not fight you anymore,' says the Blue Dragon Knight.

`We keep losing,' says the Green Dragon Knight.

`And it's costing us a fortune in armour, not to say a lot of bruises!' says the Red Dragon Knight.

You are turned away, unless you have the SCOUTING *Axe*, in which case turn to **521**. Otherwise, turn to **276**.

131

On the island is a community of sea gypsies. They hail you, but then they seem to recognize you. Rapid activity takes place, and within seconds a huge sail has been raised, and the island scuds away. It seems they would rather not meet you a second time. Turn to **85**.

132

You play the flute like never before. The king and queen are entranced by the haunting melodies you are able to coax from the enchanted flute. Unfortunately, you have played too well. The king puts you under a spell, so that you find you cannot stop. Make a SANCTITY roll at Difficulty 11.

| Successful SANCTITY roll | turn to **413** |
| Failed SANCTITY roll | turn to **307** |

133

You are forced back by the flames. Some townsfolk, covered in wet blankets, manage to get the woman out. They are treated like heroes – you are forgotten. Such is life. Turn to **100**.

134

`The high priest is out of town,' a clerk tells you.

`Yeah, until the heat dies down!' quips a passing member of the temple. The clerk glares at her angrily.

Turn to **235**.

135

The shores of the Lake of the Sea Dragon are swept by ochre waves, and the air smells foul. A sickly, pale green seaweed is the only vegetation that can survive in the sulphurous waters of the lake. A small fishing village, Cadmium, has grown up on the shores of the lake.

Talk to a fisherman	turn to **382**
Visit the local market	turn to **292**
Hire a boat and go fishing	turn to **203**
Go north to the Coldbleak Mountains	turn to **474**
North east into the farmlands	turn to **548**
South east into open countryside	turn to **278**
South, following the Stinking River	turn to **576**
West along the road	turn to **387**

136

The Sea of Whispers. The sea is uncannily quiet and flat as a pane of glass under a grey-blue sky. At night, however, the waters seem to come alive with an eerie whispering. One of your crew tells you that the sounds you heard at night are the sea centaurs speaking to one another across the waves. Roll two dice:

Score 2-4	Storm	turn to **639**
Score 5-7	An uneventful voyage	turn to **507**
Score 8-10	An unusual catch	turn to **337**
Score 11-12	A strange dream	turn to **108**

137

The merchantman appears to be from Golnir. It keeps well away from you, no doubt fearing piracy. Turn to **559**.

138

If you have the codeword *Ague*, turn to **115**. If not, read on. You take a stroll through the streets. Marlock City is teeming with people.

Explore the Barracks area	turn to **15**
Visit the Street of Entertainers	turn to **129**
Enter the residential quarter	turn to **619**

139

You are spotted by a spear-armed guard. It gives an ululating cry of alarm, and many others swarm out of the mound.

You have little choice but to run – with a pack of deadly killers close behind. Desperately, you try to lose them in the night.

Roll a die, and subtract one from the score. If the result is less than or equal to your Rank, turn to **295**. Otherwise, turn to **663**.

140

The ship drops you at Yellowport docks. You make your way to the city centre. Turn to **10**.

141

The Temple of Maka, the terrible goddess of disease and famine, is a large underground chamber accessible via an ornate entrance in the middle of the Plaza of the Gods, where all the temples stand in Yellowport.

Down below, the walls are bare earth; the ceiling is covered in the roots of growing plants, for Maka is also the goddess of the harvest, who must be kept happy else disease and famine will strike the people, their crops and their livestock, bringing ruin to all.

Become an initiate	turn to **368**
Renounce her worship	turn to **261**
Seek a blessing	turn to **481**
Ask to be cured of disease or poison	turn to **77**
Leave the temple	turn to **10**

142

All shipping in and out of Marlock City must come through the offices of the harbourmaster. Here you can buy passage to far lands, or even a ship of your own, to fill with cargo and crew.

You can buy a one-way passage on a ship to the following destinations:

Yellowport, cost 10 Shards	turn to **372**
Wishport, cost 15 Shards	turn to **455**
Sorcerers' Isle, cost 30 Shards	turn to **234**
Copper Island, cost 30 Shards	turn to **424**

If you buy a ship, you are the captain, and can take it wherever you wish, exploring or trading. You also get to name it. There are three types of ship, and four quality levels of crew. You can also buy cargo for your ship to sell in other ports.

Ship type	Cost	Capacity
Barque	250 Shards	1 Cargo Unit
Brigantine	450 Shards	2 Cargo Units
Galleon	900 Shards	3 Cargo Units

If you buy a ship, add it to the Ship's Manifest, and name it as you wish. The quality of the ship's crew is average unless you pay to upgrade it. If you already own a ship, you can sell it to the harbourmaster at half the above prices.

It costs 50 Shards to upgrade a poor crew to average, 100 Shards to upgrade an average crew to good, and 150 Shards to upgrade a good crew to excellent.

Cargo can be bought at Marlock City and sold at other ports for profit. If you own a ship you may buy as many Cargo Units as it has room for. You may also sell cargo, if you have any. Prices quoted here are for entire Cargo Units.

Cargo	To buy	To sell
Furs	190 Shards	180 Shards
Grain	190 Shards	180 Shards
Metals	700 Shards	635 Shards
Minerals	500 Shards	460 Shards
Spices	820 Shards	760 Shards
Textiles	325 Shards	285 Shards
Timber	190 Shards	180 Shards

Fill in your current cargo on the Ship's Manifest – assuming you own a ship.

If you own a ship and wish to set sail, turn to **84**. If not, you can go to the city centre. Turn to **100**.

143

To renounce the worship of Elnir, you must pay 40 Shards to the priesthood by way of compensation. A passing noble says disdainfully, 'Ha! Only those born to rule have the fibre to worship the Sky Lord. Those who renounce Elnir never reach the top!'

Do you want to change your mind? If you are determined to re-nounce your faith, pay the 40 Shards and delete Elnir from the God box on your Adventure Sheet.

When you have finished here, turn to **316**.

144

You call on the divine powers of the gods, to banish this foul, blasphe-mous travesty of life. The Ghoul shrinks back for a moment, snarling. Make a SANCTITY roll at Difficulty 10.

Successful SANCTITY roll	turn to **223**
Failed SANCTITY roll	turn to **289**

MARLOCK HARBOUR

145

King Skabb gives a cry of anger, and leaps at you in desperation, swinging a spiked mace in his hand. You must fight him, adding 3 if you have some **rat poison** to put on your weapon. If you use the poison, cross it off your Adventure Sheet.

King Skabb, COMBAT 5, Defence 7, Stamina 10

If you lose, your adventuring career will be over, unless you have a resurrection deal. If you win, turn to **554**.

146

He seems to see something he approves of because he says, 'Perhaps. But first you must prove yourself. There is a knight, a man of great evil. He is known as the Black Dragon Knight. Defeat him in battle and I will teach you. Bring me his **black dragon shield** as proof of your valour.' With that, he turns and walks away.

'But how will I find him? And then how will I find you?' you cry.

'Would you have me kill him for you as well?' he asks over his shoulder. 'As for the second, ask for me in the Blue Griffon Tavern in Caran Baru. My name is Yanryt the Son.'

Gain the codeword *Axe* and turn to **412**.

147

An old troubadour tells an epic tale of adventure and romance involving three heroes, a princess and a dragon. Afterwards, you find yourself talking to him at the bar. He tells you about the time he was captured by the Manbeasts of Nerech, and that by soothing their savage ferocity with music, he was able to escape.

If you are a Troubadour, turn to **469**. Otherwise, turn to **100**.

148

'Stop, stop, I surrender!' yells the tree. You cease your attack. 'I guess you can pass, in view of recent events!' it says grudgingly. Then it uproots itself with a great tearing sound, and shuffles out of the way. 'There you go!' mutters the tree, 'You can blooming well pass.'

You walk through the thorn bush gate. Beyond, you find several huge oaks trees whose branches are so big that they are able to support the homes of many people. Get the codeword *Apple* and turn to **358**.

149

A man accosts you as you are leaving a tavern. His breath reeks of rotting teeth, and his ear has been cut off – the mark of a man punished for piracy.

'Give me 10 Shards and I will tell you what you want to know,' he says.

Pay the money (cross off 10 Shards)	turn to **533**
Refuse to pay	turn to **468**

150

Cross off the 10 Shards. You get a berth on a merchantmen headed for Marlock City. It is a trouble-free journey.

'I pay everyone off – the Sokarans, the pirates,' says the captain. 'That way I get left alone.'

You disembark in Marlock City. Turn to **100**.

151

Inside the cave, you find Damor the Hermit, floating crosslegged in the air. 'I told you never to come back!' he shouts angrily. He waves his hand, and you are teleported back down to the bottom of the mountain before you can say a word. Turn to **244**.

152

If you have the codeword *Attar*, turn to **623** immediately.

You clamber down a ladder into a long low hall, the Venefax Market. A sign reads, 'Closed on Thursday'. Fortunately, it's not Thursday, and a stocky, barrel-chested man with piggy eyes introduces himself as Fourze, the Master of the Market.

There is not much you can buy or sell in this provincial market. Items with no purchase price listed are not available locally.

Armour	To buy	To sell
Leather (Defence +1)	50 Shards	45 Shards
Ring mail (Defence +2)	–	90 Shards

Weapons (sword, axe, etc)	To buy	To sell
Without COMBAT bonus	50 Shards	40 Shards
COMBAT bonus +1	–	200 Shards

Other items	To buy	To sell
Rope	50 Shards	45 Shards
Lantern	100 Shards	90 Shards
Climbing gear	100 Shards	90 Shards
Scorpion antidote	100 Shards	90 Shards

When you are finished, turn back to **427**.

153

You and your men are forced to surrender. The Sokarans take all your money and cargo, if you have any.

'Count yourself lucky I haven't decided to call you rebels and sell the lot of you into slavery!' says the captain.

They depart, leaving you and your crew with the bitter taste of defeat. Disconsolately, you sail on. Turn to **439**.

154

The temple of Alvir and Valmir, Divine Rulers of the House of the Sea, is right on the teeming harbour of Marlock City. Its sea-green marbled porticos are draped in a hundred silver nets. Brother and sister, Alvir and Valmir rule below the waves. Alvir brings the souls of the drowned in his nets before his sister, Valmir, for judgment.

A swaggering ship's captain emerges from the temple, saying to you in passing, 'Never, I mean never go to sea without paying your respects to the twin gods – unless ye want to sail through a world of storms!'

Become an initiate	turn to **343**
Renounce their worship	turn to **68**
Seek a blessing	turn to **275**
Leave the temple	turn to **100**

155

One of the Trading Post sailors rows you out to your ship anchored in the bay. 'Welcome aboard, Cap'n,' says the mate. The sky is clear and the smell of the sea fills your heart with wanderlust.

Set sail into the Sea of Whispers	turn to **136**
Return to the Trading Post	turn to **195**

156

The priest looks you over. `I'm afraid we have no one skilled enough to cure you. However, I believe the temple of Maka in Yellowport might be able to help. And the holy waters at Blessed Springs are known to be efficacious in this kind of case.'

Turn to **100**.

157

You try to prove your loyalty to the new regime, but they don't believe a word of it. They beat you into unconsciousness, and leave you lying in the gutter. They rob you of all the money you had, but leave your possessions untouched. You come round with only 3 Stamina points. Turn to **10**.

158

The Three Rings Tavern is a comfortable inn near the city centre. The tavern costs you 1 Shard a day. Each day you spend here, you can recover 1 Stamina point if injured, up to the limit of your normal unwounded Stamina score.

Pay 3 more Shards and buy some drinks	turn to **147**
Leave the tavern	turn to **100**

159

Your mind falls into a waking dream, and you walk lazily into the waters. The mer-folk, laughing and singing, take you down to their undersea home of living coral, where they stop you from drowning with their faery magic. They keep you for several weeks, until you are no longer an amusement to them.

You wake up, as if from a long sleep, with only a shadowy memory of your ordeal, to find yourself washed up in the harbour of Yellowport. You have lost all the possessions you were carrying (erase them from your Adventure Sheet) but you still have your money.

Turn to **10**.

If there is a tick in the box, turn to **461** immediately. If not, put a tick there now, and read on.

You learned the password 'Rebirth' in the library of Dweomer.

'My, aren't we the wise one,' carps the door sarcastically. 'Still, a job's a job, eh?' it mutters.

The door lifts straight up, and you step into the shadows of the Tomb of the Wizard King. It is lit by still-burning torches that give off an eerie eldritch glow. In the middle of the large round chamber, a sarcophagus lies, surrounded by a pentacle drawn in blood. You notice the blood still seems fresh!

Make a MAGIC roll at Difficulty 10.

Successful MAGIC roll	turn to **674**
Failed MAGIC roll	turn to **309**

161

The governor is a seasoned veteran of many battles, a hardy man. He is quick to react, and calls his guards before you can kill him. You are subdued by sheer numbers.

'Take this dirty rebel assassin to the dungeons!' sneers Marloes Marlock.

The guards take all your money and possessions. Cross them off and turn to **454**.

162

With the golems out of the way, you can get on with business. You reach forward to strip the armour off the idol of Tyrnai. Make a THIEVERY roll at Difficulty 12.

Successful THIEVERY roll	turn to **509**
Failed THIEVERY roll	turn to **228**

163

You hold up the **pirate captain's head**. The guildmaster looks up expectantly, but his face quickly darkens.

'This is not Amcha!! Everyone knows he has only one eye. This poor fellow is probably some beggar you killed in an alley somewhere. You think you can swindle the guild with this pathetic ruse! Out! Get out! And don't come back until you bring me the head of Amcha One-eye!'

The guildmaster has you removed by his guards, and you are dumped into the street. Turn to **100**.

164

The dank tunnels, running with rivulets of foul water, take you deeper into the unknown. You mark the twisting passages with chalk so that you can find your way back.

Shortly, you come out into a large, rough-hewn cavern, wreathed in shadows that dance and flicker in the light you have brought.

A sound makes you start in surprise. Make either a SCOUTING or a THIEVERY roll (your choice) against Difficulty 11.

Successful SCOUTING/THIEVERY roll	turn to **247**
Failed SCOUTING/THIEVERY roll	turn to **42**

165

A Sokaran war galley hails you and draws up alongside. 'We're coming aboard for an inspection!' yells the captain of the galley. His men attempt to grapple your ship.

Let them	turn to **552**
Try to escape	turn to **444**

166

You are on the road between Marlock City and the Shadar Tor. Along most of the length of the road, a thin sliver of a shanty town has grown up. Tents and lean-tos line the way. You find out that the people living here are refugees from Trefoille. The city was burnt to the ground during the recent civil war, in which the old king was overthrown. Roll a die:

Score 1 or 2   A pick-pocket! You lose 10 Shards

Score 3 or 4   Nothing happens

Score 5 or 6   You find a **lantern** by the side of the road

When you are finished, you can:

Go to Marlock City	turn to **100**
Head for the Shadar Tor	turn to **35**

167

You lose your pursuers in the treacherous rocky passes of the mountains. Eventually, you reach the safety of the foothills.

Turn to **474**.

168

As you stretch out your hand, you loose your footing, and plummet to the ground, right between the two golems! They turn their heads with a grating rumble, and open their mouths to speak. The sound that comes out is a bell-like gonging that alerts the temple. You pick yourself up and fall back on the last resort of the rogue – running for your life! Warrior priests swarm out of the temple in pursuit.

Roll one die, and subtract one from the total.

If the result is less than or equal to your Rank, turn to **395**, otherwise turn to **551**.

If there is a tick in the box, turn to **443** immediately. If not, put a tick there now, and read on.

You see a couple of Sokaran warships, pursuing two other ships. Your first mate says, 'See the Red Pennants on them thar ships? They be pirates, running from the Sokarans!'

The warships catch up and a bitter battle ensues. You can intervene if you wish.

Help the Sokarans	turn to **286**
Help the pirates	turn to **394**
Ignore the battle	turn to **443**

170

Becoming an initiate of Lacuna gives you the benefit of paying less for blessings and other services the temple can offer. It costs 60 Shards to become an initiate. You cannot do this if you are already an initiate of another temple. If you choose to become an initiate, write 'Lacuna' in the God box on your Adventure Sheet – and remember to cross off the 60 Shards. Once you have finished here, turn to **615**.

171

You have soon laid the figures out like three logs on the village green. They are badly hurt, but still alive. Now that you can get a better look at them, you see that they are dusted all over with flour, giving them a spectral appearance.

You summon the other villagers. At first they are loath to venture out and inspect the three strangers, but the fact that you survived convinces them there are no ghosts to worry about.

'Why, it's Old Megan!' cries a man as he claps eyes on one of the three. 'And here's Bradok the miller, and Lame Pootmar! Why are they all covered in flour? Where're the ghosts?'

You shake your head and sigh at the stupidity of yokels. 'There weren't any ghosts,' you explain. 'It was these three all along.'

Turn to **671**.

172

'Thank you, thank you,' coughs the scholar. He gives you a **vial of yellow dust** as a reward. Note it on your Adventure Sheet.

'I found this at an ancient archaeological site I have been studying,' he says. 'I believe it needs to be thrown into the holy waters at the village of Blessed Springs, although quite what happens then, I have no idea.'

He thanks you again and takes his leave. Turn to **100**.

173

You find yourself washed up on a rocky shore, battered and cold, but lucky to be alive. You haul yourself up the beach on to land. Fortunately for you, you find the village of Blessed Springs. Turn to **510**.

174

You advance, weapon at the ready. As you draw closer, something rushes out of the cave with a shrieking cry. It is the gorlock, a beast with legs like a bird, a body like a reptile, with two short forelimbs and a beaked, lizard-like head. Its two legs do indeed have backward-pointing feet. You'll have to fight.

Gorlock, COMBAT 4, Defence 6, Stamina 7

If you win, turn to **315**. If you lose, your bones will join the others at the entrance of the cave.

175 ☐

If there is a tick in the box, turn to **673** immediately. If not, put a tick there now, and read on. You are trekking across the aptly named Curstmoor. A great rolling expanse of blasted heath stretches before you. Grey clouds hang over a mournful, dirty-water coloured plain, studded with rocky outcrops and low hills. A raven flutters to the ground nearby, eyeing you curiously. His brothers caw loudly into the echoing sky. Dusk falls, and in the dim twilight, a herd of horses comes streaking out of the night, straight at you. As they near, it seems to you that their hooves are not touching the ground, and from their manes trail wispy clouds of sparks, like tiny stars.

Get out of their way   turn to **390**

Mount one of them   turn to **66**

176

The crew are very nervous about your orders. They drop anchor in a bay, and will row you to shore, but they absolutely refuse to come with you. In fact, they won't even wait for you to come back.

If you insist on going ashore, your crew will sail for Yellowport and meet you there. 'If you ever make it back,' adds the first mate ominously.

If you want to go ashore, note on your Adventure Sheet that your ship is now docked in Yellowport, and turn to **32**. Otherwise, turn to **85** and choose again.

177

You can leave possessions and money here to save having to carry them around with you. You can also rest here safely, and recover any Stamina points you have lost. Record in the box anything you wish to leave. Each time you return, roll two dice:

```
ITEMS AT TOWNHOUSE
```

Score 2-9	Your possessions are safe
Score 10-11	A break-in. Any money left here has gone
Score 12	Raiding nomads take all your possessions

Turn to **400**.

178

A pale woman in black leather brushes past you in the street, casting you an enigmatic look. Make a THIEVERY roll at a Difficulty of 10.

Successful THIEVERY roll	turn to **635**
Failed THIEVERY roll	turn to **198**

179

You claim that you have come to swear allegiance to Nergan, the rightful king of Sokara. Captain Vorkung is not convinced. He narrows his eyes suspiciously.

'You'd better leave – now. Before I decide you are a spy, and have you shot!'

One of the archers looses a shaft, and an arrow thuds into the ground at your feet, quivering menacingly.

You realize it is time to leave, and climb down the mountain. Turn to **474**.

180

You step through the archway. Immediately the symbols on the stone begin to glow with red-hot energy; your hair stands on end and your body tingles. A crackling nimbus of blue-white force engulfs you, the sky darkens and rumbles, thunder and lightning crash and leap across the heavens.

Suddenly, your vision fades, and, momentarily, everything goes black.

When your sight returns, you find yourself outside the gates of a huge, fortified city. A guard starts in surprise at the sight of you. Then he shakes his head as if to clear it, sure he must have imagined what he just saw!

The gates open, and a troop of heavy cavalry canter past.

'Make way for the Marlock City militia!' says the guard.

When they have passed, you walk into the city. Turn to **100**.

181

The Green Man Inn costs you 1 Shard a day. Each day you spend here, you can recover 1 Stamina point if injured, up to the limit of your normal unwounded Stamina score.

When you are ready, turn to **195**.

182

Your ship, crew and cargo are lost to the deep, dark sea. Cross them off your Adventure Sheet. Your only thought now is to save yourself. Roll two dice. If the score is greater than your Rank, you are drowned. If the score is less than or equal to your Rank, you manage to find some driftwood, and make it back to shore. Lose Stamina points equal to the score of one die roll and, if you can survive that, turn to **591**.

183

You find a shadowy natural alcove in the rocky wall of a tunnel. Desperately, you squeeze yourself into it, using all your skill to hide in the darkness.

Several ratmen run past, but others sniff you out with their highly developed sense of smell. You are overwhelmed by sheer numbers. Turn to **308**.

184

The Blue Griffon Tavern is frequented by soldiers and mercenaries. The tavern costs you 1 Shard a day. Each day you spend here, you can recover 1 Stamina point if injured, up to the limit of your normal unwounded Stamina score.

If you have the codeword *Axe* or if you have a **black dragon shield**, and want to find Yanryt the Son, turn to **451**.

If not, but you want to spend a further 3 Shards buying drinks all round at the bar, and listen for rumours, turn to **341**. Or you can return to the town centre: turn to **400**.

185

You tell him who you are, and that General Grieve Marlock's brother, the Governor of Yellowport, is your personal friend. His eyes widen as recognition dawns on his fat, greedy face.

`Ah, er… my lord!,' he cries. `I was merely jesting! Umm… We were, I mean to say, perhaps you need an escort?'

`I think we require a levy in order to carry out the important mission the governor has entrusted to me,' you say. `Sixty Shards ought to do it, Captain!'

The Sokaran captain hands over the 60 Shards (add it to your Adventure Sheet) and leads his men off your ship.

You sail on. Turn to **439**.

186

You pass the leash over to the man in the palanquin, who leans out and hands you 75 Shards. You leave the slave market.

Turn to **400**.

187

You tell the high priest that you wish to renounce the worship of Nagil. He brings out a small wax dummy, and carves your name into it. Then he sets fire to it. The wax melts into a puddle on the floor and the priest steps into it, leaving the imprint of his foot.

`Such is the fate of those who would deny Nagil, the Lord of Death,' he says.

When you ask if you must pay compensation to the temple, he shakes his head, saying, `It is you who loses, not we.'

Do you want to reconsider? If you are determined to renounce your faith, delete Nagil from the God box on your Adventure Sheet. You must lose any outstanding resurrection arrangements. When you have finished here, turn to **100**.

188

You are thrown into a stinking prison cell.

`Well, well, we meet again, my old friend,' says a half-dead old man with white hair.

You recognize the poor old man whom you met the last time you were thrown into the dungeons! He launches into the same old story about the gorlock, the creature with the backward-pointing feet. By the end of it, you are looking forward to being sold into slavery and sent to work in the tin mines of Caran Baru. Turn to **118**.

189

There is nothing in your limited knowledge of undersea wildlife to help you.

Swim back to the Shadar Tor	turn to **35**
Fight your way to the **golden net**	turn to **121**
Try magic	turn to **592**

190

You are sailing along the coast off Blessed Springs and Fort Brilon. Gulls cluster around the ship, looking for food. Their cries echo across the vasty seas. Roll two dice:

Score 2-4	Storm	turn to **38**
Score 5-9	An uneventful voyage	turn to **209**
Score 10-12	A shipwreck	turn to **504**

191

The provost marshal is a rich and powerful man, cunning and capable.

`I have need of someone like you,' he says. `A group of rebels, loyal to the old king, are hiding out in the Coldbleak Mountains. Their leader, Nergan Corin, is dangerous to us, as he is the heir to the old throne and a rallying point for the rebels. Penetrate their stronghold and slay

Nergan Corin, and you will be richly rewarded. I can promise you 500 Shards and a title if you succeed.'

If you take the mission, gain the codeword *Artery*.

If you have the codeword *Ambuscade*, turn to **375**. Otherwise, the provost marshal dismisses you. Turn to **10**.

192

During your short trip upward, the old man regales you with tales of your destiny and fate, continuously arguing with himself as he does so.

You reach a hill crowned with a circle of large obsidian standing stones.Despite the bitter wind that blows across these hills the stones are unweathered and seem almost newly lain.

'Here are the Gates of the World.' says the mad old man.

The stones are laid in such a way that they form three archways, each carven with mystic symbols and runes of power.

'Each gate will take you to a part of the world of Harkuna, though I know not to where,' explains the old man. Abruptly, he turns around and sets off down the hill, babbling to himself. His voice fades as he descends the hill, leaving you alone with the brooding stones and the howling wind.

Turn to **65**.

193

You find yourself washed up on a rocky shore, battered and cold, but lucky to be alive. You head inland until you come to a road. Turn to **621**.

194

You know what the strange swellings on the dead bodies mean. They have been injected with the eggs of the ker'ilk, hideous lobster-like beings of the deep. Soon the eggs will hatch, and the young will feed on the bodies of the sailors. You also know that the adults never stray far from their eggs, and warn your men that the ker'ilk are nearby.

Your warning is timely – several horrific-looking creatures, like giant lobsters, all spines and pincers, surge out of the waters. Your men, however, are ready. A battle ensues – you must fight one of the creatures.

Ker'ilk, COMBAT 4, Defence 9, Stamina 8

If you win, turn to **519**. If you lose, you'll end up as food for ker'ilk young, unless you have a resurrection deal.

195

Gain the codeword *Aspen* if you do not already have it.

The Trading Post is a small village, set up here by enterprising settlers from the mainland. Its main export appears to be furs from the forest.

The Mayor, a fat genial fellow, who greets you personally, insists that one day the Trading Post will be a thriving town. There is not a lot here yet, however: a small market, a quay, the settlers' houses, and a shrine to Lacuna the Huntress, goddess of nature.

Visit the shrine to Lacuna	turn to **544**
Visit the market	turn to **452**
Visit the quayside	turn to **332**
Visit the Green Man Inn	turn to **181**
Climb the hill that overlooks the town	turn to **11**
Go inland, into the forest	turn to **257**

196

If you were wounded by the ghoul you have been infected with a disease (ghoulbite). Note that, until you can find a cure, you must subtract one from your SANCTITY, COMBAT and CHARISMA (no ability score can drop below one). If you were already suffering from ghoulbite, there are no further effects. In any case, you hack off the hideous head and leave. Note you have a **ghoul's head** and turn to **100**.

197

The blessing of Sig costs 10 Shards if you are an initiate, 30 Shards otherwise. If you buy the blessing, cross off the money and mark 'THIEVERY' in the Blessings box on your Adventure Sheet. The blessing works by allowing you to reroll any failed THIEVERY attempt once. When you use the blessing, cross it off your Adventure Sheet. You can then make a second try at the roll. You can have only one blessing for each ability at any one time. Once your THIEVERY blessing is used up, you can return to any branch of the temple of Sig to buy a new one. When you are finished here, turn back to **235**.

198

Musing to yourself about the strange woman, you pause at the end of an alleyway to buy roast chestnuts as you watch her striding off into the evening smog enveloping the city.

'That'll be a Shard,' grunts the chestnut vendor.

You reach for your money pouch. Then your hands fumble in panic. The pouch has gone! After a moment the truth dawns on you. You stare grimly in the direction that the black-garbed woman went, but there is no sign of her now.

'I'll have them chestnuts back then!' growls the vendor when he sees you can't pay. Lose all the money you were carrying and turn to **10**.

199 ☐

If there is a tick in the box, turn to **634** immediately. If not, put a tick there now, and read on. A strange, vaguely humanoid shape, flickering with energy, soars down to attack you. You must fight.

Storm demon, COMBAT 3, Defence 6, Stamina 8

If you win, it fades away, leaving a clear blue jewel, worth 200 Shards. Note the money on your sheet directly.

If you lose, it's the end of you, unless you have a resurrection deal. If you still live, there's nothing else up here, so you climb down again. Turn to **658**.

200

You have acquired an old map of the Forest of the Forsaken in Golnir (in *Cities of Gold and Glory*), showing a safe path that leads to the Tower of Despair. It seems to conflict with the location of the Tower on the regular map of Golnir. Which is correct?

You can turn to **200** in *The War-Torn Kingdom* whenever you wish, providing you own the map, but remember, always note the paragraph you were at before turning here.

Return to the paragraph you came from (if you have only just bought the map, you were in Yellowport market, so return to **30**).

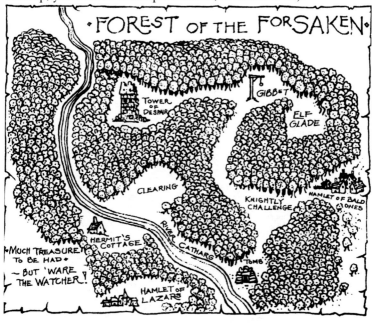

201

The road between the Citadel and Caran Baru is chock-a-block with troops and carts. It looks like there is a war in the north.

Head for the citadel turn to 271

Go south to Caran Baru	turn to **400**
Head west	turn to **276**
Head east	turn to **60**

202

Gingerly, you open the door. It leads to a curtained alcove, through which you observe the room beyond. It is a long, low hall – clearly an ancient Uttakin temple, from a time when the Masked Lords of Uttaku ruled all of Harkuna, but now part of the sewers of Yellowport.

A cheap wooden chair has been placed on the altar to act as a throne. On it sits a large and extremely ugly ratman. He has a tacky amulet around his neck, and a rusty iron hoop for a crown. About four ratmen are kneeling before him, engaged in conversation.

'But, Skabb...' one of the rat men is saying.

'That's Great King Skabb to you, dung-breath!!' bellows the rat on the throne.

Charge in to the attack	turn to **428**
Sneak in to assassinate the king	turn to **595**
Use sorcery to get close to Skabb	turn to **24**
Bluff your way in	turn to **336**

203

You can hire a fishing boat for 15 Shards a day. It comes with a fishing net.

Pay 15 Shards and go fishing	turn to **267**
Don't go fishing	turn to **135**

204

There are simply too many of them, and you are beaten into submission. Your end is grisly indeed – killed, boiled with herbs and garlic, and eaten by the cannibal cultists of Badogor the Unspoken! Your adventures end here – unless you have a resurrection deal.

205

The runes are written in Old Shadar, an ancient language from thousands of years ago. You realize that the runes form a spell that will give you the power to breathe underwater for a few hours.

Use the spell and swim out to sea	turn to **493**
Go down to the beach	turn to **97**
Take the road to Trefoille	turn to **602**
Take the road to Marlock City	turn to **166**

206

The crew absolutely refuses to sail into the Unbounded Ocean. 'There's no land out there, and the seas are infested with Demons of the Deep. If we go too far, we'll fall off the edge of the world!' says the first mate.

You have no choice but to reconsider your destination. Turn back to **507** and choose again.

207 ☐

If there is a tick in the box, turn to **137** immediately. If not, put a tick there now, and read on.

The look-out cries, 'Ship on the starboard bow!'

You spot a crippled merchant ship, limping towards Marlock City. It looks like a trading vessel from the Feathered Lands.

Assist	turn to **293**
Attack	turn to **464**

208

Using your sorcerous powers you breathe a cloud of greenish vapour over the ratmen. Coughing and gasping, they sink into an enchanted slumber – all but King Skabb. Standing on the altar, he is able to keep his head above the vapours. Turn to **145**.

209

You are sailing in the coastal waters off Fort Brilon, and Blessed Springs.

Sail north along the coast of Nerech	turn to **249**
Sail south to Scorpion Bight	turn to **430**
Sail east into the Sea of Whispers	turn to **136**

210

They fall back for a moment, but your invocation fails to take hold, and they close in. You must fight them one at a time.

1st Storm Demon, COMBAT 4, Defence 7, Stamina 8

2nd Storm Demon, COMBAT 4, Defence 7, Stamina 8

3rd Storm Demon, COMBAT 4, Defence 7, Stamina 8

If you win, turn to **54**. If you lose, you are tossed off the top of the peak, and end up as a messy paste on the ground below. That's the end of you, unless you have a resurrection deal.

211

When he emerges, you are waiting for him. Make a THIEVERY roll at Difficulty 11.

Successful THIEVERY roll	turn to **58**
Failed THIEVERY roll	turn to **304**

You are dissolved in the acid, until all that is left of you is a pile of yellow dust. Vayss scoops you up and puts you into a bottle on his shelf.

Cross off all the possessions and money you were carrying, and turn to **31**.

Each creature bursts open in death, spilling a black inky cloud into the water. The sac in which this ink is kept falls free from its body. You can take the **ink sacs** if you wish; note up to three of them on your Adventure Sheet. You also find coral jewellery worth about 45 Shards which you can take as cash. You swim down and take the **golden net** (note it on your Adventure Sheet) and swim for the Shadar Tor as fast as you can.

Take the road to Trefoille	turn to **602**
Take the road to Marlock City	turn to **166**

You try to stop the panic but your men are too far gone. They are already diving over the side, trying to swim back to your ship. Unfortunately, they are even more vulnerable in the sea, and the ker'ilk take them at will. Soon you are all overwhelmed, and you are taken alive to be injected with eggs – a most horrible end. Your adventures are over, unless you have a resurrection deal with a temple.

Caran Baru market consists of several covered arcades – much of its stock is for miners and soldiers, and it is run with business-like efficiency by the Sokaran military. Items with no purchase price listed are not available locally.

Armour	*To buy*	*To sell*
Leather (Defence +1)	50 Shards	45 Shards
Ring mail (Defence +2)	100 Shards	90 Shards
Chain mail (Defence +3)	200 Shards	180 Shards
Splint armour (Defence +4)	400 Shards	360 Shards
Plate armour (Defence +5)	800 Shards	720 Shards
Heavy plate (Defence +6)	–	1440 Shards

Weapons (sword, axe, etc)	*To buy*	*To sell*
Without COMBAT bonus	50 Shards	40 Shards
COMBAT bonus +1	250 Shards	200 Shards
COMBAT bonus +2	500 Shards	400 Shards
COMBAT bonus +3	–	800 Shards

Magical equipment	*To buy*	*To sell*
Amber wand (MAGIC +1)	–	400 Shards
Ebony wand (MAGIC +2)	–	800 Shards
Cobalt wand (MAGIC +3)	–	1600 Shards
Selenium wand (MAGIC +3)	–	1600 Shards

Other items	*To buy*	*To sell*
Mandolin (CHARISMA +1)	300 Shards	270 Shards
Lockpicks (THIEVERY +1)	–	270 Shards
Holy symbol (SANCTITY +1)	–	100 Shards
Compass (SCOUTING +1)	500 Shards	450 Shards
Rope	50 Shards	45 Shards
Lantern	100 Shards	90 Shards
Climbing gear	100 Shards	90 Shards
Bag of pearls	–	100 Shards
Rat poison	60 Shards	50 Shards
Silver nugget	–	150 Shards

| **Platinum earring** | – | 800 Shards |
| **Wolf pelt** | 100 Shards | 90 Shards |

When you are finished, turn back to **400**.

216

The cry goes up throughout the palace, 'Murder! Assassin!' and the hunt is on – for you. You will need all your skill to get out of the palace alive. Roll one die, subtracting one if you are a Rogue, Troubadour or a Wayfarer. If you score less than or equal to your Rank, turn to **407**. Otherwise, turn to **566**.

217

You come across a forest glade. Birds twitter in the trees, and woodland animals frolic playfully about. In the middle of the glade stands a mighty willow, ancient beyond reckoning. The trunk is hollow, and a wooden door has been set in the entrance. You step into the glade.
Make a SANCTITY roll at Difficulty 9.

| Successful SANCTITY roll | turn to **356** |
| Failed SANCTITY roll | turn to **646** |

218

The militia take you alive. You lose all your money and possessions. Cross them off your Adventure Sheet. Then you are thrown into the dungeons of Yellowport. Turn to **454**.

219

Your ship, crew and cargo are lost to the deep, dark sea. Cross them off your Adventure Sheet. Your only thought now is to save yourself. Roll two dice. If the score is greater than your Rank, you are drowned. If the score is less than or equal to your Rank, you manage to find some driftwood, and make it back to shore. Lose Stamina points equal to the score of one die roll and, if you can survive that, turn to **436**.

220

The temple of Alvir and Valmir is built like an upside-down galleon. Alvir and Valmir are brother and sister, King and Queen of the Land beneath the Waves, masters of the sea. Their servants and soldiers are the souls of the drowned, and when seas are rough and storm-tossed, sailors say that Alvir and Valmir are arguing again.

If you have the codeword *Anchor*, turn to **531**.

Otherwise, you notice a sign on the door, which says: 'Wanted: brave adventurer – apply to the high priest.'

Become an initiate	turn to **294**
Renounce worship	turn to **624**
Seek a blessing	turn to **448**
Talk to the high priest	turn to **411**
Leave the temple	turn to **10**

221

One of the militiamen recognizes you and shouts, 'That's the one who assassinated Marloes Marlock!' You turn tail and flee with fifteen militiamen on your heels. Roll one die. If you score less than or equal to your Rank, turn to **57**. Otherwise, turn to **252**.

222

Your ship is sailing in the coastal waters near Marlock City. Roll two dice:

Score 2-4	Storm	turn to **124**
Score 5-9	An uneventful voyage	turn to **420**
Score 10-12	Sea battle	turn to **169**

223

The ghoul staggers back, howling at the night sky, and gnashing its teeth. Suddenly, brownish ichor spills from its eyes and the flesh begins to shrivel on its bones. It collapses in on itself, leaving only a mound of putrescent matter, atop of which rests its head, now lifeless, empty eye-sockets staring at the moon. You grab the head, and set off. Note you have a **ghoul's head** and turn to **100**.

224

Using your wilderness-honed sense of direction you dart through the maze of tunnels. Soon the sounds of pursuit fade, until they are but a dim echo. Heaving a sigh of relief, you press on. Turn to **580**.

225

You find a cave, with piles of human bones outside it. However, it is quite empty without signs of habitation. The beast that lived here is dead or departed. You make your way back down to Blessed Springs. Turn to **510**.

226

You take a stroll through the streets. Marlock City has a busy night life.

Explore the barracks area	turn to **15**
Go to the Street of Entertainers	turn to **129**
Search the residential quarter	turn to **619**

227

Cross off 5 Shards. The mad beggar takes the money and swallows the lot in one gulp. 'A gourmet meal!' he babbles.

If you want to bless him, turn to **632**. If not, he wanders off ranting and you head back to the city centre, turn to **10**.

228

A stone slab at the base of the idol shifts ominously as you put your foot on it. A wickedly barbed spear springs out of the ground, straight into your leg. Lose 5 Stamina points.

If you still live, you remove the chain mail and sling it over your shoulder. Note the **gold chain mail of Tyrnai** on your Adventure Sheet. Because it is made of gold, it is useless if worn as armour.

As you glance at the jaguar-headed idol, its eyes seem to turn to look at you. Make a SANCTITY roll at Difficulty 8.

Successful SANCTITY roll	turn to **625**
Failed SANCTITY roll	turn to **279**

229

The guildmaster welcomes you warmly. He has no further missions for you, though he treats you with respect because you brought Amcha to justice. If you are completely broke, however, without a Shard in your pocket or in the bank, he will give you 200 Shards. If you have any money at all, he will not help.

Turn to **100**.

230

You are caught in a narrow defile, and seized by many men. You are hauled before Captain Vorkung, who sentences you to be hanged. Sentence is carried out immediately. Your adventures are over, unless you have a resurrection deal.

If you do have a resurrection deal, turn to the paragraph you have noted. Also, through a quirk of magical fate, somehow the **royal ring** has travelled with you through the lands of the dead. Retain it on your Adventure Sheet.

231

You notice that the figures have left footprints on the damp grass and cannot, therefore, be ghosts.

Step out and confront the figures	turn to **23**
Stay hidden and follow when they leave	turn to **541**

232 ☐

If there is a tick in the box, turn to **151**, immediately. If not, put a tick there now, and read on.

The interior of the cave is cool and refreshing, a paradise compared with the savage heat of your gruelling climb. You find a man, floating cross-legged in the middle of the air! He is dressed only in a loincloth, and is painfully thin. His face is shrouded in a great luxuriant growth of glossy black hair, a beard like no other you have ever seen.

At the sight of you, he gives an exasperated sigh, and says, `I am Damor the Hermit. A HERMIT. That means I like to live alone – got that? Alone! So go away!'

`I nearly died getting here, old man!' you reply testily.

`Yes, you'd have to be pretty tough to get through the curse I put on the path, I suppose,' he says somewhat apologetically.

If you have the codeword *Anthem*, turn to **285**. Otherwise, turn to **480**.

233 ☐

If there is a tick in the box, turn to **412**. If not, put a tick there now, and read on.

You are on the cobbled road between Yellowport and Trefoille. It is well-kept by the Sokaran military.

You spot a man up ahead, striding towards you. Suddenly, five or six bandits appear from the wayside to assault him. The lone figure executes a series of movements, almost faster than the eye can see, and you see his sword flashing in the sun. Moments later, the bandits are lying dead or dying around him.

You stop to compliment him on his swordsmanship.

The man, a grizzled veteran of many campaigns, regards you with steely grey eyes and says, 'I have learned much of the arts of war in my time, it is true.'

Impressed by his skill and demeanour, you venture to ask him to teach you some of these arts. He looks you up and down critically.

If you are a Warrior, turn to **146**. Otherwise, turn to **567**.

234

The ship's captain says, 'I'll take you to Dweomer, on the Sorcerers' Isle but it's a dangerous place. You'd better be sure you can handle it – if you're not at least a Master of your profession, I'd advise against. It's up to you, though.'

You must have Over the Blood-Dark Sea to travel to Sorcerers' Isle. If you want to go, cross off the 30 Shards and turn to 26. Otherwise, if you are in Marlock City, turn back to **142**; if you are in Yellowport, return to **555**.

235

The temple of Sig the Cunning, patron of vagabonds, troubadours, lovers, thieves and rogues, is a ramshackle warehouse in the poor quarter. Inside, however, there is so much wealth, it makes you gasp – the idol of Sig, a saturnine two-faced young human of indistinct sex, is covered in gems. 'As you can see, we have been made rich by generous, er, donations!' says a black-robed priest.

Seek an audience with the high priest	turn to **113**
Become an initiate	turn to **437**
Renounce worship	turn to **563**
Seek a blessing	turn to **197**
Leave the temple	turn to **100**

236

You find Fourze inside, desperately trying to get out of his suit and run off. At the sight of a hardened adventurer, rather than a timid villager, he surrenders and confesses all. He terrified people with the monster disguise to keep them away from the farm. He and his men were kidnapping villagers, chaining them in the cellar below and selling them to a slaver from Caran Baru, for work in the slave mines. You find Haylie, and several other villagers down below in the cellar.

'Don't hurt me,' begs Fourze, 'I'm only trying to make a few Shards.'

'What! By selling your own people into slavery,' says one of the villagers, giving him a good kick.

You lead them back to Venefax. Turn to **414**.

237

You explain what a tree-lover you are, and that your heart has always been at home in forests. You portray yourself as the greenest adventurer ever. Make a CHARISMA roll at Difficulty 10. Add 3 to the dice roll if you are a Wayfarer, and add 1 if you are an initiate of Lacuna.

Successful CHARISMA roll	turn to **391**
Failed CHARISMA roll	turn to **410**

238

The vile-looking creature shoots toward you with a terrifying predatory speed. You have no choice but to fight it.

Repulsive One, COMBAT 5, Defence 10, Stamina 10

You must subtract 2 from your dice rolls for this fight, as you are unused to underwater combat. If you win, turn to **53**. If you lose, your adventuring days are over, unless you have a resurrection deal.

239

The climb is long and hard, but at last you heave yourself up on to the top of Devil's Peak – a flat expanse of weathered black rock. If you have the codeword *Altitude*, turn to **126**. Otherwise, turn to **199**.

240

You sail into the teeming harbour of Marlock City. Sokaran warships escort you in.

'Troubled times,' comments a sailor.

Turn to **100**.

241

To renounce the worship of Elnir, you must pay 40 Shards to the priesthood by way of compensation. The high priest says nothing – he merely regards you with a mild contempt, as if he expected you to fail in the worship of Elnir. Do you want to change your mind?

If you are determined to renounce your faith, pay the 40 Shards and delete Elnir from the God box on your Adventure Sheet. When you have finished here, turn to **100**.

242

You fight the Sokarans to a standstill. The Sokaran captain orders the retreat; he and his marines pull back to their galley. You and your crew are too tired to pursue, and the Sokarans pull away.

'I'll get you next time!' yells the captain.

You sail on. Turn to **439**.

243

You cannot find any hidden panels – Lauria did say that the real treasure was upstairs. You call to her, but she doesn't reply.

Go upstairs	turn to **386**
Wait downstairs	turn to **534**

You have come to the foothills of the Spine of Harkun. The great mountains rise up majestically before you, their snowcapped peaks wreathed in clouds. You find a clear, cold stream, where you drink your fill and replenish your water supply.

Climb upwards	turn to **536**
Head south	turn to **518**
Head east to Disaster Bay	turn to **495**
West to the citadel	turn to **271**

The footprints cross a stream, and there you lose them. After an hour's fruitless searching by moonlight, you are forced to give up and go back to the village. There you are admonished for being reckless.

'What if the ghosts had taken you with them back to their graves?' says one man grimly.

The next day you are ready to resume your journey.

Follow the river north	turn to **576**
Follow the river south	turn to **82**
East into the countryside	turn to **278**
West to the main road	turn to **558**

If you have already successfully stolen the **gold chain mail of Tyrnai** for the Temple of Sig, turn to **467**. If not, read on.

The Temple of Tyrnai, the God of Battle, Chaos and Strife, is built like a small fortress in one corner of the city, near the barracks. Its heavy wooden gates are flanked by iron statues of bull-headed men wielding clubs. The workmanship is uncannily lifelike. Inside, the god is represented by a stone idol of a jaguar-headed warrior. A beautiful suit of gold chain mail adorns the idol.

Become an initiate	turn to **636**
Renounce his worship	turn to **514**
Seek a blessing	turn to **107**
Make resurrection arrangements	turn to **33**
Try to steal the chain mail	turn to **305**
Leave the temple	turn to **400**

The sound was the click of a secret door sliding open in the wall of the cavern. With a swift motion, you step up beside it, back to the wall. A figure emerges but you are able to ambush the ambusher – a deft blow to the back of the head sends the dark figure crashing to the ground.

Another steps forth, however, shouting in a guttural voice. You realize the figures are ratmen – manlike creatures that stand on two legs, but which have the tail and hairy features of a gigantic rat.

You must fight the ratman. If you have some **rat poison**, you can apply it to the blade of your weapon and add 3 to your dice rolls, for this fight only. If you use the **rat poison**, cross it off your Adventure Sheet.

Ratman, COMBAT 3, Defence 6, Stamina 6

If you win, turn to **423**. If you lose, turn to **308**.

If you have a **willow staff**, turn to **319** immediately. If not, read on.

The Oak Druid, who asked you to take the oak staff to the Willow Druid, has nothing more to say to you.

You head back to the Trading Post. Turn to **195**.

'Nerech's a dangerous place – even its coastal waters, Cap'n,' says the first mate. 'The men probably won't follow you there if they don't think you're good enough to lead them!'

If your Rank is 4 or more, turn to paragraph **50** in *The Plains of Howling Darkness*.

If your Rank is less than 4, the first mate advises you against making the ocean journey. If you take his advice, turn back to **209**.

If you insist on making the trip, you need to make a CHARISMA roll at Difficulty 11 to convince the crew to follow you.

| Successful CHARISMA roll | *The Plains of Howling Darkness* **50** |
| Failed CHARISMA roll | turn to **209** |

The city of Trefoille is a terrifying vision of apocalyptic destruction. It had once been a thriving crossroads town, but now it is a burnt-out hulk.

It was almost razed to the ground when it declared for the king, and tried to hold out against the army of Grieve Marlock during the recent civil war. It was sacked by the general's mercenaries. General Marlock is now trying to rebuild it. Craftsmen are hard at work everywhere.

If you have the codeword *Amends*, and want to visit Oliphard the Wizardly, turn to **656**. Otherwise there is nothing here but ashes and rubble.

Take the road to the Shadar Tor	turn to **602**
Take the road to Marlock City	turn to **377**
Head into the Curstmoor	turn to **175**
Take the road north	turn to **558**
Take the road to Yellowport	turn to **233**

251

If you have the codeword *Avenge*, turn to **622** immediately. If not, read on.

The last time you were here, you only had a few minutes to grab some loot. This time, the sea dragon returns almost straight away, and you are forced to climb out of the hole in the roof without getting anything except a pouch of 50 Shards. You crawl out on to the island in the middle of the lake and hitch a boat ride back to Cadmium.

Turn to **135**.

252

You lead them a merry chase through the backstreets of Yellowport but unfortunately for you, you run smack dab into another patrol. You are captured and thrown into the dungeons to await your fate but not before the militiamen take all your money and possessions. Turn to **454**.

253

To renounce the worship of Lacuna, you must pass an ordeal of judgment. This entails the high priestess throwing several silver daggers at you, while you remain motionless.

'If Lacuna sees it in her heart to forgive you, the daggers will all miss,' she claims.

Submit to the ordeal	turn to **313**
Remain an initiate after all	turn to **615**

254

You ask for a kiss. `Oh no!' cry the mer-folk, `A kiss is not so easily won! Tell us a tale to stir our hearts   then we may reward you.'

Make a CHARISMA roll at Difficulty 9.

Successful CHARISMA roll	turn to **12**
Failed CHARISMA roll	turn to **281**

255

The provost marshal takes you to an empty side chamber, away from prying ears. Over a glass of fine wine you tell him of your adventures in the Coldbleak Mountains. When you give him the Royal Ring of the House of Corin, he knows that Nergan is dead. Cross the **royal ring** off your Adventure Sheet.

Marloes Marlock is pleased indeed. He pays you 500 Shards, and awards you the title Protector of Sokara. Note it in your Titles and Honours box. The title will give you instant respect and command obedience in Sokara.

Also, after completing such a difficult test, you find the experience has taught you much – gain 1 Rank and roll one die. The result is the number of Stamina points you gain permanently. Note the increase on your Adventure Sheet.

Return to **10** and choose again.

256

The king is overjoyed with the news. `Excellent! At this rate, I will be able to take my rightful place in the throne room of Old Sokar.'

He rewards you with the title King's Champion. Note this in the Titles and Honours box on your Adventure Sheet. The title comes with a cash gift of 500 Shards as well.

You also go up one Rank. Roll one die – the result is the number of Stamina points you gain permanently. Note the increases on your Adventure Sheet.

The king has another mission for you. He explains that an army of steppe Nomads, Trau, Mannekyn people, and Sokaran troops still loyal to Nergan, have gathered on the steppes, and are moving to siege the Citadel of Velis Corin, which guards the Pass of Eagles through the Spine of Harkun. Nergan tells you that an alliance of northern nations has declared war on the new Sokaran regime. A certain General Beladai leads the Northern Alliance, and King Nergan has joined forces with him. He asks you to travel to the Steppes and talk to General Beladai.

'An adventurer like yourself might be able to steal into the citadel, and bring about its downfall from within, or some such. If the citadel falls, we will have Sokara at our mercy.'

If you want to take up this mission for the King, record the codeword *Assault*. When you are ready, you are led back down to the foothills of the mountains. Turn to **474**.

257

The trees are closely packed, leaning together as if in conference, whispering quietly among themselves. Birds twitter in the distance, and slivers of sunlight lance down through the musty gloom.

As you proceed along a forest track, you think you hear a rustling in the bushes. Later, you spot a shadowy figure darting through the trees— or was it your imagination? An animal snuffling sound right behind you makes you spin around, but there is nothing there.

Make a SCOUTING roll at Difficulty 10.

Successful SCOUTING roll	turn to **630**
Failed SCOUTING roll	turn to **36**

258

Becoming an initiate of the Three Fortunes gives you the benefit of paying less for blessings and other services the temple can offer. It costs 75 Shards. You cannot already be an initiate of another temple. If you choose to become an initiate, write 'The Three Fortunes' in the God box on your Adventure Sheet. Once you have finished here, turn to **86**.

259

Fort Brilon, named after a Sokaran king of the first dynasty, is the southernmost castle on the fortified wall that keeps out the rabid, manbeasts. What the soldiers fear most is what they call 'Death Duty' – going out on patrols beyond the wall, into Nerech itself. Roll one die.

Score 1 or 2   Thief steals one item from you (your choice)
Score 3 or 4   Nothing happens
Score 5 or 6   Find a **manbeast's helmet**

When you are ready, you can head:

East into Nerech	*The Plains of Howling Darkness* **365**
North west to Fort Estgard	turn to **472**
West into the farmlands	turn to **548**
South to Blessed Springs	turn to **466**

260

You are shocked to find that you cannot damage the tomb guardian at all! You have no choice but to run for the door. Roll one die – if the result is less than or equal to your Rank, you make it back out into the Forest: turn to **47**. Otherwise, the whirlwind guardian catches you, and buffets you against the stone walls until you are dead: your adventures are over unless you have a resurrection deal.

261

To renounce the worship of Maka, you must pay 15 Shards to the priesthood by way of compensation.

A man, lying on a pallet, groans, 'I renounced the goddess, and look at me now...' He is ravaged by disease. Do you want to change your mind? If you are determined to renounce your faith, pay the 15 Shards and delete Maka from the God box on your Adventure Sheet.

When you have finished here, turn to **141**.

262

You charge into the burning building in search of the child's mother. You see her lying unconscious at the bottom of the stairs. Desperately, you try to get to her but a burning beam has fallen across your way and the smoke is making you choke.

Roll a die and subtract one from the result. If you score less than or equal to your Rank, turn to **546**. Otherwise, turn to **133**.

263

You are passing through a wooded glade when you hear a horrendous trumpeting noise. Suddenly, a massive bear-like form about the size of a large bull appears in front of you. It looks rather like a huge hairy toad, with a gaping, toothy mouth.

The creature breathes a billowing cloud of noxious, sulphurous gas at you. You feel your head swim as you start to fall asleep.

Roll one die, and subtract one from the total. If the total is greater than your Rank, turn to **491**. Otherwise, turn to **72**.

264 ☐

If there is a tick in the box, turn to **131**. If not, put a tick there now, and read on.

A large island made of reeds and plants, which grow out of a massive floating bed of kelp, drifts aimlessly across the waters. As you draw near, you see that a number of people have made their home there. The inhabitants hail you, and invite you ashore. Turn to **537**.

265

If you have the title Unspeakable Cultist, turn to **404**. If not, read on.
You hear a muffled cry of distress from a dark alley.

Investigate	turn to **361**
Walk on	turn to **10**

266

'You rebel swine,' slurs one of them.

'Not showing proper respect to the army,' says another. 'That can't go unpunished!'

They wade into you, intent on beating you into submission. Make a

COMBAT roll at Difficulty 12.

    Successful COMBAT roll   turn to **76**

    Failed COMBAT roll   turn to **498**

267

You row out on to the lake, spread the net, and wait to see what happens.

After an hour or so, a great bubbling and frothing of the waves disturbs your solitude. A massive scaly head, the size of your boat, erupts out of the ochre-coloured water on the end of a long, sinuous neck. Great luminous green eyes look down at you. The creature is covered in brown scales, with a bright red crest running from the head down its thick, ropy neck.

`I am Vayss the Sea Dragon,' it says in a rich, creamy voice, tinged with evil greed. `To fish in my lake, you have to pay tribute – to wit, one silver nugget. Pay now, or face my wrath.'

    Hand over a **silver nugget**   turn to **505**

    Unable or refuse to pay   turn to **582**

268

The goblin-folk swarm over you. You try to put up a fight, but there are too many of them. Everything goes black...

You wake up, spluttering, face down on a beach! A wave has just soaked you.

`Going for a swim, are we?' asks an old woman who is gathering shells on the beach. You learn from her that a month has passed since your adventure in the faery mound, and you can remember none of it.

If you were wounded, you are now back to full Stamina. However, you realize you have lost all the money and items you were carrying. Cross them off your Adventure Sheet. Instead, you have a **wolf pelt** that you are wearing, some **rat poison** and a **silver nugget**. The old lady tells you that you are on the delta of the River Grimm. Turn to **579**.

269

You find a natural alcove in the wall of a tunnel. Desperately, you squeeze yourself into it, and fade into the shadows. The ratmen come bundling past, whooping and yelling. None of them spot you, and once they have gone you step out, smiling to yourself. Turn to **580**.

270

You make a swift inspection of the casements, walls and furnishings, searching for secret panels where treasure might be concealed. Make a THIEVERY roll at a Difficulty of 12.

Successful THIEVERY roll	turn to **59**
Failed THIEVERY roll	turn to **243**

271

You arrive at the Pass of Eagles, a thin chasm sliced right through the Spine of Harkun, as if Tyrnai himself had split the mountains with his sword.

A vast citadel has been built right across the southern end of the pass, bottling it up, so that none can travel into Sokara without passing through the castle. Its white walls and flag-topped towers shine brightly in the sunlight.

Enter the citadel	*The Plains of Howling Darkness* **400**
Go to the western foothills	turn to **3**

The eastern foothills   turn to **244**
South on the road to Caran Baru   turn to **201**
Take the road to Fort Mereth   turn to **518**

THE CITADEL of VELIS CORIN

272

If you have the codeword *Aloft*, turn to **649** immediately. If not, read on.

The chief administrator is not happy to see you.

'What are you doing here?' he demands. 'You should be at Devil's Peak, north of here! The storm demons still threaten our city. Come back when you have succeeded.'

Turn to **100**.

273

You find the city is in turmoil. A rebel group, loyal to the old king, led an uprising against the army. Vicious fighting ensued and the streets ran with blood before the rebellion was brutally put down. Unfortunately, much damage was done during the battle. If you own a town house in Yellowport it has been looted; any possessions you may have cached there have gone. Make a note of this paragraph number, turn to **300**, cross off anything you had stored there, and return here to read on.

If you have the codeword *Artefact* and the **Book of the Seven Sages**, turn to **40**. If not, turn back to **10** and choose from the options listed there.

274

Desperately, you try to sneak behind a pile of coins but the dragon spots you. 'A sneaky little thief, eh! Can't have that, oh no, not at all!' hisses the dragon, and it breathes a cloud of billowing acidic gas all over you. You watch in horror as the coins in front of you begin to melt, and then the cloud engulfs you.

If you have an **amulet of protection**, turn to **298**. Otherwise, turn to **212**.

275

If you are an initiate it costs only 5 Shards to propitiate the twin gods of the sea. A non-initiate must pay 20 Shards. Cross off the money and mark Safety from Storms in the Blessings box on your Adventure Sheet. The blessing works by allowing you to ignore any one storm at sea. When you use the blessing, cross it off your Adventure Sheet. You can only have one Safety from Storms blessing at any one time. Once it is used up, you can return to any branch of the temple of Alvir and Valmir to buy a new one. Turn to **154**.

276

You are wandering across the wilderness of north-western Sokara. There is a magnificent castle nearby, with many different pennants flying from its towers.

Visit the castle	turn to **611**
Head west to the River Grimm	turn to **123**
Travel north to the mountains	turn to **3**
Head north-east	turn to **201**
Head east into the Bronze Hills	turn to **110**
Go south into the Forest of Larun	turn to **47**

277

A patrol of militiamen – mercenaries in the pay of the dictator, General Grieve Marlock – stop you in the street.

If you have the codeword *Assassin*, turn to **221** immediately.

If not, but you are a Protector of Sokara, they greet you politely, and salute. You return to the city centre without incident – turn to **10**.

Otherwise, they decide you will be arrested unless you pay 15 Shards as 'taxes'. If you refuse, or don't have 15 Shards, turn to **538**. If you hand over the money, cross it off and the militiamen leave you alone – turn back to **10**.

278

You are crossing an open expanse of flinty ground. A few herds of sheep roam the low hills. Roll a die.

Score 1 or 2   You get lost – turn to **82**.

Score 3 or 4   Nothing happens

Score 5 or 6   A shepherd gives you a **wolf pelt**

When you are ready, you can go:

To Venefax	turn to **427**
West to the Stinking River	turn to **310**
North to the lake	turn to **135**
East	turn to **87**

279

What you have just done is probably a sacrilege, desecrating the Temple of Tyrnai, but you don't care. You sneak out of the temple unseen, and head back to town with your prize. Who else could have stolen a holy relic from right under the noses of the warrior priests of Tyrnai! Turn to **400**.

280

There are too many wolves to contend with. You withdraw before they get angry. Turn to **3**.

281

Your tale of valour and derring-do falls on an unappreciative audience. The mer-folk slip beneath the waves with snorts of derision, leaving you alone on the desolate beach. There is nothing for you to do but return to the clifftop tor.

Take the road to Trefoille	turn to **602**
Take the road to Marlock City	turn to **166**

282

If you have the codeword *Armour*, turn to **246** immediately. If not, read on.

The Temple of Tyrnai, the God of Battle, Chaos and Strife, is built like a small fortress in one corner of the city, near the barracks. Its heavy wooden gates are flanked by iron statues of bull-headed men wielding clubs. The workmanship is uncannily life-like. Inside, the god is represented by a stone idol of a jaguar-headed warrior. A beautiful suit of gold chain mail adorns the idol.

Become an initiate	turn to **636**
Renounce worship	turn to **514**
Seek a blessing	turn to **107**
Make resurrection arrangements	turn to **33**
Leave the temple	turn to **400**

283

'What goes on here?' you ask. 'Why do you behave so oddly?

The villagers seem quite frightened of you, but one old fellow has nerve enough to reply.

'This banquet is for the ghosts of three travellers who lost their way in a storm, fell into our millpond and were drowned.'

'When was this?' you ask.

'Seven years since. They come every year on this night, and if we didn't placate them with victuals and treasure there'd be a mess of trouble.'

'How do you know that?'

'Old Megan told us,' he says. 'She knows about such things.'

Stay out at night and watch for the ghosts	turn to **590**
Follow the river north	turn to **576**
Follow the river south	turn to **82**
Head east into the countryside	turn to **278**
Go west to the main road	turn to **558**

284

You find an open window and squeeze through into a long hall. Your foot, however, snags on a thin wire stretched across the floor. The wire triggers a loud bell-like gonging that alerts the temple. You have little choice but to run for your life as warrior priests swarm out of the temple and the iron statues at its gates come to life to join in the chase.

Roll a die, and subtract one from the total. If the result is less than or equal to your Rank, turn to **395**. Otherwise, turn to **551**.

285

You remember a bard in a tavern told you about Damor the Hermit, and that he knew the secret of the Greatest Story Ever Told so you ask him about it.

'Ahh,' says Damor. 'I have waited for one such as you.' He tells you the secret of the Greatest Story. 'Well, my young adventurer, destiny beckons, for it is fated that your life will be the Greatest Story Ever Told.'

As you consider this, you feel a sense of momentary enlightenment. Gain 1 Rank and roll one die. The result is the number of Stamina points you gain permanently.

'Right, that's that,' says Damor. 'Now, go away and don't come back!'

For a few hours, he lifts the curse that soured your water so you can make it down again safely. Turn to **244**.

286

When you and your crew join the fray, the battle is short lived. The pirates are overpowered, though they fight to the last man, preferring death to enslavement or execution. The Sokaran leader, an admiral in the navy, thanks you gravely for your help. He rewards you with a share of the pirate's booty. You get 400 Shards and 1 Cargo Unit of spices, if you have room for it in your ship's hold. You sail on. Turn to **420**.

287

You wait for an hour. At dusk, something emerges. It is the gorlock, a beast with legs like a bird, a body like a reptile, with two short forelimbs and a beaked, lizard-like head. You see that its two legs do have backward-pointing feet. The beast heads off into the hills, and you creep forward. Turn to **315**.

288

You end up dead in an alleyway with your throat cut. Your adventures are over, unless you have a resurrection deal.

289

There is a pause, as if you are both waiting for something to happen. You realize the gods have not heard your prayer, as does your enemy. It snarls triumphantly, and slashes you across the chest. Lose 2 Stamina. If you still live, you have no choice but to fight it. Turn to **617**.

290

If you have the codeword *Cutlass*, turn to **403** immediately. If not, but you have the codeword *Amcha*, turn to **512**. Otherwise read on.

The guildmaster, a tall, gaunt man welcomes you.

'The guild, in Golnir and Sokara, is plagued by privateers on the high seas. Amcha One-eye is the worst of these lawless dogs – he has cost us thousands of Shards! Bring me the head of Amcha One-eye, and I will reward you! He and his cut-throat crew operate from the Unnumbered Isles – now called the Kingdom of the Reavers because of the pirates who have made their base there. The isles lie to the south.'

If you want to take up the quest, note the codeword *Amcha*. When you are ready, turn to **100**.

291

Becoming an initiate of Elnir gives you the benefit of paying less for blessings and other services the temple can offer. It costs 60 Shards to become an initiate. You cannot become an initiate of Elnir if you are already an initiate of another temple. If you choose to become an initiate, write 'Elnir' in the God box on your Adventure Sheet – and remember to cross off the 60 Shards.

Once you have finished here, turn to **316**.

292

The local market is very small – only two commodities are available for trade.

Item	To buy	To sell
smoulder fish	60 Shards	55 Shards
silver nugget	160 Shards	150 Shards

When you are finished, turn back to **135**.

293

The merchantman has suffered a lot of damage, and the remaining crewmen are half dead with thirst. You give them water, and help to repair the ship. The captain, a woman dressed in multi-coloured feather robes, and an ornate headdress, is most grateful. She tells you her name is Moon of Evening and that she comes from Smogmaw, the city at the Misty Estuary, in far off Ankon-konu. She tells you to visit her, if you are ever in Smogmaw, so that she can repay the debt.

Note the codeword *Aid*. You sail on. Turn to **559**.

294

Becoming an initiate of Alvir and Valmir gives you the benefit of paying less for blessings and other services the temple can offer. It costs 40 Shards to become an initiate. You cannot do this if you are already an initiate of another temple. If you choose to become an initiate, write Alvir and Valmir in the God box on your Adventure Sheet – and remember to cross off the 40 Shards. Once you have finished here, turn to 220.

295

The scorpion men cannot keep up with you, and you leg it all the way back to the road. Maybe you can come back and try again later. Turn to **492**.

296

Make a MAGIC roll at Difficulty 9.

Successful MAGIC roll	turn to **494**
Failed MAGIC roll	turn to **352**

297

Decide which armour and weapon you will use in the fight. They will be the ones you are betting with.

Roll a die, and check the table below. The result is the knight you must fight.

Score 1 or 2	Blue Dragon Knight
	COMBAT 3, Defence 8, Stamina 6
Score 3 or 4	Green Dragon Knight
	COMBAT 4, Defence 8, Stamina 8
Score 5 or 6	Red Dragon Knight
	COMBAT 5, Defence 8, Stamina 10

Because it is not a duel to the death, your weapons are padded, so any Stamina you lose is not permanent – it is recovered after the fight.

If you win, turn to **19**. If you are reduced to 0 Stamina, you pass out, turn to **370**.

298

The **amulet of protection** dissolves in a flash of smoke; cross it off your Adventure Sheet.

It does protect you, however, and you are obscured by the smoke long enough to get into hiding. The amulet leaves a residue of yellow powder, which the dragon thinks is all that is left of you. He scoops it up and puts it into a bottle, beside the others on his rocky shelf.

Turn to **16**.

299

Fort Mereth, named after an ancient hero, is the northernmost of the forts that guard Sokara from the ravening manbeasts of Nerech. A fortified wall stretches right across the peninsula. Roll a die.

Score 1 or 2	Get in a fight with a drunken soldier.
	Soldier, COMBAT 4, Defence 6, Stamina 7
	If you win, you can take his **axe**
Score 3 or 4	Nothing happens
Score 5 or 6	Opportunity to buy a **mandolin (CHARISMA +1)** for 100 Shards.

When you are ready, you can travel:

East into Nerech	*The Plains of Howling Darkness* **20**
South east to Fort Estgard	turn to **472**
South into the farmlands	turn to **548**
West on the road to Caran Baru	turn to **458**
West on the road to the citadel	turn to **518**

300

You can leave possessions and money here to save having to carry them around with you. You can also rest here safely, and recover any Stamina points you have lost.

```
ITEMS AT TOWN HOUSE




```

Record in the box anything you wish to leave. Each time you return, roll two dice:

Score 2-9	Your possessions are safe
Score 10-11	A thief. All the money you left here has gone
Score 12	Burglars! Lose all the possessions you left here
Turn to **10**.	

301

A barque, heading for the Isle of Druids to buy furs, is prepared to take you. Cross off 15 Shards. The journey, across the Sea of Whispers, is uneventful, and you dock at the Trading Post on the island a week or so later. Turn to **195**.

302

You can explore:

The poor quarter	turn to **93**
The harbour area	turn to **587**
The area around the palace	turn to **277**

303

Cross off the **salt and iron filings** from your Adventure Sheet. As fast as you can, you lay out a line of the powder in front of you. The ghoul gives a moaning wail and shrinks back, unable to cross the line of salt and iron filings. Quickly you run around the ghoul, encircling it with the powder. The creature lunges for you but it cannot cross the line – you keep it at bay at every turn. Soon it is completely trapped. Casually, you sit on a tombstone, and wait for sunrise. When it comes, the ghoul is burnt to a crisp. You take the rotting, charred head and make your way back to town.

Note you have a **ghoul's head** and turn to **100**.

304

He spots you before you can get the jump on him. 'Stinking assassin!' he yells, drawing his sword. You must fight him.

Man with eyepatch, COMBAT 5, Defence 8, Stamina 12

If you win, turn to **92**. If you lose, he kills you, and your adventuring days are over, unless you have a resurrection deal.

305 ☐

If there is a tick in the box, turn to **367** immediately. If not, put a tick there now, and read on.

Make a MAGIC roll at Difficulty 11.

Successful MAGIC roll	turn to **609**
Failed MAGIC roll	turn to **528**

306

Something doesn't feel right about the pearls. You realize a minor enchantment has been put on them – they are in fact tiny pebbles, made to look like pearls. You squeeze them in the palm of your hand, and they revert to their natural state. 'By the twin gods!' exclaims the young man. 'Look at that! They were pebbles all along!'

You stare at him for a long while, fingering your weapon. The Sea Gypsy shifts uneasily from foot to foot, coughing nervously and hands you another bag of pearls. This time you are sure they are real. Note the **bag of pearls** on your Adventure Sheet.

You take your leave, and resume your journey. Turn to **85**.

307

It feels like you are playing the flute for an eternity. But at last they tire of your music…

You wake up with a scream. You realize you are not aboard your ship! You find out that you are in the temple of Alvir and Valmir in Yellowport. A priest tells you that your crew brought you here three months ago because they could not wake you from your sleep.

Your ship and crew are long gone now – note that you no longer own a ship. The priests, however, have been looking after all your possessions. Among them is a **silver flute (+2 CHARISMA)**. While you have the flute, it adds 2 to your CHARISMA. Note that it is worth 500 Shards, and that you can sell it at any market if you like.

You leave the temple. Turn to **10**.

308

The ratmen beat you into unconsciousness, and then toss you down an underground sewer outlet. You are washed up on the beaches outside Yellowport, where you come to. You have 1 Stamina point left, and the ratmen have taken all the items and money that you were carrying. Cross them off your Adventure Sheet. Groggily, you make your way back into the city. Turn to **10**.

309

As you move closer to the sarcophagus, your foot crosses the edge of the pentacle by a few millimetres – it is enough. The lid of the sarcophagus explodes into the air with a deafening crash, and a pillar of black smoke erupts from the stone coffin! The smoke hurtles towards you, like a miniature tornado.

You must fight the tomb guardian. If you have a weapon with a +1 COMBAT bonus or greater, turn to **43**. Otherwise, turn to **260**.

310   ☐

If there is a tick in the box, turn to **614** immediately. If not, read on.

The Stinking River has cut its way through the high ground here. On the edge of the chasm that overlooks the river lies the village of High Therys.

The locals are behaving very oddly. You watch the villagers lay out a fine feast on the village green. A pig is set roasting on a spit, loaves of freshly baked bread are piled beside bowls overflowing with fruits, butter and cheese. Then the innkeeper comes with huge bottles of wine and beer. Lastly, the richest merchants of the village bring coffers full of silver which they set beside the table.

To your amazement, instead of sitting down to dine, the villagers then scurry home and start closing the shutters on their windows. Turn to **283**.

311

He narrows his eyes angrily at your refusal. If your ship is a galleon and you have a good or excellent crew, turn to **335**, immediately. If not, read on.

'In that case, I have no choice but to seize your ship!' More of his men swarm on to your ship, and a battle ensues.

Roll three dice if you are a Warrior, or two dice if you belong to any other profession. Add your Rank to this roll. If your crew is poor quality, subtract 2 from the total. If the crew is good, add 2; if it is excellent, add 3.

Score 0-4	Calamity. You are killed	
Score 5-9	Crushing defeat.	
	Lose 1-6 Stamina	turn to **153**
Score 10-13	A draw	turn to **242**
Score 14+	Outright victory	turn to **62**

312

'Nerech's a dangerous place – even its coastal waters, Cap'n,' says the first mate. 'The crew probably won't follow you there if they don't think you're good enough to lead them!'

If your Rank is 4 or more, turn to paragraph **50** in *The Plains of Howling Darkness*.

If your Rank is less than 4, the first mate advises you against making the ocean journey. If you take his advice, turn to **507**.

If you insist on making the trip, you need to make a CHARISMA roll at Difficulty 11 to convince the crew to follow you.

Successful CHARISMA roll	*The Plains of Howling Darkness* **50**
Failed CHARISMA roll	turn to **507**

313

You stand against the wall as the high priestess draws back her arm, and hurls a stream of daggers at you. Roll two dice. If the total is higher than your Defence, a dagger hits you and you lose 1-6 Stamina points (roll a die to see how many). If the two dice score less than or equal to your Defence, the daggers all miss. Either way, if you survive then you are free to leave. Delete Lacuna from the God box on your Adventure Sheet and turn to **400**.

314

The runes mean nothing to you.

Go down to the beach	turn to **97**
Take the road to Trefoille	turn to **602**
Take the road to Marlock City	turn to **166**

315

With the gorlock out of the way, you are free to investigate its lair. Inside the cave, you find 500 Shards, a **mace** and a **silver nugget**. Turn to **510**.

316

The temple of Elnir is an imposing edifice of grey stone, inlaid with yellow marbling. Elnir is the god of the sky and of kingship. He is the ruler of the gods.

'His dreams are the clouds before a storm,' says a passing priest.

Become an initiate of Elnir	turn to **291**
Renounce his worship	turn to **143**
Seek a blessing	turn to **388**
Leave the temple	turn to **10**

317

It is the same craft you got the magic spear from, with the silver-skinned demon inside – still dead you presume. You examine it again, but there is nothing else of interest on board. The figure still lies there unmoving. You sail on. Turn to **85**.

318

A scorpion man scuttles out of the brush to confront you. It resembles a huge scorpion, but with a human head and torso. It holds a sword and shield in its human arms. The creature's eyes blaze with an unearthly yellow light, and it scrabbles toward you with frightening speed, whipping its sting up and around at you. You must fight it.

Scorpion Man, COMBAT 3, Defence 6, Stamina 8

If you win, turn to **657**. If you lose, you are finished, unless you have a resurrection deal.

319

You give the **willow staff** to the Oak Druid of the City of Trees. Cross the **willow staff** off your Adventure Sheet.

'Ah, thank you,' the druid intones, going on, 'a willow staff, eh? I see.'

As a reward, the druid lets you train with the City of Trees' best hunters and trackers. Gain 1 Rank, and roll one die. The result is the number of Stamina points you gain permanently.

When you are ready, you leave the City of Trees and return to the Trading Post. Turn to **195**.

320

You learn from their conversation that they are from the jungles of distant Ankon-Konu, the Feathered Lands, and that they have come here to find new sacrifices for their god, and new members for their cult. The chef pronounces the cauldron is ready, and they remove the net that holds you.

Fight	turn to **204**
Shout 'Badogor!' repeatedly	turn to **101**
Join their cult	turn to **61**

321

The Black Dragon Knight comes out to meet you. His armour is of black steel, and you think you can see glowing red eyes through the slits in his full-face helm. You must fight him.

Black Dragon Knight, COMBAT 5, Defence 9, Stamina 11

If you win, turn to **417**. If you lose, you are dead, unless you have a resurrection deal.

322

The repulsive one recognizes you from your last undersea trip! Turn to **238**.

323

A few locals are discussing recent events – it seems some hideous beast has made its lair in a cave on the hill that overlooks the village.

'It's a gorlock,' says a farmer. 'And it's amassed quite a bit of treasure by all accounts – lifted from its victims. A brave adventurer like yourself could get rich if you killed it. You'd be doing us a favour as well.'

You ask what a gorlock looks like, but no one knows.

'Nobody's come back to tell the tale!' says the innkeeper.

You leave the tavern. Turn to **510**.

324

Heavy black clouds race towards you across the sky, whipping the waves into a frenzy. The crew mutter among themselves fearfully. If you have the blessing of Alvir and Valmir, which confers Safety from Storms, you can ignore the storm. Cross off the blessing and turn to **559**. Otherwise the storm hits with full fury. Roll one die if your ship is a barque, two dice if it is a brigantine, or three dice if a galleon. Add 1 to the roll if you have a good crew; add 2 if the crew is excellent.

Score 1-3	Ship sinks	turn to **607**
Score 4-5	The mast splits	turn to **83**
Score 6-20	You weather the storm	turn to **559**

325

Your ship, crew and cargo are lost to the deep, dark sea. Cross them off your Adventure Sheet. Your only thought now is to save yourself. Roll two dice. If the score is greater than your Rank, you are drowned. If the score is less than or equal to your Rank, you manage to find some driftwood and make it back to shore. Lose Stamina points equal to the score of one die roll and, if you can survive that, turn to **173**.

326

You follow the footprints to the mill, where you see an old lady and two men brushing flour off their clothes.

'Another successful year's haunting!' laughs the woman.

Quietly you creep back and tell the villagers what you have discovered. Brimming with outrage, they go straight to the mill and seize the three miscreants.

'Old Megan!' cries one of the villagers when he sees who is the ringleader of the three. 'So, you've been masquerading as a ghost these seven years, eh? Well, tomorrow we'll take you to the gallows and then you can play the part for real.'

Turn to **671**.

327

You have already cleaned the ratmen out of the tunnels below the city but the old well will make a good cache for equipment and money that you don't want to carry with you. It has an advantage over a town house as there is no risk of burglary or fire. You may also rest here as long as you like, restoring any lost Stamina points. Note 'Secret cache, Yellowport – *The War-Torn Kingdom* **327**' on your Adventure Sheet so that you can come here whenever you are in Yellowport.

To go back to the city above, turn to **10**.

```
ITEMS IN CACHE




```

328

You are not sure where to start looking for the ghoul, so you wander around, looking for stories, strange murders – anything that might put you on its trail.

Make a SCOUTING roll at Difficulty 12.

Successful SCOUTING roll	turn to **419**
Failed SCOUTING roll	turn to **360**

329

'Still haven't found him?' he says. 'Did you try the Castle of the Dragon Knights to the west of the Bronze Hills?' As he turns and leaves, he says, 'When you have better tidings, I will return here.'

You follow him, but he is nowhere to be seen. Turn to **400**.

330

You must have *Cities of Gold and Glory* before you can travel to Wishport. Turn back to **65** and choose again if you do not have this book. Otherwise, read on.

You step through the archway. Immediately the symbols on the stone begin to glow with red-hot energy, your hair stands on end and your body tingles. A crackling nimbus of blue-white force engulfs you, the sky darkens and rumbles, thunder and lightning crash and leap across the heavens. Suddenly, your vision fades, and everything goes black.

When your sight returns, moments later, you find yourself at the gates of Wishport. You join the throng of merchants and peasants making their way into the city. Turn to **217** in *Cities of Gold and Glory*.

331 ☐

If there is a tick in the box, turn to **627** immediately. If not, put a tick there now and read on.

You fall into conversation with Pyletes, a kindly old scholar priest of Molhern, the God of Knowledge.

`Many years ago, the Book of the Seven Sages was stolen from us,' he croaks. `News suggests that the scorpion men are in possession of it. I need a young adventurer like yourself to travel to Scorpion Bight and return the book to me. In return I can show you how to improve the skill of your choice.'

If you take up the quest, gain the codeword *Artefact*. Now turn back to **10**.

332

The quayside at the Trading Post is a simple affair, without the harbour facilities or the shipwrights of large ports. There are no ships available to buy here, but if you already own a ship, you can buy and sell cargo.

Cargo	To buy	To sell
Furs	135 Shards	130 Shards
Grain	220 Shards	210 Shards
Metals	600 Shards	570 Shards
Minerals	400 Shards	310 Shards
Spices	900 Shards	820 Shards
Textiles	325 Shards	285 Shards
Timber	120 Shards	100 Shards

Prices are for single Cargo Units. Fill in your current cargo on the

Ship's Manifest.

You can buy a one-way passage to Yellowport from here at a cost of 15 Shards: turn to **74**.

If you own a ship and wish to set sail, turn to **155**. If not, turn to **195**.

333

You are on the east bank of the River Grimm. Roll one die.

Score 1 or 2	A water sprite curses you – lose a Blessing, if you have one
Score 3 or 4	Nothing happens
Score 5 or 6	Catch a **smoulder fish** while fishing

When you are ready, you can:

Cross to the west bank	*Cities of Gold and Glory* **99**
Head east into the Forest of Larun	turn to **47**
Follow the river north	turn to **123**
Follow the river south	turn to **99**

334

To renounce the worship of Lacuna, you must pay 40 Shards in compensation to the shrine. 'If you forsake the love of the goddess, you will never survive the rigours of the wilderness,' warns the priestess.

If you still want to renounce the worship of Lacuna, cross off the 40 Shards and delete 'Lacuna' from the God box on your Adventure Sheet.

When you are finished, turn to **195**.

335

The captain eyes your crew, and your marines. They are a tough-looking lot, seasoned sailors and veterans of quite a few battles at sea.

'Bah!' he exclaims, 'It's not worth the trouble. I'll let it pass this time.'

With that, he returns to his ship, and departs. Turn to **439**.

336

You step in, saying, 'I have a message for King Skabb...'

The ratmen stare at you in amazement.

'A human! Get it!' screams Skabb.

The four ratmen charge toward you with a roar, wielding swords before you can say anything more. Soon they have been joined by many others and you have little choice but to turn and flee for your life! Desperately, you race down the sewer tunnels, with an army of ratmen in hot pursuit.

Lose them in the tunnels	turn to **79**
Try some magic	turn to **296**
Hide	turn to **127**

337 ☐

If there is a tick in the box, turn to **37** immediately. If not, put a tick there now and read on.

The crew have been using a net to catch fish. This time they have caught a sea centaur, a strange-looking creature, with a top half like a man, and a bottom half like a sea horse. It struggles feebly, clutching at the net with webbed fingers, trying to saw it apart with a long, serrated dagger made of some sea shell.

'We'll have to kill it, Cap'n. They're terrible bad luck to have on board,' says the first mate.

One of the sailors is already readying his cutlass.

| Give the order to kill it | turn to **522** |
| Spare it | turn to **604** |

338

You climb down the ladder into a house with herbs and plants hanging on the walls, and shelves lined with pots, pans and bottles of all sorts. The healer, an old woman, can cure you of poison but is unable to cure disease, lift curses or heal wounds. It will cost you 25 Shards to get cured, if you are poisoned. If you pay, you can restore your abilities to normal. When you are ready, turn back to **427**.

339

You find a burned-out house in the poor quarter where a trader has set up a stall, selling ash and debris. The merchant, a weaselly-looking old woman, is screeching, 'Ashes, ashes from the house of a sorceress! Fifteen Shards a packet!'

If you want to buy some, cross off 15 Shards and note the **ashes** on your Adventure Sheet. When you are ready, you head back to the centre of town. Turn to **100**.

340

Make a SCOUTING or THIEVERY roll (your choice) at Difficulty 10.

Successful roll	turn to **239**
Failed roll	turn to **34**

341

You hear an interesting story about one of Baroness Ravayne's knights, in Golnir. Apparently he is plotting against her!

`Intrigue and treachery in the court of the baroness...' mutters a man before his voice fades into a whisper.

You leave the tavern. Turn to **400**.

342

The alchemist's shop is lined with potions, jars of exotic substances, herbs, and so on. Alembics and beakers bubble and boil, full of strange-ly-coloured liquids. The alchemist, a tall, gangly fellow with a beak of a nose, sells potions. You can buy as many as you can afford – each one costs 50Shards.

Potion of strength (COMBAT +1)
Potion of comeliness (CHARISMA +1)
Potion of intellect (MAGIC +1)
Potion of godliness (SANCTITY +1)
Potion of stealth (THIEVERY +1)
Potion of nature (SCOUTING +1)

A potion can be used just before an ability roll or a fight to add 1 to the relevant ability for that one roll or fight only. Each potion can be used only once. The alchemist can make you a special potion for 250 Shards, but he needs an **ink sac**. If you pay the money, and have an **ink sac** (cross it off your Adventure Sheet) he will make you a **potion of restoration**. It can be used only once to heal all lost Stamina points, cure poison and disease. Turn to **510**.

343

Becoming an initiate of Alvir and Valmir gives you the benefit of paying less for blessings and other services the temple can offer. It costs 40 Shards to become an initiate. You cannot become an initiate of Alvir and Valmir if you are an initiate of another temple. If you choose to become an initiate, write Alvir and Valmir in the God box on your Adventure Sheet and cross off the 40 Shards. Turn to **154**.

344

You must make either a COMBAT or a MAGIC roll (your choice) at Difficulty 14 to slay him. If you fail the roll, turn to **161** immediately. If you are successful, read on.

You cut him down, or enchant him so that he obeys your every command and falls on his own sword. Note the codeword *Assassin*.

Hurriedly, you flee the palace. Turn to **216**.

345

A ship, impaled on some rocks, is breaking up. Nothing remains save for rotten timbers. However, a little bottle is bobbing in the waves. Inside, a message reads, 'Never sail at night through rocky waters.' You sail on. Turn to **209**.

346

Your ship, crew and cargo are lost to the deep, dark sea. Cross them off your Adventure Sheet. Your only thought now is to save yourself. Roll two dice. If the score is greater than your Rank, you are drowned. If the score is less than or equal to your Rank, you manage to find some driftwood, and make it back to shore. Lose Stamina points equal to the score of one die roll and, if you can survive that, turn to **453**.

347

The road is nearly blocked by wagons and supply convoys. A troop of soldiers forces its way through the throng – the men bang heads indiscriminately to clear people out of the way. Roll a die.

Score 1 or 2   Banged on the head! Lose 1 Stamina

Score 3 or 4   Nothing happens

Score 5 or 6   Mistaken for a beggar – receive 10 Shards from a passing priest

When you are ready, you can go:

North to Caran Baru	turn to **400**
East into the Coldbleak Mountains	turn to **474**
South along the road	turn to **387**
West into the Forest of Larun	turn to **47**

348

You remember what the fishermen say: the root of a certain seaweed, when crushed, gives off a cloud of toxic fluid. This sap is harmless to humans but is known to paralyse marine creatures for a short while. Fortunately, the seaweed grows in abundance here. You swim down with a handful of the roots, squeezing its sap into the waters. The hideous creatures shoot towards you, but are paralysed the instant they enter the cloud of reddish fluid that billows around you.

You take the **golden net** (note it on your Adventure Sheet) and swim back to the Shadar Tor as fast as you can.

Take the road to Trefoille	turn to **602**
Take the road to Marlock City	turn to **166**

349

You are too fast to get caught, and run off into the shadowy backstreets of Caran Baru. Cursing your luck, you consider your next move. Turn to **400**.

350

You are restored to life at the Temple of Nagil in Marlock City. Your Stamina is back to its normal score. The possessions and cash you were carrying at the time of your death are lost. Also remember to delete the entry in the Resurrection box now it has been used.

`Nagil has taken you from the barge of souls that sails to the lands of the dead, and returned you to us,' declares the high priest.

You leave the temple. Turn to **100**.

351

One day, a new slave is brought in to work beside you. Much to your astonishment, it is Lauria, the thief who left you in the lurch when you burgled a wizard's house in Yellowport.

`Sorry about the last time,' she says, `Business, you know. Now's my chance to make it up to you.'

She explains that she has discovered an escape route. This time, she promises to set up a diversion while you make for a tunnel where a cave-in has left an opening to the outside. Lauria says she will meet you there later.

| Go along with her plan | turn to **662** |
| Escape on your own | turn to **565** |

352

You mutter an enchantment that is intended to give you the appearance of a ratman but you get some of the intricate syllables wrong, and take on the appearance of a particularly wealthy merchant! At the sight of you, the ratmen redouble their efforts, and you are overwhelmed by sheer numbers. Turn to **308**.

353

The guard recognizes you, and shouts at the top of his lungs, `It's the stinking traitor who murdered Nergan. Shoot to kill!'

Several archers pop up from behind the rocks overhead, and start shooting at you. An arrow embeds itself in your shoulder. Lose 3 Stamina points. If you still live, you realize you made a bad mistake in coming back here, and you run for your life. As you climb down, you are shot at again. Roll a die.

Score 1 or 2   You are hit twice, lose 6 Stamina

Score 3 or 4   Hit once, lose 3 Stamina

Score 5 or 6   Missed completely, no wounds

After that, if you are still alive, you make it back to the foothills of the mountains. Turn to **474**.

You throw, muttering a prayer for forgiveness to the gods.

The weapon soars through the air. It turns, and catches the sunlight, sparkling like a flashing star, before sinking beneath the water with barely a splash. No ripples appear. Your heart feels uplifted, and the curse is no more! Delete the curse and its effects, and lose the codeword *Appease*.

Turn to **378**.

To find out how well your investments have done, roll two dice. You can add 1 to the dice roll if you are an initiate of the Three Fortunes. Also add 1 if you have the codeword *Almanac*, add 2 if you have the codeword *Brush*, and add 3 if you have the codeword *Eldritch*.

Score 2-4	Lose entire sum invested
Score 5-6	Loss of 50%
Score 7-8	Loss of 10%
Score 9-10	Investment remains unchanged
Score 11-12	Profit of 10%
Score 13-14	Profit of 50%
Score 15+	Double initial investment

Now turn to **46**, where you can withdraw or leave the sum written in the box there after adjusting it according to the result rolled.

You are pious enough to be allowed to enter the sacred grove. You step in and knock on the door.

A kindly old druid opens the door and greets you.

You hand him the **oak staff** (cross it off your Adventure Sheet).

'Thank you!' says the druid, 'An oak staff, eh! That's an interesting message, to be sure.'

He hands you 50 Shards as payment and a **willow staff**, saying, 'Please take this staff to the Oak Druid in the City of Trees, on the Isle of Druids. I'm sure he'll reward you, too. Good day and thanks again!'

With that he shuts the door.

You head back into the forest.

Turn to **47**.

The moon begins to rise, making the ghosts seem to glow. They sit hunched over their feast like vultures, occasionally stirring their hands in the pile of silver coins and tittering eerily.

Confront them	turn to **23**
Stay hidden and follow when they leave	turn to **541**

358

'Welcome to the City of Trees,' says a passing woman dressed in the garb of a druid.

The city has been built amid the branches of several mighty oaks. Ladders run up and down the trees to houses that perch like nests in the branches. You are not allowed into any houses, but the druids allow you to barter at the market.

Items with no purchase price listed are not available locally.

Armour	To buy	To sell
Leather (Defence +1)	50 Shards	45 Shards
Ring mail (Defence +2)	–	90 Shards

Weapons (sword, axe, etc)	To buy	To sell
Without COMBAT bonus	50 Shards	40 Shards
COMBAT bonus +1	250 Shards	200 Shards

Magical equipment	To buy	To sell
Amber wand (MAGIC +1)	500 Shards	400 Shards
Ebony wand (MAGIC +2)	1000 Shards	800 Shards
Cobalt wand (MAGIC +3)	–	1600 Shards

Other items	To buy	To sell
Mandolin (CHARISMA +1)	–	270 Shards
Silver holy symbol (SANCTITY +2)	800 Shards	750 Shards
Gold compass (SCOUTING +2)	900 Shards	800 Shards
Rope	50 Shards	45 Shards
Lantern	100 Shards	90 Shards
Silver nugget	–	150 Shards

When you are finished, if you are a Wayfarer by profession, turn to **645**. Otherwise you leave the City of Trees: turn to **678**.

359

A wandering tinker accosts you, selling **lanterns** for 50 Shards each. You can buy no more than three. Turn to **10**.

360

You have no luck in tracking down the ghoul. The next day, you hear a rumour doing the rounds in the taverns. A ghoul was found and

destroyed by an adventuring priestess of Tyrnai – apparently, the
temple of Nagil rewarded her handsomely. Looks like you were pipped
at the post. Turn to **100**.

361 ☐

If there is a tick in the box, turn to **55** immediately. If not, put a tick
there now, and read on.

You find a huddled, moaning figure on the ground. As you approach,
a net is thrown over you from behind. You glimpse a face painted with
white bone dust and big red circles around the eyes just before a terrific
blow on the back of your head slams you into unconsciousness.

Turn to **508**.

362

The sea dragon dives deep to the bottom of the lake. You are pulled
along at a terrific rate through the murky waters. You think your lungs
are about to burst when at last the creature surges upwards, breaking
the surface.

You find yourself in a cave inside a small rocky island, somewhere on the surface of the lake. A hole in the roof lets in a shaft of bright sunlight, that reflects off the water, casting dappled yellow light all over the walls.

Part of the cave is dry ground, heaped with the dragon's treasure hoard – sparkling coins, swords, armour and the like. You notice a rocky ledge, lined with a number of bottles, full of yellow dust.

The dragon pulls itself on top of its hoard – you have a few seconds to try to hide. Make a THIEVERY roll at a Difficulty of 10.

Successful THIEVERY roll	turn to **16**
Failed THIEVERY roll	turn to **274**

363

You collapse a rotting beam, just inside the cabin. The roof falls in, and a cloud of debris fills the water, obscuring you completely. You grab the gems, but it is not long before the magic of the sea centaurs takes you over. You live on for a hundred years, as a sea centaur. Your adventure ends here.

364

'The Violet Ocean's a dangerous place, Cap'n,' says the first mate. 'The crew probably won't follow you there if they don't think you're good enough!'

If your Rank is 4 or more, turn to paragraph **66** in *Over the Blood-Dark Sea*.

If your Rank is less than 4, the first mate advises you against the ocean journey. If you take his advice, turn to **85**.

If you insist on making the trip, you need to make a CHARISMA roll at Difficulty 11 to convince the crew to follow you.

Successful CHARISMA roll	*Over the Blood-Dark Sea* **66**
Failed CHARISMA roll	turn to **85**

365

Sul Veneris wakes up the moment you remove the stake. He rips the other stakes out of the ground, and soars into the air, with a shout like a clap of thunder. He swings his hammer around his head, and bolts of lightning leap forth to strike the storm demons.

As he rises into the clouds in pursuit of the demons, a bolt of lightning streaks from his hand and strikes you full force! You are thrown backwards, but to your amazement you are unhurt. In fact, you feel empowered by the blast. Gain 3 points of Stamina permanently.

You have freed Sul Veneris, the Lord of Thunder. Record the codeword *Aloft* before climbing down to the bottom. Turn to **658**.

366

'The Violet Ocean's a dangerous place, Cap'n,' says the first mate. 'The crew probably won't follow you there if they don't think you're good enough!'

If your Rank is 4 or more, turn to paragraph **66** in *Over the Blood-Dark Sea*.

If your Rank is less than 4, the first mate advises you against the ocean journey. If you take his advice, turn to **439**.

If you insist on making the trip, you need to make a CHARISMA roll at Difficulty 11 to convince the crew to follow you.

Successful CHARISMA roll	*Over the Blood-Dark Sea* **66**
Failed CHARISMA roll	turn to **439**

367

You have attempted to steal the chain mail before. This time, security has been doubled with warrior priests of Tyrnai in abundance. Inside the temple, there are two more of the bullheaded iron golem guards, and you realize there is no way you can succeed.

You head back to the city centre. Turn to **400**.

368

Becoming an initiate of Maka gives you the benefit of paying less for blessings and other services the temple can offer. It costs 50 Shards to become an initiate. You cannot become an initiate of Maka if you are already an initiate of another temple. If you choose to become an initiate, write 'Maka' in the God box on your Adventure Sheet – and remember to cross off the 50 Shards.

Once you have finished here, turn to **141**.

369

If you have a **boar's tusk**, turn to **612**. If not, read on.

The priestess, dressed in ceremonial leather armour, and carrying a silver bow, recognizes you, and welcomes you. She offers you the usual services.

Become an initiate of Lacuna	turn to **618**
Renounce the worship of Lacuna	turn to 334
Seek a blessing	turn to **52**
Leave the temple	turn to **195**

370

You come round, back to your Stamina score before the fight started. You lose the weapon and armour you were using – cross them off your Adventure Sheet. The Dragon Knights compliment you on your bravery.

'Until the next time!' says your recent opponent.

You take your leave, somewhat bruised. Turn to **276**.

371

With a war cry, you leap to the attack. Your first blow rips away a great chunk of its body!

Suddenly, a voice pipes up from inside the Gob-gobbler. 'Help, help, lads, this one's a real fighter!'

You realize the Gob-gobbler is a man disguised as a monster. But then two thugs – bandits, by the look of them – run out of the woods to attack you. You must fight them one at a time.

First bandit, COMBAT 3, Defence 4, Stamina 6

Second bandit, COMBAT 2, Defence 3, Stamina 7

If you win, turn to **422**. If you lose, you are dead, unless you have a resurrection deal.

372

Cross off the 10 Shards. A sleek yacht takes you on a trouble-free journey to Yellowport. Turn to **10**.

373

If you are an initiate it costs only 10 Shards to purchase Tyrnai's blessing. A non-initiate must pay 25 Shards. Cross off the money and mark 'COMBAT' in the Blessings box on your Adventure Sheet. The blessing works by allowing you to try again when you make a failed COMBAT roll. It is good for only one reroll. When you use the blessing, cross it off your Adventure Sheet. You can have only one COMBAT blessing at any one time. Once it is used up, you can return to any branch of the temple of Tyrnai to buy a new one.

When you are finished, turn to **526**.

374

You sense that sorcery is afoot. You make a few magical divinations which tell you that the path is cursed: it will sour the water supply of anyone that travels upon it. However, you can tell that the curse affects only the path. There is just enough room to squeeze your way up beside it, hugging the rock face. You find your water returns to a state that is drinkable.

Eventually, the path leads to a bubbling well of spring water in the rocks, just at the opening of a cave. You refill your canteen, then explore the cave. Turn to **232**.

375

You tell the provost you have important news, best heard by him alone. He takes you to a side chamber without his guards.

If you want to attempt to slay the provost marshal, turn to **344**.

Otherwise, you tell him some old news and he throws you out: turn to **10**.

376

You manage to slip out of your chains, and sneak off into the tunnels. You make it to the outside, but a troop of guards and a pack of dogs finally track you down. The fate of all escaped slaves is death – you are executed. Your adventuring days are over, unless you have a resurrection deal.

377

The road between Marlock and Trefoille is well maintained with regular guard posts. The Sokarans are nothing if not efficient. Roll a die.

Score 1-2   Bad omen – lose one Blessing

Score 3-4   Uneventful journey

Score 5-6   Find a **sword** (ordinary weapon)

When you are ready, you can go:

To Trefoille   turn to **250**

To Marlock City   turn to **100**

North into the Curstmoor   turn to **175**

378

You find a wide pool of bubbling, electric blue water. It gives off a strong invigorating scent, like crushed pine leaves.

If you have the codeword *Appease*, turn to **593** immediately. If not, but you have a **vial of yellow dust**, turn to **556**. Otherwise, you can bathe in the waters, turn to **598**, or leave, turn to **510**.

379

The scholar is in no condition to resist now that your work has been done for you by the ruffians. You take his purse. Inside you find 100 Shards. Happy with a good bit of banditry, you decide to call it a night. Turn to **100**.

380

'By the Larcenous One!' exclaims the high priest joyfully. 'You are indeed an accomplished rogue.'

Erase the **golden chain mail of Tyrnai** from your Adventure Sheet. The high priest teaches you secret knowledge of Sig, the God of Deception. You get a 300 Shard reward and you go up 1 Rank. Roll 1 die; the result is the number of Stamina points you gain permanently.

If you are under Tyrnai's curse, turn to **564**. Otherwise, turn to **100**.

381

You dart down a side tunnel but are horrified to meet several ratmen coming to meet you while your pursuers close in behind. You are caught in a vice and, though you fight with desperate bravery, you are overcome. Turn to **308**.

382

'Fishing?' you ask. 'Surely nothing can live in these poisonous waters.' The fisherman shows you a bright yellow fish with grey stripes, saying, 'Only the smoulder fish has adapted to the sulphur – it feeds on the local seaweed. Mind you, the smoulder fish is totally inedible.'

`Why hunt it then?'

`Well, each fish is worth quite a bit to sorcerers and the like. We have a standing quota to fill each month for the magical colleges at Dweomer. The sulphur-laden organs burn in a particular way – a very useful ingredient in certain magics, I am told.'

`And where does all this sulphur come from?'

`Scholars say there is an underground volcanic vent. Others believe it is the breath of the sea dragon. Personally, I always drop a silver nugget into the waters once a month to appease the dragon, for his favourite metal is silver.' Turn to **135**.

383

After a while Fourze circles around, heading across country. Make a SCOUTING roll at Difficulty 9.

Successful SCOUTING roll	turn to **585**
Failed SCOUTING roll	turn to **263**

384

Guildmaster Vernon is pleased to see you. You hand him the **copper amulet** and he exclaims joyfully, `The amulet of King Skabb! Well done, indeed!'

Cross the **copper amulet** off your Adventure Sheet. You are given 450 Shards as a reward.

Note the codeword *Acid* and turn to **10**.

385

The king is taken totally by surprise, and you cut him down. He falls dead at your feet.

`Long live General Marlock,' you mutter under your breath.

You take the king's **royal ring** as proof of your act. Note it on your Adventure Sheet and get the codeword *Ark*.

Although you manage to talk your way out of the stockade, the body is discovered as you are heading down the mountain path. Vengeful soldiers set off in pursuit.

Make a SCOUTING or a THIEVERY roll (your choice) at Difficulty 9.

Successful roll	turn to **167**
Failed roll	turn to **230**

386

There is no sign of Lauria, but you do find an open trunk and a window with a knotted rope dangling from it. So, she found the treasure and then made her escape, leaving you behind to face the music. You allow yourself a tight-lipped smile as you hear her voice echoing leadenly from far off in the fog: 'There's a thief at Master Talanexor's house! Quick!'

You'll settle the score with Lauria at a future date. For now, you just have time to escape before a patrol arrives. Gain the codeword *Ashen* and turn to **10**.

387

You are on a road between Caran Baru and Trefoille. You come to the Weary Pilgrim Tavern, a waystation between the cities. The tavern costs you 1 Shard a day. Each day you spend here, you can recover 1 Stamina point if injured, up to the limit of your normal unwounded Stamina score.

If you want to spend 3 Shards buying drinks all round so you can glean rumours, turn to **666**. To leave, you can go:

South	turn to **558**
North	turn to **347**
West into the Forest of Larun	turn to **47**
East to the lake	turn to **135**

388

If you are an initiate it costs only 10 Shards to purchase Elnir's blessing. A non-initiate must pay 25 Shards. Cross off the money and mark 'CHARISMA' in the Blessings box on your Adventure Sheet. The blessing works by allowing you to try again when you make a failed CHARISMA roll. It is good for only one reroll. When you use the blessing, cross it off your Adventure Sheet. You can have only one CHARISMA blessing at any one time. Once it is used up, you can return to any branch of the temple of Elnir to buy a new one. Turn to **316**.

389

Driving one of the creatures back with your sword, you leap on to the forecastle shouting, 'To me, men!' They rally around you, organizing themselves into a fighting unit and a battle ensues. You must fight one ker'ilk.

Ker'ilk, COMBAT 4, Defence 9, Stamina 8

If you win, turn to **519**. If you lose, you end up as food for ker'ilk young – unless you have a resurrection deal.

390

The horses rush past you. They seem to gallop through the air, whinnying and neighing, bellowing at the twilight sky. Soon they disappear from your sight. You make camp, and the next day continue your journey.

Go north across country	turn to **560**
Head east to the road	turn to **558**
Go to Trefoille	turn to **250**
Go to Marlock City	turn to **100**
Head west towards the River Grimm	turn to **99**

391

'Umm, well, I suppose I could let one such as you through,' says the tree thoughtfully. Then it uproots itself with a great tearing sound, and shuffles out of the way. 'There you go!' says the tree, 'You may pass.'

You walk through the thorn bush gate. Beyond, you find several huge oak trees whose branches are so big that they are able to support the homes of many people. Get the codeword *Apple* and then turn to **358**.

392

You pass your hands over the mad beggar, mumbling a prayer to the gods.

The beggar cries out, 'A cloud has been lifted from my mind! The curse is dispelled! I remember all!'

His name, he tells you, is Akradai, the Azure Prince of the Horde of the Thundering Skies, nomads of the steppes. 'I was cursed with madness by Shazir of the Ruby Citadel but now you have cured me!' he says. 'I am forever in your debt!'

He leaves, with a parting cry, 'Seek me on the steppes and I shall reward you.'

Gain the codeword *Azure*. Turn to **10**.

393

You hear a sound behind you. You spin around just as a another man, a beefy, disreputable-looking thug, comes for you with a long dagger. `Get him!' yells the man with the eyepatch. You must fight.

Thug, COMBAT 3, Defence 6, Stamina 13

If you lose, you are dead, unless you have a resurrection deal. If you win, turn to **476**.

394

When you and your crew join the fray, the battle is short-lived. The Sokarans are overpowered, and taken as slaves by the pirates.

The pirate captain, Verin Crookback, is a short, bull-chested man. He walks like a hunchback, because of a crippling wound he took to the shoulder blade, many years ago. He thanks you for your help and rewards you with a share of the booty from the Sokaran warships – only 50 Shards. He also hands you a **silver medallion**.

`If you ever go to the Kingdom o' the Reavers,' he says, `flash this about, one of the lads'll recognize it. Villains, the lot of them, but they'll honour one who carries the medallion. Someone will bring you to me. I'll help you, if you need it.'

The pirates take their leave, and you sail on. Turn to **420**.

395

You make it out of the temple with your pursuers close behind. However, you manage to lose them amid the alleys of Caran Baru, hiding inside a barrel of rotting food – garbage from the army barracks. You emerge stinking, but safe.

Turn to **400**.

396

The market square in Marlock City is huge. Armed guards stand around the edge to enforce General Marlock's will. Merchants and traders from all over Harkuna hawk their goods in a dozen languages.

Items with no purchase price listed are not available locally. The general has imposed a sales tax on all trade; the tax has been included in all the prices listed.

Armour	To buy	To sell
Leather (Defence +1)	70 Shards	25 Shards
Ring mail (Defence +2)	120 Shards	70 Shards
Chain mail (Defence +3)	220 Shards	160 Shards
Splint armour(Defence +4)	420 Shards	340 Shards
Plate armour (Defence +5)	–	700 Shards
Heavy plate (Defence +6)	–	1420 Shards

Weapons (sword, axe, etc)	To buy	To sell
Without COMBAT bonus	70 Shards	20 Shards
COMBAT bonus +1	270 Shards	180 Shards
COMBAT bonus +2	–	380 Shards
COMBAT bonus +3	–	780 Shards

Magical equipment	To buy	To sell
Amber wand (MAGIC +1)	520 Shards	380 Shards
Ebony wand (MAGIC +2)	–	780 Shards
Cobalt wand (MAGIC +3)	–	1580 Shards

Other items	To buy	To sell
Mandolin (CHARISMA +1)	300 Shards	250 Shards
Lockpicks (THIEVERY +1)	300 Shards	250 Shards
Holy symbol (SANCTITY +1)	220 Shards	80 Shards
Compass (SCOUTING +1)	520 Shards	430 Shards
Rope	70 Shards	25 Shards
Lantern	120 Shards	70 Shards
Climbing gear	120 Shards	70 Shards
Bag of pearls	–	80 Shards
Rat poison	80 Shards	30 Shards
Silver nugget	–	190 Shards

To return to the city centre, turn to **100**.

397

Your ship is thrown about like flotsam and jetsam. When the storm subsides, you take stock. Much has been swept overboard. You lose 1 Cargo Unit, if you had any, of your choice. Also, the ship has been swept way off course and the mate has no idea where you are. 'We're lost at sea, Cap'n!' he moans.

Turn to **90**.

398 ☐

If there is a tick in the box, turn to **225** immediately. If not, put a tick there now, and read on.

You make your way up the hill. After a while, you spot a cave set into the hillside, a little further up. Judging by the human bones, dumped near the entrance, this is the lair of a dangerous beast. Fresh tracks, of some large, two-legged, three-toed creature, lead from the cave into some nearby trees. It seems it is not at home, at the moment.

If you have the codeword *Apache*, turn to **463** immediately. If not, make a MAGIC or a SCOUTING roll (your choice) at Difficulty 11.

Successful roll	turn to **577**
Failed roll	turn to **486**

399

You were asked by the Governor of Yellowport to assassinate Nergan Corin. It is a good time to make the attempt. If you want to have a go, make a COMBAT or a THIEVERY roll at Difficulty 12. If you succeed, turn to **385**. If you fail, turn to **581**.

If you would rather join the rebels and kill the governor instead, record the codeword *Ambuscade*. If you join the rebels, when you are ready, the king wishes you well, and you are led out of the stockade, and back down to the foothills of the Coldbleak Mountains. Turn to **474**.

400

Caran Baru is a medium-sized town, that acts as a way-station between the citadel to the north, and the rich towns of the south. It is a garrison town; many supplies, arms and soldiers move through Caran Baru on the north-south trail. Shops, traders, temples and the like have sprung up here to serve the needs of the military. There is also a sizeable mining community, for the mines of Sokara lie in the Bronze Hills just outside town, and a slave market where poor unfortunates, sold into slavery, are bought for work in the mines.

You can buy a town house in CaranBaru for 200 Shards. Owning a house gives you a place to rest, and to store equipment. If you buy one, tick the box by the town house option.

If you have the codeword *Barnacle*, turn to **418** immediately. Otherwise, pick from the following options.

Visit the marketplace	turn to **215**
Visit the merchants' guild	turn to **112**
Visit the slave market	turn to **473**
Visit the temple of Tyrnai	turn to **282**
Visit the temple of Lacuna	turn to **615**
Visit the temple of the Three Fortunes	turn to **86**
Visit your town house ☐ (if box ticked)	turn to **177**
Visit the Blue Griffon Tavern	turn to **184**
Follow the road north to the citadel	turn to **201**
Go west into the Bronze Hills	turn to **110**
Travel north east into the country	turn to **60**
Take the east road to Fort Mereth	turn to **458**
Head south east into the mountains	turn to **474**
Take the south road	turn to **347**

CARAN BARU

401

Cross off the 60 Shards. The captain gives you a satisfied smile.

'Harbour duties all paid up. You may proceed,' he says mockingly.

He and his men leave the ship. Several of your crew curse or spit in disgust.

You sail on. Turn to **439**.

402

Your ship draws away, leaving the Sokarans behind. Your crew jeer at them, and you spot the captain shaking his fist at you in rage, before they disappear from sight. Turn to **439**.

403 ☐

If there is a tick in the box, turn to **229** immediately. If not, put a tick there now and read on.

You dump the head of Amcha One-eye on the guildmaster's desk. He stares at in horror for a moment and then a look of joy crosses his features.

'At last! We are rid of that scourge of commerce! Well done, well done indeed!'

Cross **Amcha's head** off your Adventure Sheet. The guildmaster pays for you to have special training. You can choose which area you would like to improve – you gain one point on one ability of your choice (for example, +1 COMBAT).

When you are ready, you return to the city. 'Come back anytime,' yells the guildmaster as you go. Turn to **100**.

404

One of the cultists of Badogor the Unspoken is feigning distress in the hope of luring a sacrificial victim for dinner. He sits up when he recognizes you as a member of the cult, and says, rather disconsolately, 'Ah, hallo, friend. We were hoping for a big banquet tonight.'

Two more cultists step from the shadows, holding a net. 'Oh well, perhaps another will come along,' one of them says optimistically.

They treat you as one of their own – even giving you a share of the cult's recent income. You get 20 Shards.

'May you never speak his name,' they intone in parting.

You return to the city centre. Turn to **10**.

405

The merchants' guild of Yellowport is a large building of granite, plushly decorated inside to show off its wealth. Here you can bank your money for safe-keeping – or invest it in guild enterprises in the hope of making a profit. You hear that the guildmaster is looking for adventurers.

Visit the guildmaster	turn to **122**
Make an investment	turn to **46**
Check on investments	turn to **355**
Deposit or withdraw money (note that you are in Yellowport)	turn to **605**
Return to the town centre	turn to **10**

406

You know that the **Book of the Seven Sages** that Pyletes wanted you to get lies within the mound. If you don't want to go for it now, you can leave by turning to **492**. Otherwise, you wait until nightfall, then creep towards the mound.

Make a THIEVERY roll at Difficulty 9.

Successful THIEVERY roll	turn to **449**
Failed THIEVERY roll	turn to **139**

407

You hide in the kitchen pantry, and then, disguised as a kitchen scullion, sneak out unnoticed. The skill and daring of your exploit will be forever remembered! Long live the rightful king! Turn to **10**.

408

You decline. They look at you inscrutably, and then sink beneath the waves with the body of their companion. Turn to **507**.

409 ☐

Becoming an initiate of Nagil gives you the benefit of paying less for services the temple can offer. You cannot do this if you are already an initiate of another temple. To become an initiate you have to pass a priestly exam.

If you want to take the exam, make a SANCTITY roll at Difficulty 10 unless there is a tick in the above box, in which case it is Difficulty 15.

If you succeed, you become an initiate: write Nagil in the God box on your Adventure sheet and turn to **71**.

If you fail, put a tick in the box (unless one is already there) and turn to **100**.

410

`Oh, what a load of rotten leaves!' exclaims the tree, `Anyone can see you're as bad as the next human. In fact, I'd say you're probably a... a lumberjack! Now, get lost!'

| Leave the forest | turn to **678** |
| Attack the tree | turn to **570** |

411

The high priest tells you that the **golden net** of the twin gods has been stolen. The repulsive ones have taken it to their palace beneath the sea in the Sunken City of Ziusudra. The repulsive ones worship the fish-god Oannes, who struggles with Alvir and Valmir for control of the sea.

`We must have that golden net, or the repulsive ones will use it against us. If you return it to us, we will reward you,' says the high priest. `The Sunken City lies under the coastal waters off the Shadar Tor.'

If you take the mission, gain the codeword *Anchor*. When you are finished, turn to **220**.

412

You are on the cobbled road between Yellowport and Trefoille. You meet a few merchants and pilgrims, but all in all it is an uneventful journey.

| Head for Yellowport | turn to **10** |
| Head for Trefoille | turn to **250** |

413

You are so devout that the king's spell cannot affect you for more than a few seconds. The queen, recognizing your faith in the gods, thanks you for entertaining them.

You wake up in the cabin aboard your ship. You are musing about the strange nature of your dream when you realize you have something in your hand. It is a **silver flute (+2 CHARISMA)**. While you have the flute, it adds 2 to your CHARISMA. Note that it is worth 500 Shards, and you can sell it at any market if you like. Turn to **507**.

414

Haylie runs into her mother's arms for a tearful reunion. Lynn, the mother, gives you a suit of **chain mail (Defence +3)** and a **sword** (an ordinary weapon).

`These have been in the family for generations. It's all I have to give,' she says.

Fourze is hauled off to the local magistrate for judgment – he will probably be sold into slavery.

Gain the codeword *Attar* and turn to **427**.

415

You cannot continue. You sink to your knees, gasping for water and pass out. Death is not long in coming. It is all over, unless you have a resurrection deal.

416

`The Violet Ocean's a dangerous place, Cap'n,' says the first mate. `The crew probably won't follow you there if they don't think you're good enough!'

If your Rank is 4 or more, you can take the ship south-west, turn to paragraph **77** in *Over the Blood-Dark Sea*. Or you can head south east, turn to **66** in *Over the Blood-Dark Sea*.

If your Rank is less than 4, the first mate advises you against the ocean journey. If you take his advice, turn back to **559**.

If you insist on making the trip, you need to make a CHARISMA roll at Difficulty 12 to convince the crew to follow you. If you succeed, you can take the ship south west (turn to paragraph **77** in *Over the Blood-Dark Sea*) or south east (turn to **66** in *Over the Blood-Dark Sea*.) If you fail, turn back to **559**.

417

The other knights are amazed by your skill, and they seem quite pleased that the Black Dragon Knight is dead.

`He was an evil man,' says the Green Dragon Knight.

You take the **black dragon shield** – note it on your Adventure Sheet. As you watch, the rest of your opponent's body dissolves into a foul-smelling smoke, armour and all.

Lose the codeword *Axe*.

You leave the castle. Turn to **276**.

418

You have heard that the man with the velvet eyepatch should be in Caran Baru. If you want to search for him now, turn to **117**. If not, turn to **400** and choose from the options there.

419

The trail of gruesome murders, and tales of terror leads you to an old cemetery in a near-deserted part of the old quarter. It is early morning, a few hours from daylight, so you haven't much time before it goes into hiding.

At the gates of the cemetery, you find a small girl, hunched over, sobbing. When she sees you, she backs away, terrified.

Make a CHARISMA roll at Difficulty 10.

Successful CHARISMA roll	turn to **553**
Failed CHARISMA roll	turn to **45**

420

Your ship is sailing in the coastal waters beside Marlock City. You notice an unusual number of Sokaran warships patrolling the area.

`The pirates are getting bolder and bolder – that's why the navy's out in force,' says the first mate.

Sail west	*Cities of Gold and Glory* **119**
Sail into Marlock City	turn to **142**
Sail east along the coast	turn to **120**
Sail south into the Violet Ocean	turn to **502**

421

The storm demons shrink back with a wailing, mournful cry, like wind in the trees. The power of your faith is enough to repel them. You work free one of the stakes holding down Sul Veneris. Turn to **365**.

422

The bandits are dead. The man inside the suit surrenders. It is Fourze, the master of the market. He terrified people with the monster disguise, and used a large pair of bellows full of gas to put his victims to sleep. Then he sold them to a slaver from Caran Baru, for work in the slave mines. You find Haylie, and several other villagers in the cellar of an old farm nearby.

'Don't hurt me,' begs Fourze, 'I'm only trying to make a few Shards!'

'What! By selling your own people into slavery!' says one of the villagers, giving him a good kick.

You lead them back to Venefax. Turn to **414**.

423

The ratmen lie defeated at your feet. You find 15 Shards on the bodies, and a note which says: 'Parti! Kitchuns. Tonite. Rank and file rats only. No offsirs and no king allowed!'

The rest of the cavern is bare, so you press on down the tunnels ahead.

After a while you come to a cleaner area of the sewers, a part of the old city now buried under Yellowport. It dates from the period when all of Harkuna was ruled by the Masked Ones of Uttaku, before the people overthrew them.

You come to two rotten wooden doors. Names have been scratched on to them by some half-literate ratman. One says 'Thrown Rum'; the other says 'Kitchuns'. You can hear gravelly rat voices from behind both doors.

Enter the 'kitchuns'	turn to **572**
Enter the 'thrown rum'	turn to **202**

424

The ship's captain says, 'I'll take you but you should be warned – it's a dangerous place we're travelling to. You'd better be sure you can handle it – if you're not at least a Master of your profession, I'd advise against. It's up to you, though.'

You must have *Over the Blood-Dark Sea* to travel to Copper Island. If you still want to go, cross off the 30 Shards and turn to **99** in that book. If you decide not to go, turn back to **142** if you are in Marlock City or **555** if you are in Yellowport.

425

The woman tells you her name is Lauria. She leads you stealthily through winding cobblestoned streets to a town house standing at the back of a small tree-lined square.

A yellowish fog is descending with the coming of night. Lauria waits until it is thick enough to shroud your activities from any stray passers-by, then jemmies a downstairs window. Within seconds the two of you are inside.

`You've got the easy job,' she says. `Stay down here and keep watch. The stuff we're after is upstairs.'

She bounds silently up to the next floor.

Stay on watch	turn to **534**
Search the ground floor	turn to **270**

426

`Ah, I see that you are a student of the arcane arts,' says Oliphard the Wizardly. `There is something I need. If you can get it for me I will teach you how to advance as a mage. It was Vayss the Sea Dragon who turned me into powder. He stole my **magic chest** in which I store all my magical equipment. Without it, I am virtually powerless. Meet me in Trefoille when you have it.'

`Where is Vayss?' you ask.

`Why, in the Lake of the Sea Dragon, of course,' he replies.

Record the codeword *Avenge*. As he leaves, Oliphard gives you an **amulet of protection**. Note it on your Adventure Sheet. Now turn to **378**.

427

If you have the codeword *Attar*, turn to **578** immediately. If not, read on.

Venefax is a strange-looking village. It looks like a single gigantic building. All the houses are joined together to form a jumbled mass, and none of the houses have doors. The only way in is through holes in the rooftop. Ladders lead up to the roof, which in effect forms a network of streets that the inhabitants travel across to get to certain buildings.

`We had to build it that way, for defence,' says a passing farmer.

'You see, the scorpion men from the south cannot climb, so they can't get inside the town!'

Visit the market	turn to **152**
Visit the Scorpion's Sting tavern	turn to **497**
Visit the village healer	turn to **338**
Chat to villagers on the rooftop	turn to **63**
Go south into Scorpion Bight	turn to **492**
Take the road north to Blessed Springs	turn to **87**
South west on the road to Yellowport	turn to **621**
North into open countryside	turn to **278**

428

With a martial cry you draw your weapon and charge. You manage to cut down two of the ratmen before they can react. The remaining two officers draw their swords while King Skabb ducks down behind his throne. You must fight them, both at once, as if they were one opponent. If you have some **rat poison**, you can smear it on your weapon blade to add 3 to your dice rolls. Cross the **rat poison** off your Adventure Sheet after use.

Two ratmen, COMBAT 8, Defence 11, Stamina 12

If you win, turn to **145**. If you lose, turn to **308**.

429

The gloomy wreck is filled with coral-encrusted skeletons of its drowned crew. You find the captain's cabin. Inside, a figure still sits in a chair, a chest of gems at its feet. With a thrill of horror, you realize it is a ghost, an undead remnant of a pirate captain, steeped in evil, its nacreous, fish-gnawed flesh still pulsing with a kind of half-life.

| Swim straight in and grab the chest | turn to **89** |
| Try to steal it without being seen | turn to **363** |

430

You are sailing in the waters around Scorpion Bight.

'I wouldn't want to put into land in these parts,' says your navigator. 'The scorpion men'll take all we've got, and our lives too, given half a chance!'

Roll two dice:

Score 2-4	Storm	turn to **586**
Score 5-7	An uneventful voyage	turn to **85**
Score 8-9	A ship of bizarre design	turn to **56**
Score 10-12	A floating island	turn to **264**

431

You notice that Oliphard has erected his pavilion over a verdigris trapdoor set into the floor.

'Ah, you have the key, I see!' says Oliphard. 'Please, be my guest – use the door.'

You open it up and climb some short stairs into a square chamber with three doors.

'They are doors of teleportation – step through and you will be taken to whatever land is displayed!' says Oliphard.

The first door leads to a teeming city of merchants – Metriciens in Golnir. Turn to paragraph **48** in *Cities of Gold and Glory* if you enter this door.

The second door leads to a huge mountain: Sky Mountain in the Great Steppes, far to the north. Turn to paragraph **185** in *The Plains of Howling Darkness* if you enter this door.

The third door leads to Dweomer, the City of Sorcerers, on Sorcerers' Isle. Turn to paragraph **100** in *Over the Blood-Dark Sea* if you open this door.

If you don't want to step through any of the doors, turn to **656** and choose again.

432

The militiamen are down. The tall gentleman watches you like a snake with its eyes on a mongoose. You have no time to bother with him now.

'We'll meet again, perhaps,' he says in a voice like slithering murder. 'Remember my name: Talanexor the Fireweaver.'

'Remember my name,' you call back as you lope off, 'Lauria the Housebreaker.'

Let the conniving vixen get into trouble. She nearly played you for her patsy, after all. Turn to **10**.

433

You rush in, taking the ruffians by surprise. A couple of good buffets around the head, and they run off. The scholar lies groaning on the ground.

Help him up	turn to **172**
Rob him	turn to **379**

434

You can leave possessions and money here to save having to carry them around with you. You can also rest here safely, and recover any Stamina points you have lost. Record in the box anything you wish to leave. Each time you return, roll two dice:

Score 2-10	Your possessions are safe
Score 11	A thief. All the money you left here has gone
Score 12	Earthquake! Lose all possessions you left
	here and the town house (erase the tick at **100**)

When you are ready, turn to **100**.

ITEMS IN TOWN HOUSE

435

Becoming an initiate of Tyrnai gives you the benefit of paying less for blessings and other services the temple can offer. To qualify as an initiate you must have a COMBAT score of at least 6. You cannot become an initiate of Tyrnai if you are already an initiate of another temple.

If you choose to become an initiate (and meet the qualification) write 'Tyrnai' in the God box on your Adventure Sheet.

Turn to **526**.

436

You find yourself washed up on a rocky shore, battered and cold, but lucky to be alive. You haul yourself up the beach on to land. Fortunately for you, you are near the Trading Post on the Isle of Druids. Turn to **195**.

437

Becoming an initiate of Sig gives you the benefit of paying less for blessings and other services. Also, you can add 1 to your THIEVERY score, as Sig will watch over your pilfering activities and keep you safe from the law. It costs 50 Shards to become an initiate. You cannot become an initiate of Sig if you are an initiate of any other temple.

If you choose to become an initiate, write 'Sig' in the God box on your Adventure Sheet and cross off the 50 Shards.

Turn to **235**.

438

The climb is too arduous for you. The air becomes too thin to breathe, and you cannot find the footholds you need to pull yourself up. You are forced to abandon the attempt and climb back down.

Turn to **244**.

439

Your ship is sailing in the coastal waters beside Yellowport.

Sail into Yellowport Harbour	turn to **555**
Sail north east towards Scorpion Bight	turn to **430**
Sail south west along the coast	turn to **120**
Sail south into the Violet Ocean	turn to **366**

440

Becoming an initiate of Elnir gives you the benefit of paying less for blessings and other services the temple can offer. It costs 60 Shards to become an initiate. You cannot become an initiate of Elnir if you are already an initiate of another temple.

If you choose to become an initiate, write 'Elnir' in the God box on your Adventure Sheet, and cross the 60 Shards off your Adventure Sheet.

Turn to **568**.

441

You clamber up on to the battlements of the Temple of Tyrnai with relative ease and manoeuvre yourself into a position overlooking the golem guards at the gate. Now you have to reach down without being noticed.

Make a THIEVERY roll at Difficulty 11.

Successful THIEVERY roll	turn to **22**
Failed THIEVERY roll	turn to **168**

442

You set out to explore the city of Yellowport at night, unwholesome though it is with its reeking air and dusty ochre streets.

Head for the rough part of town	turn to **21**
Go to the wealthy area	turn to **178**
Explore the merchants' storehouses	turn to **265**

443

You are witness to a major sea battle, involving at least 40 warships, between the Sokaran navy, and a pirate fleet. Arrows fill the air, and smoking fireballs are launched from catapults mounted on some of the ships. The shrieks of the dying carry across the waves. You decide it would be better not to get involved in such a conflict. Turn to **420**.

444

You try to make a run for it. Roll two dice and add your Rank. Subtract 1 from the total if you have a poor crew. Add 1 if you have a good crew or add 2 if you have an excellent crew.

Score 1-7	The galley overtakes you	turn to **51**
Score 8+	You outrun them	turn to **402**

445

You climb up, and squeeze through an open window into a long hall. Thin wires are stretched across the room, but you are an able enough rogue to crawl though without touching any of them and setting off possible traps or alarms.

Inside the temple, it is cool and dark, filled with an unearthly stillness. Suddenly, the temple doors are flung open, and two figures lumber into the room. You realize with a thrill of horror that the bull-headed iron statues outside the gates have come to life! They are golems, set here to guard the temple.

Run for your life	turn to **349**
Fight them	turn to **569**

446 ☐

If there is a tick in the box, turn to **226** immediately. If not, put a tick there now and read on.

You set out that night on your quest. Make a MAGIC roll at a Difficulty of 10.

Successful MAGIC roll	turn to **511**
Failed MAGIC roll	turn to **328**

447

You find yourself washed up on a rocky shore, beneath towering cliffs. You are battered and cold, but lucky to be alive. Eventually, you find a path up the cliff. You climb up, to find yourself at the Shadar Tor. Turn to **35**.

448

If you are an initiate it costs only 5 Shards to propitiate the twin gods of the sea. A non-initiate must pay 20 Shards. Cross off the money and mark 'Safety from Storms' in the Blessings box on your Adventure Sheet. The blessing works by allowing you to ignore any one storm at sea. When you use the blessing, cross it off your Adventure Sheet. You can only have one 'Safety from Storms' blessing at any one time. Once it is used up, you can return to any branch of the temple of Alvir and Valmir to buy a new one. Turn to **220**.

449

You creep past a scorpion man guard, which is dozing at the entrance to one of the burrows. The stench inside the mound is foul – a kind of acrid, rotting vegetable smell. You head for the centre of the mound, past tunnels, rooms and egg chambers, avoiding the inhabitants by skulking in the shadows.

Finally, you come to a room which is more like the laboratory of a sorcerer than a scorpion den: jars, alembics and scrolls lie all over the place. A scorpion man is at work at a desk. Unlike others of his kind, he wears rudimentary clothing.

Suddenly, what you took for a stuffed animal's head, mounted on the wall, says, 'There is an intruder, master.'

The scorpion man wheels round and charges straight at you!

Make a MAGIC roll at Difficulty 9.

Successful MAGIC roll	turn to **503**
Failed MAGIC roll	turn to **105**

450

A wooden stockade encloses the springs. At the gate, two militiamen stand on guard, and a priest, dressed in blue robes, sits behind a desk.

'Thirty-five Shards to enjoy the divine spa,' says the priest.

Pay 35 Shards and enter	turn to **378**
Cannot or will not pay	turn to **510**

451

You ask the innkeeper about Yanryt the Son. He looks at you oddly, clearly unsettled by your question.

'Some say he is the son of a mortal woman, and the god Tyrnai. But he has not been here for some time...' Suddenly he stops, and stares in amazement at the corner of the tavern.

You turn to look, and there, hunched over a stoop of ale, is Yanryt the Son, He greets you.

If you have a **black dragon shield**, turn to **575**. If not, turn to **329**.

452

The Trading Post has a small market place in the village square, where half a dozen stalls sell a few goods. Items with no purchase price listed are not available locally.

Armour	To buy	To sell
Leather (Defence +1)	50 Shards	45 Shards
Ring mail (Defence +2)	–	90 Shards
Chain mail (Defence +3)	–	180 Shards

Weapons (sword, axe, etc)	To buy	To sell
Without COMBAT bonus	50 Shards	40 Shards
COMBAT bonus +1	–	200 Shards

Magical equipment	To buy	To sell
Amber wand (MAGIC +1)	–	400 Shards

Other items	To buy	To sell
Mandolin (CHARISMA +1)	300 Shards	270 Shards
Lockpicks (THIEVERY +1)	–	270 Shards

Holy symbol (SANCTITY +1)	–	100 Shards
Compass (SCOUTING +1)	500 Shards	450 Shards
Rope	50 Shards	45 Shards
Lantern	100 Shards	90 Shards
Climbing gear	–	90 Shards
Bag of pearls	–	100 Shards
Rat poison	–	50 Shards
Pickaxe	–	90 Shards
Silver nugget	–	150 Shards

When you are finished, turn to **195**.

453

You find yourself washed up on a long, sandy beach, battered and cold, but lucky to be alive. You head inland until you realize you have arrived at the rivermouth delta of the River Grimm.

Turn to **579**.

454 ☐

If there is a tick in the box, turn to **188**. If not, put a tick there now, and read on.

You are thrown into a stinking prison cell. Your cellmate, a half-dead old man with long white hair tells you his tale: 'The lair of the gorlock! A hideous beast that has backward-pointing feet – Krine and I, fleeing with our stolen treasure sought refuge in its cave near Blessed Springs. The tracks led us to believe it had just left its cave, but we didn't know about its feet – in fact it was at home. It took Krine but I managed to escape with my life, only to be taken by the militia. I will never live to see the treasure but you, forewarned, may defeat the gorlock and take the riches it guards...'

Gain the codeword *Apache*.

A few days later, you learn your own fate. You are to be sold into slavery, and taken to Caran Baru to work in the tin mines. Turn to **118**.

455

A merchant ship, sailing for Wishport, will take you for 15 Shards. You must have *Cities of Gold and Glory* before you can travel to Wishport. If you do not want to make the trip, turn back to **142**. Otherwise, pay the 15 Shards and read on.

You have an uneventful journey and arrive in Wishport safely. Turn to *Cities of Gold and Glory* **217**.

456

'Ah, welcome, welcome,' says Marloes Marlock.

If you have the codeword *Ambuscade*, turn to **375**. If not, but you have the codeword *Ark* and the **royal ring**, turn to **255**.

Otherwise, you tell him you have not yet completed your mission. You are thrown out immediately before you have time to say more.

'Come back when you have better news, you worthless dog,' screams the provost marshal.

Turn to **10** and choose again.

457

They are unimpressed with your musical ability. The king waves his hand irritably. Suddenly, you wake up in your cabin, puzzled by your peculiar dream. If you have a blessing of 'Safety from Storms' it is now gone; delete it from your blessings box. There are no other effects.

Turn to **507**.

458

The road between Caran Baru and Fort Mereth is another military highway for transporting troops and supplies.

North into the country	turn to **60**
South to the farmlands	turn to **548**
South west to Caran Baru	turn to **400**
North east to Fort Mereth	turn to **299**

459

Cross off 50 Shards. The little Mannekyn creature is handed over to you on a leash. Its wings have been tied together to stop it flying away.

'Who are you, then?' it pipes in a squeaky voice.

Just then, a palanquin, carried by four bearers, arrives. A man leans out and hails you, 'You there! I've come to buy that flying monkey but I see I am too late. Nevertheless, I will give you 75 Shards for it.'

`Don't sell me to that popinjay – free me instead,' chitters the Mannekyn.

| Free it | turn to **659** |
| Sell it | turn to **186** |

460

You climb down an old disused well in the poor quarter of Yellowport. If you have the codeword *Acid* or a **copper amulet**, turn to **327** immediately. If not, read on.

It is dank, dark and smelly down below. If you do not have a light source, such as a **lantern** or a **candle**, you will have to return to the city: turn to **10**. If you are a Mage you can use sorcery to create light. If you have a light source, read on.

You follow a tunnel into the darkness. Turn to **164**.

461

You say the password `Rebirth' to the door.

`Sorry,' says the Demon Door. `The password changes once it has been used.' adds the door smugly. `I can't open for you.'

You will just have to leave.

North to the Bronze Hills	turn to **110**
West to the river Grimm	turn to **333**
South to the country	turn to **560**
East to the road	turn to **387**

462

What service do you seek at the temple of the Twin Gods of the Sea?

Become an initiate	turn to **294**
Renounce worship of Alvir and Valmir	turn to **624**
Seek a blessing	turn to **448**
Leave the temple	turn to **10**

463

You remember the words of the old man you shared a prison cell with. This must be the lair of the gorlock that is said to have backward-pointing feet, so that the tracks it leaves will always show the opposite direction of travel! You realize that this means the gorlock must be inside the cave.

Challenge the beast to combat	turn to **174**
Wait for it to leave the cave and sneak in	turn to **287**

464

The ship, already crippled by a storm, and with only half its crew, is easy meat for your hardy men. The strangely dressed foreigners surrender without much of a fight. You get 100 Shards as booty, and 1 Cargo Unit of spices, if you have room to take it.

Now turn to **559**.

465

Several hideous creatures, which resemble giant lobsters, surge out of the water to attack you! You and your crew are taken by surprise, and things look bleak . Some of your men are quickly killed, their bodies torn in two by powerful mandibles. The others begin to panic.

Make a CHARISMA roll at Difficulty 10.

Successful CHARISMA roll	turn to **389**
Failed CHARISMA roll	turn to **214**

466

The road between Blessed Springs and Fort Brilon is patrolled by troopers of the Sokaran army. The fort is well-supplied from Blessed Springs, and traffic abounds.

Visit Fort Brilon	turn to **259**
Head for Blessed Springs	turn to **510**
Set off north into the farmlands	turn to **548**

467

The heavy wooden gates of the temple of Tyrnai are guarded by a couple of veteran warriors – the old iron bullmen are gone. Inside, the god is represented by a stone idol of a jaguar-headed warrior. He appears to be naked.

Suddenly, a priest shouts, 'It's the thief! The blasphemous devil has had the nerve to return here!'

A score of warrior priests of Tyrnai boil out of the back rooms of the temple. You had better run for your life!

Roll a die. If the score is less than or equal to your Rank, turn to **395**, otherwise, turn to **551**.

468

You are walking down a side alley when a figure steps out of a doorway to block your path; it is a man with a velvet eyepatch.

His one good eye glitters with evil humour from a face ravaged with the scars of many a fight.

'I hear you are looking for me,' he says in a silky voice.

Make a THIEVERY roll at Difficulty 11.

Successful THIEVERY roll	turn to **393**
Failed THIEVERY roll	turn to **14**

469

He tells you of his life-long quest to find the 'Greatest Story Ever Told'. It is said that the god, Sig, in his aspect as the Divine Bard, passed this knowledge to a mystic called Damor the Hermit. He lives alone in a lost cave, awaiting the day when he can pass on the story to the one who finds him.

'I am too old now to pursue the quest — so I pass it on to you. I believe he can be found in the foothills of the Spine of Harkun, the mountains to the north. If you find Damor, you will become a great Troubadour!'

Acquire the codeword *Anthem*. Turn to **100**.

470

You grab the woman's wrist and give it a painful twist. You are not being cruel for the sake of it — she was about to steal your money.

'Oh, let me go,' she pleads, showing you the little infant son she's carrying in her other arm. 'I need the money for my starving children and my poor crippled husband.'

Yellowport is full of wretches like this. With a snarl, you push her away, tossing a coin after her for good measure (cross 1 Shard off your Adventure Sheet).

Later, strolling down by the canal, you find a small bundle lying on the slick cobblestones. It is a doll wrapped in swaddling clothes to make it look like a baby. Turn to **10**.

471

If you have the codeword *Animal*, turn to **369**. If not, read on.

The priestess, dressed in silken robes, and wearing a wreath of oak leaves, says, 'I have need of an adventurer like yourself. For arcane reasons involving the secret mysteries of Lacuna, I need the tusk of a boar. A were-boar, in fact. I believe they can be found in the Forest of the Forsaken, in northern Golnir. Hunt down a were-boar, and bring me a **boar's tusk**. In return, I will teach you how to be a better scout.'

If you accept the mission, acquire the codeword *Animal*.

Turn to **544**.

472

If you have the codeword *Dotage*, turn to **667** immediately. If not, read on.

Fort Estgard is one of three forts along the wall that runs right along the border. Their purpose is to defend Sokara against the ravening manbeasts of Nerech, which are constantly trying to break through to raid the interior. The commander of the fort desperately wants to see you.

'My daughter, Alissia, has been kidnapped by the man-beasts!' he says. 'They are asking that I let one of their raiding parties through, to attack the farmlands. I'm delaying my response as long as possible, but if I don't do something soon, they will kill her! Please, I need a brave adventurer to rescue her!'

If you take up the quest, record the codeword *Alissia*.

Head east into Nerech	*The Plains of Howling Darkness* **225**
North west to Fort Mereth	turn to **299**
South east to Fort Brilon	turn to **259**
West into the farmlands	turn to **548**

473 ☐

The slave market is a large, canvas-covered square. The poor unfortunate slaves, people from all over Harkuna – from the Feathered Lands, Golnir, criminals of Sokara, nomads from the steppes, are paraded in chains on a dais. Merchants and nobles bid for the slaves they want. If there is a tick in the above box, turn to **610** immediately. If not, put a tick in it now and then read on.

An unusual sale has come up: a little, furry, bat-winged humanoid. It is one of the Mannekyn People from Sky Mountain in the north and it is going for 50 Shards.

If you want to buy it, turn to **459**. If not, you head back into town. Turn to **400**.

474

The Coldbleak Mountains look as inhospitable and forbidding as their name implies, their frozen flanks climbing high into the icy clouds.

Climb into the mountains	turn to **5**
Enter Caran Baru	turn to **400**
Go west to the road	turn to **347**
Head into the farmlands	turn to **548**
Go south to the Lake of the Sea Dragon	turn to **135**

475

You slip on the rotting scraps of King Skabb's last meal and fall over with a crash. The ratmen turn to stare at you.

`A human! Get him!' screams Skabb.

The ratmen charge toward you with a roar. Soon they have been joined by others and you have no choice but to flee for your life! You race down the sewer tunnels, with an army of ratmen in hot pursuit.

Lose them in the tunnels	turn to **79**
Try some magic	turn to **296**
Hide	turn to **127**

476

`Not bad,' says the man with the eyepatch. `But now I'll finish you!' He draws his sword, and you must fight.

Man with eyepatch, COMBAT 4, Defence 6, Stamina 12

If you win, turn to **92**. If you lose, you are dead unless you have a resurrection deal.

477

You cannot get away fast enough. With one gulp Vayss the Sea Dragon gobbles you up. Your adventuring days are over, unless you have a resurrection deal.

478

Resurrection costs 200 Shards if you are an initiate, 600 Shards if not. It is the last word in insurance. Once you have arranged for resurrection you need not fear death, as you will be magically restored to life here at the temple.

To arrange resurrection, pay the fee and write 'Temple of Nagil (*The War-Torn Kingdom* **350**)' in the Resurrection box on your Adventure Sheet. If you are later killed, turn to **350** in this book. You can have only one resurrection arranged at any one time. If you arrange another resurrection later at a different temple, the original one is cancelled – cross it off your Adventure Sheet. You will not get a refund!

Turn to **71**.

479

They seem quite alarmed to see you charge forward undaunted. As your first blow lands solidly and you hear a satisfying grunt of pain, you know for a fact that these are no ghosts that you are facing, but people of flesh and blood. Fight them one at a time:

First Trickster, COMBAT 2, Defence 3, Stamina 3

Second Trickster, COMBAT 2, Defence 3, Stamina 2

Third Trickster, COMBAT 2, Defence 3, Stamina 2

If you win, turn to **171**. If you lose, you are dead, unless you have a resurrection deal.

480

'Well, tell you what – I'll teach you a few tricks, and then you can go away. What do you say?'

You've got nothing to lose so you accept. Damor was once a Troubadour, and he instructs you in its arts. Gain 1 CHARISMA point permanently. Afterwards, for a few hours, he lifts the curse that soured your water so you can make it down the mountain path safely. Turn to **244**.

481

If you are an initiate it costs only 10 Shards to purchase Maka's blessing. A non-initiate must pay 20 Shards. Cross off the money and mark 'Immunity to Disease and Poison' in the Blessings box on your Adventure Sheet.

The blessing works by allowing you to ignore any one occasion when you would normally suffer from disease or poison – for instance, the venomous bite of a snake. When you use the blessing, cross it off your Adventure Sheet. You can have only one 'Immunity to Disease and Poison' blessing at any one time. Once it is used up, you can return to any branch of the temple of Maka to buy a new one.

Turn to **141**.

482

If you are an initiate it costs only 10 Shards to purchase Lacuna's blessing. A non-initiate must pay 25 Shards. Cross off the money and mark 'SCOUTING' in the Blessings box on your Adventure Sheet.

The blessing works by allowing you to try again when you make a failed SCOUTING roll. It is good for only one reroll. When you use the blessing, cross it off your Adventure Sheet. You can have only one 'SCOUTING' blessing at any one time. Once it is used up, you can return to any branch of the temple of Lacuna to buy a new one.

When you are finished here, turn to **615**.

483

The tavern costs you 1 Shard a day. Each day you spend here, you can recover 1 Stamina point if injured, up to the limit of your normal unwounded Stamina score.

If you want to spend 3 Shards buying drinks all round at the bar, and listen for rumours, turn to 323.

Otherwise, turn to **510**.

484

You sail for days without sight of land. Soon you have run out of water, and the crew start dying of thirst. You lose 1-6 Stamina (the roll of one die) and several of your men. Reduce your crew to poor quality (unless it is already poor, in which case nothing happens).

Eventually, you find a familiar stretch of coast. Roll one die.

Score 1 or 2	turn to **120**
Score 3 or 4	turn to **430**
Score 5 or 6	turn to **136**

485

Your ship, crew and cargo are lost to the deep, dark sea. Cross them off your Adventure Sheet. Your only thought now is to save yourself. Roll two dice. If the score is greater than your Rank, you are drowned. If the score is less than or equal to your Rank, you manage to find some driftwood, and make it back to shore. Lose Stamina points equal to the score of one die roll and, if you can survive that, turn to **193**.

486

Everything indicates the cave is empty so you approach carefully, on the look out for attack from behind. Suddenly, something rushes out of the cave, taking you by surprise! It is a gorlock, a beast with legs like a bird, a body like a reptile, with two short forelimbs and a beaked, lizard-like head. You see that its two legs end in backward-pointing feet – the tracks it leaves will always show the wrong direction of travel!

It bites at you savagely, and you lose 4 Stamina points. If you still live, you will have to fight.

Gorlock, COMBAT 4, Defence 6, Stamina 7

If you win, turn to 315. If you lose, your bones will join the others at the entrance of the cave.

487

Make a SCOUTING roll at Difficulty 11.

Successful SCOUTING roll	turn to **348**
Failed SCOUTING roll	turn to **189**

488

You collapse, dying. A priest of Tyrnai, however, heals you so that you come round with 1 Stamina point left. It is not out of kindness that he has done this. The priests take all your money and possessions (cross them off your Adventure Sheet) and sell you into slavery. You are set to work in the tin mines outside the city. Turn to **118**.

489

Later, in your cabin, you examine the pearls more closely. To your horror, they lose their pearly sheen and return to their natural state – tiny pebbles. Some enchantment had been laid upon them to make them look like pearls. Cursing the young Sea Gypsy, you vow to be more careful next time. Turn to **85**.

490

When you hit the guardian, you tear away great wispy chunks of its smoky essence. Eventually, it dissolves into nothingness.

Inside the sarcophagus you find the mouldering bones of a long-dead wizard. In his skeletal hands you find the Book of Excellence. As you scan the pages, you learn all sorts of new tricks – add one to the ability of your choice (such as SCOUTING or COMBAT) permanently. Once you have read it, the book disappears with a flash.

You thread your way out of the Tomb of the Wizard King, back into the Forest of Larun. Turn to **47**.

491

You succumb to the insidious breath of the beast. Death has claimed you. Your adventuring days are over, unless you have a resurrection deal.

492

You are on a rough track that runs between Venefax and the territories of the scorpion men, slogging your way through hot, dry scrubland. A hawk circles overhead, cawing harshly.

Go north to Venefax	turn to **427**
Go south into Scorpion Bight	turn to **318**

493

Gills grow out of your cheeks as soon as you have read the runes aloud! You make your way down a track to the beach, and swim out to sea. The gills work perfectly, and you find yourself swimming in the eerie silence of a submarine world.

Suddenly, a hideous form looms out of the murk. It is rather like a giant squid, but it carries a spear in one of its many tentacles and wears rudimentary armour. Great black eyes shine with an implacable alien intelligence.

If you have the codeword *Anchor*, turn to **116**. Otherwise, turn to **238**.

494

You dodge down a side tunnel, and mutter an enchantment intended to give you the appearance of a ratman. Your pursuers come bundling around the corner. One of them stops to shout at you, 'Where'd the human go?'

Nonchalantly, you point down the tunnel, and the ratmen go haring off down it, whooping and yelling. You turn and walk the other way, a smile on your face.

Turn to **580**.

495

You arrive at Disaster Bay, where you find a community of fishermen. Judging by their wealth, they also make a living by other means – you suspect by looting the ships that get wrecked in the stormy waters of the bay.

A man offers to take you by boat, safely through the bay, and north to the port of Yarimura, on the Great Steppes; it will cost you 50 Shards.

Pay to go to Yarimura	*The Plains of Howling Darkness* **25**
Head north to the mountains	turn to **244**
Head for the road	turn to **518**
Head for Fort Mereth	turn to **299**

496 ☐

If there is a tick in the box, turn to **317** immediately. If not, put a tick there now, and read on.

You manoeuvre your ship as close as possible, and then take a rowboat over to the craft. Climbing inside, you find yourself in a small cabin which is lit by winking red and green lights set into the walls. A figure lies sprawled beside an ornate couch. The figure, although manlike, appears to have silver skin, and a great big round head, with one black, glittering eye that seems to fill its whole face. Whatever it is appears to be dead.

Quickly you search the craft, and find a kind of spear that fires steel balls from one end. It counts as a **magic spear (COMBAT +2)**.

Worried that you may be meddling with a ship of demons, you head back quickly, and sail on. Turn to **85**.

497

The tavern costs you 1 Shard a day. Each day you spend here, you can recover 1 Stamina point if injured, up to the limit of your normal unwounded Stamina score.

If you want to spend 3 Shards buying drinks for the locals, and ask them about the scorpion men, turn to **525**.

Otherwise, turn to **427**.

498

There are too many of them, and they give you a good hiding. 'Maybe that'll teach you some respect,' one of them says, as they swagger off, leaving you groaning in the gutter. You are reduced to only 1 Stamina point. You decide to call it a night. Turn to **100**.

499

You board your ship, which is docked in the harbour. The crew gives a drunken cheer as you come on board.

'Where are we bound, Cap'n?' says the first mate.

Return to shore   turn to **555**
Set sail   turn to **29**

500

You are restored to life at the war-god's temple in Yellowport. Your Stamina is back to its normal score. The possessions and cash you were carrying at the time of your death are lost. Cross them off your

Adventure Sheet. Also remember to delete the entry in the Resurrection box now it has been used.

The high priest, pale and wan after the effort of interceding with the god to bring you back to life says, 'You have returned from beyond the dark mirror of death. Tyrnai has granted you another chance. Strive to seek battle in his name!'

Turn to **526**.

501

If you didn't have enough money in the bank to cover the ransom demand, turn to **288**. Otherwise, your captors take the money and run. You are released into Yellowport, turn to **10**.

502

'The Violet Ocean's a dangerous place, Cap'n,' says the first mate. 'The crew probably won't follow you there if they don't think you're good enough!'

If your Rank is 4 or more, turn to paragraph **77** in *Over the Blood-Dark Sea*.

If your Rank is less than 4, the first mate advises you against making the ocean journey. If you take his advice, turn back to **420**.

If you insist on making the trip, you need to make a CHARISMA roll at Difficulty 12 to convince the crew to follow you.

Successful CHARISMA roll	*Over the Blood-Dark Sea* **77**
Failed CHARISMA roll	turn to **420**

503

Your magical awareness tells you something is wrong. You realize that the scorpion man is an illusion – a magically created disguise! The illusion falls away under your keen magical sight, and a rather fat little fellow is standing before you, dressed in a dirty, food-stained tunic.

'Ah...' he says, realizing his subterfuge has been uncovered, He drops to his knees, pleading, 'Please don't kill me! Please don't kill me!'

You manage to calm him down enough to find out his story. His name is Kaimren the Portly, a minor sorcerer. He came here in the guise of a scorpion man, and swiftly rose to power using his magical skills. He had planned to use the scorpion men as an army.

Fearfully, he hands you the **Book of the Seven Sages**, which he stole to further his campaign of conquest. Note it on your Adventure Sheet.

Then Kaimren leads you through a secret tunnel, out of the mound, and back to the village of Venefax, where you hand him over to the Venefax authorities for trial.

Record the codeword *Afraid* and turn to **427**.

504　☐

If there is a tick in the box, turn to **345** immediately. If not, put a tick there now, and read on.

The lookout spots a ship, its back broken on some rocks near the shore. The vessel will not last long before it is washed away.

Ignore it	turn to **209**
Explore the wreck	turn to **39**

505

Cross the **silver nugget** off your Adventure Sheet.

'Excellent,' says the dragon, catching the nugget in one of its clawed forelimbs.

With that, it rolls over, and dives down into the lake. At the last second, its tail whips up out of the water, inches from your face.

You could reach out and grab it, if you wanted to.

Catch the tail	turn to **362**
Leave it well alone	turn to **561**

506

The Gold Dust Tavern is a plush inn beside the city gates. The tavern costs you 1 Shard a day. Each day you spend here, you can recover 1 Stamina point if injured, up to the limit of your normal unwounded Stamina score.

If you want to spend a further 3 Shards buying drinks all round at the bar, and listen for rumours, turn to **331**. Otherwise, turn to **10**.

507

You are sailing across the Sea of Whispers with a clear, blue sky and a salty wind to help you on your way.

Dock at the Isle of Druids	turn to **195**
Sail west towards Scorpion Bight	turn to **430**
Sail north west into coastal waters	turn to **190**
Sail north into coastal waters	turn to **312**
Sail south into the Violet Ocean	turn to **13**
Sail east into the Unbounded Ocean	turn to **206**

508

You come round inside a disused warehouse, enmeshed in the net. You have been stripped of all your possessions – they are in a tidy pile nearby. Several men surround you. They are dressed in furs and robes that are adorned with hundreds of multi-coloured feathers. Each man wears a necklace of animal skulls and has his teeth sharpened to needle-like points.

'Hallo,' the leader says reasonably. 'We are the Unspeakable Ones. It is our way to eat people in sacrifice to our god'.

He points to a squat wooden idol of a grossly fat half-man, half-ape with ivory needles for teeth. You notice the name 'Badogor the Unspoken' inscribed on a plaque at the base of the idol.

'Badogor the Unspoken? Who's he?' you ask.

'Do not speak his name!' shouts the cannibal, 'Or you will be forever cursed!'

You notice a large cauldron of boiling water into which another cultist is tossing herbs and garlic. He stares at you and licks his lips.

Turn to **320**.

509

You spot a pressure pad at the base of the idol just in time – who knows what unpleasant trap that would have set off! Quickly, you remove the chain mail and sling it over your shoulder. Note the **gold chain mail of Tyrnai** on your Adventure Sheet. As it is pure gold, it is useless as armour.

The eyes of the jaguar-headed idol seem to turn to look at you. Make a SANCTITY roll at Difficulty 10.

Successful SANCTITY roll	turn to **625**
Failed SANCTITY roll	turn to **279**

510

The village of Blessed Springs, nestling at the foot of a tall hill, has grown up around the holy waters, a special spring said to have healing powers. It has been fenced off by the villagers, and a priesthood appointed to supervise the supplicants who come to bathe, or drink of the spring's waters. There is no market, but an alchemist has set up shop here.

Visit the Holy Waters	turn to **450**
Visit the alchemist's shop	turn to **342**
Visit the Blessed Ale Tavern	turn to **483**
Explore the hill	turn to **398**
Head north towards Fort Brilon	turn to **466**
South towards Venefax	turn to **87**
West into the countryside	turn to **278**
North west into the farmlands	turn to **548**

511

Your arcane knowledge tells you much about the undead. Ghouls are known to eat the flesh of the dead as well as the living. They like to make their homes in crypts and graveyards and they never venture out during the day, as sunlight burns their pallid, undead flesh. Also, they cannot abide a powder of salt and iron filings mixed together.

You can purchase these ingredients for 15 Shards at many a market stall. If you make the purchase, note you have **salt and iron filings** on your Adventure Sheet.

When you are ready, you set off to search the cemeteries of Marlock

City. Make a SCOUTING roll at Difficulty 9.

Successful SCOUTING roll	turn to **419**
Failed SCOUTING roll	turn to **360**

512

If you have a **pirate captain's head** and want to give it to the guildmaster, turn to 163. If not, read on.

'Do you have the head of Amcha the Pirate?' asks the guildmaster. 'No! Then what are you doing here? He is plying his evil trade in the seas to the south, and his base lies to the east of the Sorcerers' Isle. Now go!'

Turn to **100**.

513

One of them gives you a conch shell full of a greenish liquid. You drink it, and dive into the sea. Miraculously, you can breathe underwater! You follow the sea centaurs down into the depths until you arrive at a sunken ship, which is encrusted in barnacles and seaweed.

Suddenly, the sea centaurs swim away, leaving you alone. You notice that you are giving off a glow like the sea centaurs. Looking down, you see that the lower half of your body has turned into that of a sea centaur! You have been taken and transformed to replace their lost companion.

Explore the sunken wreck	turn to **429**
Swim back up to your ship	turn to **616**

514

To renounce the worship of Tyrnai, you must pay 50 Shards to the warrior priests, and suffer the 'Wrathful Blow'. A priest will strike you once – it is better to be struck by a priest than by Tyrnai himself!

If you are determined to renounce your initiate status, pay the 50 Shards and delete 'Tyrnai' from the God box on your Adventure Sheet. The high priest smashes you across the jaw, saying 'I'm doing you a favour – believe me!' Lose 1 Stamina point. If you earlier arranged a resurrection here, it is cancelled with no refund.

When you have finished, turn to **282**.

515

Make a MAGIC roll at Difficulty 11.

Successful MAGIC roll	turn to **205**
Failed MAGIC roll	turn to **314**

516

You pull the **wolf pelt** over you, and drop to all fours. Gingerly, you crawl in. In the dark, you now look and smell like a wolf. At the back of the cave, you find a hole in the roof. An iron ladder leads up to it.

Climb the ladder	*The Plains of Howling Darkness* **350**
Leave the cave	turn to **3**

517

If you have a **ghoul's head**, turn to **597**. If not, a priest asks which service you require.

Become an initiate	turn to **409**
Renounce worship	turn to **187**
Make resurrection arrangements	turn to **478**
Leave the temple	turn to **100**

518

You are on the road between the Citadel of Velis Corin and Fort Mereth. This is quite rarely travelled – the military guardposts are few and far between. Roll one die

Score 1 or 2	Lose 10 Shards gambling (if you have it)
Score 3 or 4	Nothing happens
Score 5 or 6	A sweet spring heals you of up to 3 Stamina points

When you are ready, you can:

Go to Disaster Bay	turn to **495**
Head for the Citadel of Velis Corin	turn to **271**
Travel to Fort Mereth	turn to **299**
Go south west into wild country	turn to **60**

519

Your crew have driven off the other ker'ilk, which dive into the sea. The ship was carrying 1 Cargo Unit of furs, which you can take if your ship has room. You clean up the dead sailors, and give them a proper burial at sea. There is nothing else of interest, so you sail on. Turn to **209**.

520

You hold up your arms and utter the mightiest prayer that you know. It has no effect.

The three white figures pelt you with a barrage of plates and knives. Something heavy hits you on the side of the head and you fall with a groan. The ghosts take advantage of this to snatch up the casket of silver and run off. Lose 2 Stamina points.

If you still live, you recover your wits to find that the three figures have vanished. But you are sure now that they were not ghosts.

Try to track them down	turn to **541**
Follow the river north	turn to **576**
Follow the river south	turn to **82**
Head east into the countryside	turn to **278**
West to the main road	turn to **558**

521

You are looking for the Black Dragon Knight on a quest that was set for you by Yanryt the Son. You ask the knights if he is here.

'The Black Dragon Knight? Yes, he is,' replies one of them. 'But he fights only to the death – there is no wager save the greatest of all for him, that is to say, life itself.'

Fight the Black Dragon Knight	turn to **321**
Don't fight and leave instead	turn to **276**

522

That night several sea centaurs emerge from the waters, their spiny skins glittering with phosphorescent flashes of light.

One of them speaks in a burbling voice. 'Where is our brother, whom you caught in your cruel nets, this day?'

'He is dead, I'm afraid', you reply, readying yourself for a fight.

The sea centaurs remain silent for a few moments, then the leader says, 'His destiny was always bleak. We would be grateful if you were to return his body to us.'

You cannot think of a reason not to, so you pass the body down to them.

'We thank you,' burbles the sea centaur. 'If you wish, we will give you the power to breathe the waters, so that you may swim down to the wreck that lies below, and take its treasures, those things that the surface-dwellers hold dear.'

Accept the offer   turn to **513**
Refuse the offer   turn to **408**

523

If you have the codeword *Assassin*, turn to **27** immediately. If not, but you have the title Protector of Sokara, you are sent in to see the provost marshal immediately: turn to **95**.

Otherwise, you have to wait several hours to be seen by one of the provost marshal's aides, a certain Captain Royzer.

If you have the codeword *Artery*, Royzer sends you in to see Marloes Marlock immediately: turn to **456**.

Otherwise, you will have to convince the captain it is worth his while to let you see the provost marshal. If you are a Warrior, Rogue or Troubadour, Royzer will let you in for the modest bribe of 5 Shards: turn to **191**.

If you are a Wayfarer, Priest or Mage, you will have to convince the captain of your loyalty to Sokara first. Make a CHARISMA roll at Difficulty 9. If you are successful, you can then bribe him: pay 5 Shards and turn to **191**.

If you fail your CHARISMA roll or do not wish to pay the bribe, Captain Royzer dismisses you rudely. Turn to **10**.

524

You struggle on. Only your iron will and hardiness keep you alive. Eventually, the path leads to a bubbling well of springwater in the rocks, just at the opening of a cave. You drink your fill, and soon you feel much better. Turn to **232**.

525

`They're vicious, evil devils,' says an old peasant. `Like huge scorpions they are, save they have the head and shoulders of a man – intelligent too, forever seeking to pillage our town, but they can't climb up the ladders!'

A soldier in the local militia speaks up, `They hate fire, too. All we have to do is sit atop the town, and pepper them with flaming arrows. They can't stand that for long. Mind you, things are getting bad. They've got a sorcerer now!'

A young man, blind in one eye and paralysed down one side, says, `They got a terrible sting as well – their venom did this to me.' There's not much else to hear, so you leave. Turn to **427**.

526

The temple of Tyrnai, the God of War, is built in the shape of a spear with a long, pillared nave, and an altar at the far end. Two massive stone warriors guard its gates.

Tyrnai is depicted here as the insensate spirit of war: a blood-drenched warrior with the head of a maddened jaguar.

Become an initiate	turn to **435**
Renounce his worship	turn to **69**
Seek a blessing	turn to **373**
Make resurrection arrangements	turn to **599**
Leave the temple	turn to **10**

527

You run off, leaving the terrible Gob-gobbler behind. The villagers of Venefax greet you with snorts of derision and contempt, and the young boy, Mikail, looks away, disappointed. It would be prudent to leave Venefax for a while.

South into Scorpion Bight	turn to **492**
North east towards Blessed Springs	turn to **87**
South west on the road to Yellowport	turn to **621**
North into open countryside	turn to **278**

528

You attempt to sneak in through the back of the temple that night. Make a THIEVERY roll at Difficulty 11.

Successful THIEVERY roll	turn to **445**
Failed THIEVERY roll	turn to **284**

529

You lose your footing, and fall. Fortunately, some bushes break your fall, and you lose only 4 Stamina points.

If you still live, turn back to **474**.

530

Your ship is thrown about like flotsam and jetsam. When the storm subsides, you take stock. Much has been swept overboard – you lose 1 Cargo Unit, if you had any, of your choice. Also, the ship has been swept way off course and the mate has no idea where you are. 'We're lost at sea, Cap'n!' he moans.

Turn to **90**.

531

If you have a **golden net**, turn to **4**. If not, turn to **462**.

532

The scorpion men's shaman falls dead with an uncannily human cry. If you were wounded in that fight, you have been poisoned by the scorpion man's venom. Subtract 1 from your COMBAT, THIEVERY and SCOUTING scores, as you are severely weakened (though no ability can drop to zero). Note that you are poisoned; you can restore your abilities to normal if you get cured. If you have some **scorpion antidote**, it will cure the poison immediately (cross off the **antidote**).

A quick search reveals what you were looking for: the **Book of the Seven Sages**. Note it on your Adventure Sheet. You steal out of the mound unnoticed and make it safely back to the village of Venefax, to the north. Turn to **427**.

533

The man takes the money, bites a coin and spits. Satisfied, he says, 'The Witches' Cauldron, that's where you'll find him.'

Later, you find the Witches' Cauldron Tavern in a maze of back-streets. Looking through a window, you spot a man with a velvet eyepatch sitting at a table, eating a meal.

Walk in and challenge him	turn to **589**
Ambush him when he leaves	turn to **211**

534

A long time passes. After a while, you risk calling up to Lauria in a whisper. Your voice sounds thick, rasping, choked with growing fear. Lauria does not reply.

Each second you remain in the house increases the risk of discovery.

Wait a little longer	turn to **119**
Go upstairs to find Lauria	turn to **386**
Leave at once	turn to **10**

535

The house of priests is an impressive building, a roundhouse of multi-coloured bricks. The myriad colours give it a bizarre and garish look, calculated to unsettle the visitor. Inside, a hundred offices teem with the administrators of the polytheistic religion of Sokara and Golnir.

If you are a Priest, turn to **9**. If not, there is little for you here, turn back to **100**.

536

If you have **climbing gear**, turn to **628**. If not, make a SCOUTING roll at Difficulty 12.

Successful SCOUTING roll	turn to **562**
Failed SCOUTING roll	turn to **438**

537

You find out that they call themselves the Gypsies of the Sea, wandering nomads of the waves, who find their islands naturally occurring in the Sea of Weeds. They make their homes upon them, and live a life of aimless drifting.

A tanned young man, full of wit and charm, explains that he makes his living from pearl diving, and selling what he finds to people like yourself. He offers you a **bag of pearls** for 25 Shards.

Buy the pearls	turn to **106**
Leave and resume your journey	turn to **85**

538

`Refusing to pay your taxes, eh!' says their leader. `That's a crime for sure!'

They close in around you. You'll have to think fast. Make a CHARISMA roll at Difficulty 11.

Successful CHARISMA roll	turn to **18**
Failed CHARISMA roll	turn to **157**

539

You roll across the eaves of the gate, and reach down to pull the plug on the other golem in one deft movement. It ceases to function before it can give the alarm. It is an easy matter to get into the temple by way of the roof.

Inside, it is cool and dark, filled with an unearthly stillness. You reach forward to strip the armour off the idol of Tyrnai.

Make a THIEVERY roll at Difficulty 12.

Successful THIEVERY roll	turn to **509**
Failed THIEVERY roll	turn to **228**

540

Sure enough, when the scholar leaves, purse bulging with Shards, the two ruffians go too. You follow at a slight distance. As you suspected, the ruffians wait for a suitable moment and then set about the scholar.

'Help, help! Thieves!' cries the scholar in a thin, reedy voice.

Return to the city centre	turn to **100**
Chase the muggers off	turn to **433**

541

Burdened by the heavy chest full of coins, the three figures have left deep footprints in the grass. Make a SCOUTING roll at a Difficulty of 10.

Successful SCOUTING roll	turn to **326**
Failed SCOUTING roll	turn to **245**

542 ☐

If there is a tick in the box, turn to **620**, immediately. If not, put a tick there now, and read on.

'By Tyrnai! It's the one who killed that pretender to the throne, Nergan Corin!' says one of them. They line up and give you a drunken salute, and then fall to slapping you on the back, and offering to buy you beers all night.

They also give you a present: a **potion of strength (COMBAT +1)**. Note it on your Adventure Sheet. When used it will add 1 to your COMBAT rating, for one COMBAT roll, or one fight only, after which it will wear off. Turn to **100**.

543

Guildmaster Vernon is too busy to see you. It seems he doesn't want to know you, now that he doesn't need you anymore. Such is life. Turn to **405** and choose again.

544

The shrine is set in a wooded grove. Birds twitter in the trees, and a deer darts away into the forest at your approach. A priestess is tending a low altar, where food and drink has been laid out in honour of Lacuna, the Goddess of the Wilderness. She is the patron of hunters, trappers, woodsman, and all those who seek oneness with nature.

Become an initiate of Lacuna	turn to **618**
Renounce the worship of Lacuna	turn to **334**
Seek a blessing	turn to **52**
Talk to the priestess	turn to **471**
Leave the temple	turn to **195**

545

You are given the cage. The trau speaks to you so quickly that you can barely distinguish the syllables.

'Let me out of here, and I'll reward you!' it says.

Free it	turn to **642**
Sell it to the mines in the Bronze Hills	turn to **651**

546

With an heroic effort, you manage to get to the woman. Gathering her up, you run for the door, and stagger out into the cool night air, smoke and flames licking at your heels. The townsfolk give you a rousing cheer and the girl thanks you effusively for saving her mother.

Later, it transpires that the woman is actually a powerful sorceress whose experiments in fire magic went slightly wrong. Her name is Elissia the Traveller and she gives you a gift: a pale moonstone. Note **moonstone of teleportation** – *The War-Torn Kingdom* 650 on your Adventure Sheet.

Elissia tells that you can use the moonstone by rubbing it, and you will be instantly teleported to the vicinity of the sunstone – which she carries on a necklace. 'I will be here in Marlock City. Whenever you are desperate, at the end of your tether, or just want to get here fast, use the moonstone and you will appear beside me. I will do everything in my power to aid you, and then my debt to you will be repaid.'

Whenever you want to use the moonstone, turn to **650** in this book. Now turn to **100**.

Your instinct was correct. The sea bed suddenly drops away, to reveal the ruins of the Sunken City of Ziusudra. Crumbling towers climb out of the hazy green depths, and shoals of flashing silverfish dart through the abandoned windows and doors of coral-encrusted buildings.

The creature you are following arrows down towards a large dome-like structure covered in waving tendrils of seaweed. It disappears through a hole in the roof of the dome.

Carefully, you swim down to the hole and look through, into the palace of the repulsive ones.

Turn to **41**.

THE SUNKEN CITY

548

You are crossing an area of fertile farmland, where much of the food is grown to feed the army. Little farmsteads dot the landscape, and the ploughed fields have the appearance of a patchwork quilt. Roll one die.

Score 1 or 2   Mistaken for a murderer! Forced to flee into the mountains – turn to **474**

Score 3 or 4   Nothing happens

Score 5 or 6   Find some **leather armour (Defence +1)**

When you are ready, you can go:

East to Fort Estgard	turn to **472**
North to the road	turn to **458**
South to Blessed Springs	turn to **510**
To the Coldbleak Mountains	turn to **474**
To the Lake of the Sea Dragon	turn to **135**

549

The priestess, dressed in a cloak made entirely of the leaves of trees, with her face smeared with moss, greets you. `A tusk!' she exclaims. `But I have no need of another.'

You ask if she might need it for the next time. `Next time? Mmm, maybe you have a point.'

She offers you 15 Shards. If you accept, cross off the **boar's tusk**. Either way, when you leave, turn to **195**.

550

If you have the **gold chain mail of Tyrnai**, turn to **380**. If not, turn to **134**.

551

You cannot escape. There are too many of them and all of them are seasoned warriors of Tyrnai. You are overpowered and given a savage beating – you are reduced to only 1 Stamina point. They take all your money and possessions. Cross them off your Adventure Sheet.

The priests do not have you sacrificed to Tyrnai – instead you are sold into slavery and set to work in the tin mines outside the city.

Turn to **118**.

552

A swaggering Sokaran captain marches on board with a complement of marines.

`I don't think you've paid your harbour duties,' he says.

`Harbour duties! We're in the middle of the sea!' you exclaim angrily.

The captain smiles smugly at you. `You'd better cough up 50 Shards, or I'll impound your ship and its cargo.'

`But that's no better than common piracy!' says your first mate, outraged.

`The duty will be 60 Shards now, for calling a captain in the Sokaran Imperial Navy a pirate!' he sneers.

Several of his men burst into laughter. If you have the title Protector of Sokara, turn to **185**. Otherwise, you can:

Hand over the money (if you have it)	turn to **401**
Refuse outright	turn to **311**

553

You convince her that you mean no harm. The little girl tells you that she was placing flowers at the grave of her father, when a horrible monster came for her. Fortunately, she was able to run away. She points to a large tomb behind which the thing was hiding.

You tell the girl to go home and then you set out warily for the tomb. Suddenly, a foul stench fills your nostrils, and a figure rises up out of the shadows! Yellow eyes glow with feral blood-lust, and the creature's talons, encrusted with dried blood, reach for you hungrily. You've found the ghoul!

Fight it	turn to **617**
Invoke the power of the gods	turn to **144**
Use some **salt and iron filings**	turn to **303**

554

King Skabb's rusty iron crown shattered when he fell, so you take the **copper amulet** from around his neck. Note it on your Adventure Sheet. You also find a chest in the corner of the room but it is clearly booby-trapped. You can open it using magic, or your skills as a thief. To pick the lock, make a THIEVERY roll at Difficulty 9. To use sorcery, make a MAGIC roll at Difficulty 9.

Successful roll	turn to **6**
Failed roll	turn to **64**
Leave the chest and return to the surface	turn to **10**

555

All shipping in and out of Yellowport must come through the offices of the harbourmaster. Here you can buy passage to far lands, or even a ship of your own, to fill with cargo and crew.

You can buy one-way passage on a ship to the following destinations:

Marlock City, cost 10 Shards	turn to **150**
Isle of the Druids, cost 15 Shards	turn to **301**
Sorcerers' Isle, cost 30 Shards	turn to **234**
Copper Island, cost 30 Shards	turn to **424**

If you buy a ship, you are the captain and can take it where you wish, exploring or trading. Three types of ship are available.

Ship type	Cost	Capacity
Barque	250 Shards	1 Cargo Unit
Brigantine	450 Shards	2 Cargo Units
Galleon	900 Shards	3 Cargo Units

If you buy a ship, add it to the Ship's Manifest, and name it as you wish. The quality of the ship's crew is poor, unless you upgrade it. If you already own a ship, you can sell it back to the harbourmaster at half the above prices.

It costs 50 Shards to upgrade a poor crew to average, and 100 Shards to upgrade an average crew to good. Excellent quality is not available in Yellowport.

If you own a ship, you can buy as many Cargo Units as it has room for. You may also sell cargo, if you have any. Prices are for single Cargo Units.

Cargo	To buy	To sell
Furs	190 Shards	170 Shards
Grain	200 Shards	180 Shards
Metals	600 Shards	500 Shards
Minerals	350 Shards	250 Shards
Spices	900 Shards	810 Shards
Textiles	350 Shards	300 Shards
Timber	180 Shards	160 Shards

Fill in your current cargo on the Ship's Manifest.

If you own a ship and wish to set sail, turn to **499**. If not, you can go to the city centre. Turn to **10**.

556

Gain the codeword *Amends*.

You scatter the powder on the surface of the waters. Cross the **vial of yellow dust** off your Adventure Sheet.

There is a flash, and a cloud of yellow smoke billows up out of the pond. When it clears, you find yourself face to face with a white-bearded bespectacled old man, floating a few feet off the water! He is dressed in long, flowing ornate robes.

He blinks at you for a moment before saying, 'Thank you, thank you. That worthless apprentice of mine! Can you imagine – I told him to throw the dust into the holy waters but the idiot couldn't even be trusted to do that!'

The old man's name is Oliphard the Wizardly. As a reward, he casts a spell that enhances your skill – add one to the ability of your choice, permanently.

If you are a Mage, turn to **426**. If not, he thanks you and says, `If you ever need some help, look for me in Trefoille.' Then he leaves. Turn to **378**.

OLIPHARD
THE WIZARDLY

557

`Who is rightful ruler of Sokara – General Grieve Marlock, or the son of the old king, Nergan Corin?' asks the soldier.

Grieve Marlock	turn to **631**
Nergan Corin	turn to **664**

558

You join the much-travelled road that connects Trefoille and Caran Baru. The traffic mostly consists of convoys of troops and supplies.

Go to Trefoille	turn to **250**
Follow the road north	turn to **387**
Go north into the Curstmoor	turn to **175**
Go east to the river	turn to **310**

559

Your ship is sailing in the coastal waters off the Shadar Tor.

Sail north west towards Marlock City	turn to **222**
Sail north east towards Yellowport	turn to **29**
Sail south into the Violet Ocean	turn to **416**

560

You are crossing the western wilderness, an expanse of wild, sparsely-populated countryside. A few trappers and woodsman make a living from the natural resources of the area.

A tall spire of rock, a towering anomaly of geology, rises up into the clouds, dominating the horizon. A local hunter tells you it is known as Devil's Peak and that the summit is infested with demons.

Climb the peak	turn to **658**
Head west to the river	turn to **99**
Head north into the Forest of Larun	turn to **47**
Go south to the Curstmoor	turn to **175**
Travel east to the road	turn to **558**

561

You are left alone, free to trawl for **smoulder fish**. Roll one die – the result is the number of **smoulder fish** you catch. When you are ready, you return to shore and give the boat back. Turn to **135**.

562

After a gruelling climb of some hours, you are halfway up the side of a mountain when you discover a thin, precarious path, leading up. You take a swig of water from your canteen and proceed up the path.

After a while you have to stop to take more water. To your horror, your water supply has turned sour and undrinkable!

Make a MAGIC roll at Difficulty 10.

Successful MAGIC roll	turn to **374**
Failed MAGIC roll	turn to **643**

563

To renounce the worship of Sig, you must pay 50 Shards in compensation to the priesthood.

`Sig will no longer watch over you!' says a priest.

If you are certain you want to renounce Sig's worship, cross off the 50 Shards, erase `Sig' from the God box on your Adventure Sheet, and lose 1 point of THIEVERY.

`The dungeons are full of would-be rogues who renounced the faith!' yells a priest as you leave.

Turn to **100**.

564

You tell the priest about the curse of Tyrnai.

`Ah, I see. Well, you have to appease the god. You need a **weapon (COMBAT +1)**, which you can buy in most markets, or acquire by some other means. Throw the weapon into the holy waters at the village of Blessed Springs, and ask for his forgiveness.'

Acquire the codeword *Appease* and turn to **100**.

565

Make a THIEVERY roll at Difficulty 10.

Successful THIEVERY roll	turn to **654**
Failed THIEVERY roll	turn to **376**

566

You are discovered hiding in the kitchen pantry. You are hauled off and thrown into the dungeons to await judgment. Lose all your money and possessions and turn to **454**.

567

`You are not worthy,' he says gruffly, and walks on without a backward glance. You sense it would not be wise to press him further.

Turn to **412**.

568

The temple of Elnir is a single spire reaching skyward. Eagles roost in its lofty belfry – they are sacred to the priests of the Skylord. Elnir is the Divine Ruler of the Heavens, patron of statesman and kings, and his sons are the stormlords.

`Thunder is the sound of the Sons of Elnir smiting the cloud demons,' says a passing peasant.

Become an initiate	turn to **440**
Renounce worship	turn to **241**
Seek a blessing	turn to **73**
Leave the temple	turn to **100**

569

You will have to fight them one at a time. They are tough opponents because their skin is made of iron.

First Golem, COMBAT 5, Defence 11, Stamina 10

Second Golem, COMBAT 5, Defence 11, Stamina 10

If you win, turn to **162**. If you lose, turn to **488**.

570

'Aargh, you fiendish human!' roars the tree, flailing its branches at you. You must fight.

Tree Guard, COMBAT 3, Defence 7, Stamina 10

If you reduce the tree to 5 or less Stamina points, turn to **148**. If you lose, you are battered into unconsciousness and wake up in the Trading Post on 1 Stamina with all your money gone – turn to **195**.

571

The merchants' guild of Marlock City is a large, many-storeyed building of marble. Inside, many clerks and scribes are at work. Here you can bank your money for safekeeping, or invest it in guild enterprises in the hope of making a profit. A sign on the guildmaster's door reads 'Help wanted'.

Visit the guildmaster	turn to **290**
Make an investment	turn to **104**
Check on investments	turn to **88**
Deposit or withdraw money	turn to **605**
Return to the town centre	turn to **100**

572

You open the door on to a large dining hall and kitchen. About thirty ratmen are standing around, eating and drinking. Everything goes quiet as they turn to stare at you with their black beady eyes.

'Er, I do have an invitation,' you stutter, holding up the note.

'And we'd love to have you for dinner,' one of them snarls.

Yelling noisily, they charge toward you. You have little choice but to turn and flee for your life! You race down the sewer tunnels, with the ratmen in hot pursuit.

Lose them in the tunnels	turn to **79**
Try some magic	turn to **296**
Hide	turn to **127**

573

To renounce the worship of the Three Fortunes, you will have to undergo a ritual.

'We must determine what the Three Fortunes have to say about the matter,' says the high priest.

Roll one die. On a 1 or a 2, you are free to go, on a 3 or 4 you must pay 25 Shards in compensation, and on a 5 or 6, they demand a sacrifice of some of your blood – lose 1 Stamina point.

Do you want to reconsider? If you are determined to renounce your faith, pay whatever price the die dictates, and delete 'The Three Fortunes' from the God box on your Adventure Sheet.

When you have finished here, turn to **86**.

574

'Ah, the saviour of the citadel. What can I do for you?' asks the general.

He can arrange for you to be healed of all your wounds, cured of poison, disease, and madness (but his court sorcerer cannot lift a curse).

If you have no weapons or armour anywhere at all, he will give you an ordinary **sword** and a suit of **chain mail (Defence +3)**. If you are completely out of money, he will give you 200 Shards.

'Any time you're in real need, just come to me,' he adds.

If you have a **coded missive**, turn to **677**. Otherwise, turn to **100**.

575

You hand him the **black dragon shield**. Cross it off your Adventure Sheet, and lose the codeword *Axe*.

'You are indeed worthy,' he says.

'And will you teach me your fighting arts?' you ask.

'You have already learned all I can teach you,' he says.

You realize that what he says is true. Your defeat of the Black Dragon Knight has taught you much. Gain 1 Rank and roll one die. The score is the number of Stamina points you can add to your unwounded total, permanently.

You look up, but Yanryt the Son has gone.

Turn to **400**.

576

You are up the Stinking River near its source: the Lake of the Sea Dragon. From here, the yellow waters rush down to the sea. The smell of the bubbling, sulphur-laden water is abominable.

Go to the Lake of the Sea Dragon	turn to **135**
Follow the river south	turn to **310**
Go west to the road	turn to **558**
East into the countryside	turn to **278**

577

You recognize the tracks as those of the legendary gorlock. You remember that it is said to have backward-pointing feet, so that the tracks it leaves will always show the opposite direction of travel! This means that the gorlock is currently inside the cave.

Challenge the beast to combat	turn to **174**
Wait for it to leave the cave	turn to **287**

578

The villagers welcome you as the one who brought Fourze to justice, and saved their people from slavery. Turn back to **427** and read on.

579

You are travelling across flatlands. The River Grimm splits into a delta here, spilling its waters into the sea. Long, sandy beaches stretch out to sea. Roll one die.

Score 1 or 2   Bitten by a crab! Lose 1 Stamina
Score 3 or 4   Nothing happens
Score 5 or 6   Find an **ink sac** washed up on the shore
When you ready, you can:

Go to Marlock City	turn to **100**
Follow the river north	turn to **99**
Travel west into Golnir	*Cities of Gold and Glory* **219**

580

You wait for things to die down, and make your way back to the door marked 'Thrown Rum'. Ignoring the kitchens, you go through. Turn to **202**.

581

You try to cut the king down, but at the last moment, he catches your wrist. His face is a mask of hate and rage. 'Traitorous viper!' he hisses, before shouting for the guards. You are forced to flee for your life.

Although you make it out of the stockade, you are caught in a narrow defile and seized by many men. You are hauled before Captain Vorkung, who looks sick and ashen-faced. He let you in to see the king in the first place.

You are sentenced to be hanged; the sentence is carried out immediately. Your adventures are over, unless you have a resurrection deal.

582

Before you have time to react, the dragon's massive tail smashes into the keel of your boat, lifting it out of the water, and breaking it in two. You are pitched into the sulphurous lake, with a rabid sea dragon closing in, intent on swallowing you whole!

Roll one die. If you score less than or equal to your Rank, turn to **637**. Otherwise, turn to **477**.

583

Your ship is thrown about like flotsam and jetsam. When the storm subsides, you take stock. Much has been swept overboard – you lose 1 Cargo Unit, if you had any, of your choice. Also, the ship has been blown way off course and the mate has no idea where you are. 'We're lost at sea, Cap'n!' he moans.

Turn to **90**.

584

'How can I come out to you? I would drown in the sea! Is that what you plan?' you ask angrily.

'Don't you know?' sighs one of them, 'the kiss of the mer-folk gives the power to breathe the waters to one of your kind for a short time!'

The others laugh mischievously.

Be kissed by the mer-folk	turn to **254**
Return to the clifftop tor	turn to **35**

585

You trail Fourze to the old farm. He goes inside, and you creep to see what he is doing.

Two rough-looking thugs are helping Fourze get into what is obviously a monster suit! It's a bit like a giant hairy toad, made of the hide of some animal stretched over a wooden framework. So much for the dreaded Gob-gobbler!

You wait by the door. As the thugs emerge, you club one to the ground, but you will have to fight the other one.

Bandit, COMBAT 4, Defence 6, Stamina 6

If you win, turn to **236**. If you lose, you are dead unless you have a resurrection deal.

586

Heavy black clouds race towards you across the sky, whipping the waves into a frenzy. The crew mutter among themselves fearfully. If you have the blessing of Alvir and Valmir, which confers Safety from Storms, you can ignore the storm. Cross off your blessing and turn to **85**. Otherwise the storm hits with full fury. Roll one die if your ship is a barque, two dice if it is a brigantine, or three dice if a galleon. Add 1 to the roll if you have a good crew; add 2 if it is an excellent crew.

Score 1-3	Ship sinks	turn to **182**
Score 4-5	The mast splits	turn to **530**
Score 6-20	You weather the storm	turn to **85**

587

While taking a stroll through the busy harbour area, you overhear a conversation between two merchants and learn the most profitable trading routes between Sokara and Golnir. Record the codeword *Almanac*.

Turn to **10** and choose again.

588

You break past the militia, leap over a table and rush out of the door. From behind you can hear muffled curses and then a fiery blast which sizzles wetly in the damp yellow fog, but you don't look back and you don't stop running until you are well clear of the house.

Turn to **10**.

589

Striding purposefully into the tavern, you walk straight up to him and say, 'I want what you've got under that eyepatch.'

His one good eye widens in surprise, and he jumps back, drawing his sword.

'We'll see about that, by Sig!' he cries.

The other people in the tavern draw back to give you room and start taking bets on the outcome of the fight.

Man with eyepatch, COMBAT 5, Defence 8, Stamina 12

If you win, turn to **92**. If you lose, the man with the eyepatch kills you – your adventuring days are over, unless you have a resurrection deal.

590

From the cover of a hedge you wait until dusk. By now all the villagers are safely indoors with their shutters tightly barred.

As the sky is turning from velvet indigo to the starlit blackness of night, you see three pale figures come loping across the green from the direction of the millpond. They must be the ghosts.

Seeing the banquet, they utter gleeful cries and start to devour what has been set out for them.

Make a MAGIC roll at a Difficulty of 11.

Successful MAGIC roll turn to **231**

Failed MAGIC roll turn to **357**

591

You find yourself washed up on a rocky shore, battered and cold, but lucky to be alive. You are almost certain you have cast away on the beaches of Scorpion Bight. You have no choice but to head inland. Turn to **32**.

592

Make a MAGIC roll at Difficulty 11.

Successful roll turn to **638**

Failed roll turn to **111**

593

You are under a curse. You remember what you were told: to lift the curse, you have to throw a weapon (any type) with a COMBAT bonus of +1 into the waters. If you have such a weapon, and want to throw it away, turn to **354**. If not, turn to **450**.

594

`Oh, it's you again,' says the tree grumpily. `All right, off you go.' The tree uproots itself and shuffles out of your way, leaving you free to visit the City of Trees once more. Turn to **358**.

595

You will have to sneak in around the hall to get behind the king. There are plenty of shadows to hide in but it will not be easy. Make a THIEVERY roll at Difficulty 11.

Successful THIEVERY roll	turn to **608**
Failed THIEVERY roll	turn to **475**

596

You thread your way through the ranks of trees. In places, the forest canopy almost blocks out the sunlight completely, and you are wandering in deep shadow, haunted by the cries of the creatures of the forest. If you have an **oak staff**, turn to **653** immediately. If not, read on.

You hack your way through the undergrowth, until you stumble across an old ruin. Creepers, and forest moss have grown over most of it, but you can see mask-like faces set into the walls, glaring down at you as if in angry outrage at your intrusion. You come to a massive stone slab, clearly a door. Set into the middle of it is a round granite face, the visage of a sleeping demon. Suddenly, an eye pops open, and regards you curiously.

`By the Tentacles of Tantallon!' exclaims the face in a gravelly voice. `A human! I haven't seen one of you lot for a hundred years.' An expression of suspicion forms on its rocky features. `What do you want, anyway?'

`Just passing through,' you comment airily.

`Well you can't pass through me unless you know the password. And that was given to me by Astrallus the Wizard King, umm... let me see, now… a thousand years ago, by Ebron! This is his tomb you know.'

If you have the codeword *Crag*, turn to **160**. Otherwise, read on.

'How do I find the password then?' you ask.

'Well,' says the demon door, 'Astrallus was a wizard, so why don't you ask some wizards?'

'Where would I find some wizards?' you ask.

'How would I know?' replies the door testily. 'I've been stuck here for a thousand years!'

You decide it is time to leave.

North to the Bronze Hills	turn to **110**
West to the River Grimm	turn to **333**
South to the country	turn to **560**
East to the road	turn to **387**

597

'You did it!' exclaims the warden happily, taking the **ghoul's head** and placing it in a jar. Cross it off your Adventure Sheet.

You can have a choice of reward: an **amber wand (+1 MAGIC)**, 500 Shards, or a free resurrection deal, if you do not already have one already. You can choose only one of these three rewards.

To arrange resurrection, write 'Temple of Nagil – *The War-Torn Kingdom* **350**)' in the Resurrection box on your Adventure Sheet. If you are later killed, turn to **350** in this book.

Finally, if you are suffering from Ghoulbite disease, turn to **156**. Otherwise, you return to town: turn to **100**.

598

You strip off, and wade into the bubbling waters. The effect is astonishing! You feel a sense of well-being coursing through your body. If you are suffering from disease or poison, you are cured instantly, and can restore your abilities to normal.

When you are ready to leave, turn to **510**.

599

Resurrection costs 200 Shards if you are an initiate, and 800 Shards if not. It is the last word in insurance. Once you have arranged for resurrection you need not fear death, as you will be magically restored to life here at the temple.

To arrange resurrection, pay the fee and write 'Temple of Tyrnai – *The War-Torn Kingdom* **500**' in the Resurrection box on your Adventure Sheet. If you are later killed, turn to **500** in this book. You can have only one resurrection arranged at any one time. If you arrange another resurrection later at a different temple, the original one is cancelled; cross it off your Adventure Sheet, you do not get a refund.

When you are finished here, turn to **526**.

600

You wait until Thursday. Lynn tells you that the disappearances happened a little way out of town, near an old farmhouse.

As you leave town, you notice Fourze, the Master of the Market, heading in the opposite direction.

Follow Fourze   turn to **383**
Head for the old farm   turn to **263**

601

The palace, the home of Protector General Grieve Marlock, is an imposing building of astonishing luxury. You get as far as a huge reception area, manned by many guards and staffed by government officials.

If you have the title Protector of Sokara, turn to **669**. If not, you are thrown out. Turn to **100**.

602

You are travelling the road between the Shadar Tor and Trefoille. You pass a convoy of masons, carpenters and builders heading for Trefoille with an escort of Sokaran soldiers.

Go to Trefoille   turn to **250**
Head for the Shadar Tor   turn to **35**

603

If you are an initiate it costs only 20 Shards to purchase The Three Fortunes' blessing. A non-initiate must pay 80 Shards. Cross off the money and mark 'Luck' in the Blessings box on your Adventure Sheet. The blessing works by allowing you to reroll any dice result once. When you use the blessing, cross it off your Adventure Sheet. You can have only one 'Luck' blessing at any one time. Once it is used up, you can return to any branch of the temple of the Three Fortunes to buy a new one. When you are finished here, turn to **86**.

604

The men mutter among themselves at your decision, but you insist. The sea centaur lies barely able to move on the deck. Nor does it speak.

That night, you see a strange glow rising up out of the depths. The sailors back away, muttering superstitiously, as several sea centaurs emerge from the waters, their spiny skins glittering with phosphorescent flashes of light.

One of the sea centaurs asks in a burbling voice, 'Where is our brother, whom you caught in your cruel nets, this day?'

'Why, here he is,' you say, indicating the half-conscious sea centaur on deck.

'Return him to us, we beg you,' one of them warbles.

Your men, anxious to be rid of the creature, hand him down to his friends.

'We thank you, landwalkers,' says the leader.

He gives you a **conch of safety from storms x 3**. When you blow it, it confers the Blessing of Safety from Storms. It can be used three times only (each time you use it reduce the number of charges by one). When it is out of charges, it becomes useless – cross it off your Adventure Sheet.

Turn to **507**.

605

You can bank money with the merchants' guild simply by writing the sum you wish to deposit in the box here. (Remember to cross it off your Adventure Sheet.) If you have banked any money with the guild in another book in the Fabled Lands series, add it now to this box and erase it from the other book.

```
┌─────────────────────────────────────────────────────────┐
│  MONEY BANKED                                             │
│                                                           │
│                                                           │
│                                                           │
│                                                           │
└─────────────────────────────────────────────────────────┘
```

To withdraw money from your account, simply transfer it from the box to your Adventure Sheet. The guild charges 10% on any withdrawals. (So if you withdrew 50 Shards, for example, the guild would deduct 5 Shards as its cut. Round fractions in the guild's favour.)

When you are ready to leave:

In Yellowport	turn to **10**
In Marlock City	turn to **100**
In Trefoille	turn to **250**
In Caran Baru	turn to **400**
If paying a ransom	turn to **501**

606

You thread your way carefully through the maze of magical symbols, until you reach the sarcophagus safely. Inside you find the mouldering bones of a long dead wizard, in whose skeletal hands you find the Book of Excellence.

As you scan the pages, you learn all sorts of new tricks . Add one to the ability of your choice (such as SCOUTING or COMBAT) permanently. Once you have read it, the book disappears with a flash.

You thread your way out of the Tomb of the Wizard King, back into the Forest of Larun.

Turn to **47**.

607

Your ship, crew and cargo are lost to the deep, dark sea. Cross them off the Ship's Manifest.

Your only thought now is to save yourself. Roll two dice. If the score is greater than your Rank, you are drowned. If the score is less than or equal to your Rank, you manage to find some driftwood to cling to and make it back to shore. Lose Stamina points equal to the score of one die roll and, if you can survive that, turn to **447**.

608

You inch your way slowly around the edge of the old temple. Suddenly, you burst out of the shadows and cut the king down, catching the ratmen by surprise.

At the sight of you standing over their dead king, the four remaining ratmen flee in terror. Without their king, they have no spirit for a fight.

Turn to **554**.

609

You recognize the two iron statues of bull-men that guard the temple. They are golems, creatures created by powerful sorcery. They will animate and attempt to kill any intruders that steal into the temple. Golems are almost impossible to defeat in combat, but they have one weakness – a ceramic plug, about the size of an apple, set into the backs of their heads. If the plug can be pulled out, the enchanted liquid that energizes the golem will pour out, and the creature will die.

That night, you resolve to try to get on to the roof of the temple, hang down from the gables above the entrance, and pull the plugs on the golems, before going for the chain mail.

Turn to **441**.

610 ☐

If there is a tick in the box, you find nothing of interest at the market — turn back to **400** immediately. Otherwise, put a tick in the box and then read on.

At nightfall, the market is kept open for a special sale. A cage with a steel floor is wheeled out. Inside is a dark, manlike shape. It seems to radiate shadows, for you can barely make it out.

The slaver says, 'A trau, ladies and gentlemen. Excellent miners, though they have to be chained with cold iron at all times.'

The price is 100 Shards. To buy the trau, cross off the money and turn to **545**. Otherwise, you leave the market, turn to **400**.

611

If you have the codeword *Anvil*, turn to **130** immediately. If not, read on.

As you draw nearer, you see that the pennants all represent different coloured dragons: the red dragon, black dragon, green dragon and so on. Outside the gates, a jousting list has been set up, and a few warriors are trying their hand against some knights who have dragon symbols on their shields.

A knight, in full plate armour, rides up and says, 'Welcome to the Castle of the Dragon Knights. It is our custom to joust against all who would come here – for a wager, of course.'

He explains that you must bet the weapon and the suit of armour that you will use for the joust. If you lose, you forfeit the weapon and armour. If you win, you get the armour and weapon of the knight you defeat. Most of your potential opponents, you note, would be using a sword and plate armour.

If you have the codeword *Axe*, turn to **521** immediately. Otherwise, you can leave (turn to **276**) or take the wager and joust (turn to **297** – you must have a weapon and at least **leather armour**).

612 ☐

If there is a tick in the box, turn to **549** immediately. If not, put a tick there now and read on.

The priestess, who is wearing the skin of a wolf, and is covered in red paint, welcomes you gleefully.

`At last, the tusk of a were-boar! Now the ceremony can go ahead.'

Cross the **boar's tusk** off your Adventure Sheet. The priestess rewards you with knowledge. Add 1 to your SCOUTING score permanently.

Turn to **195**.

613

Heavy black clouds race towards you across the sky, whipping the waves into a frenzy. The crew mutter among themselves fearfully. If you have the blessing of Alvir and Valmir, which confers Safety from Storms, you can ignore the storm. Cross off your blessing and turn to **439**. Otherwise the storm hits with full fury. Roll one die if your ship is a barque, two dice if it is a brigantine, or three dice if a galleon. Add 1 to the roll if you have a good crew; add 2 if the crew is excellent.

Score 1-3	Ship sinks	turn to **485**
Score 4-5	The mast splits	turn to **70**
Score 6-20	You weather the storm	turn to **439**

614

The Stinking River has cuts its way through the high ground here. On the edge of the chasm that overlooks the river below, lies the village of High Therys.

Just outside of town, three bodies hang on a gallows, slowly rotting. Out on the streets beyond, the villagers are having a fete. They welcome you. You can get some rest and recuperation here – restore up to 5 lost Stamina points.

When you are ready, you leave.

Follow the river north	turn to **576**
Follow the river south	turn to **82**
Head east into the countryside	turn to **278**
Go west to the main road	turn to **558**

615

Lacuna is the Goddess of the Moon, and of the Wilderness. She aids hunters, and woodsmen, and travellers in the lost places of the world. Her temple here is a long hall of oak, covered in vines and plants of all kinds. Inside, flowers fill the air with a pure and clean scent.

Become an initiate	turn to **170**
Renounce worship	turn to **253**
Seek a blessing	turn to **482**
Leave the temple	turn to **400**

616

You swim up to your ship, and haul yourself on board. The crew is astonished to see you.

'Another one of the sea devils,' says the first mate.

'We don't want any more bad luck,' says a crew member.

'Aye, we'll have to kill this one as well,' says the first mate.

You try to protest but your words come out as a bubbling, fishy warble. The first mate finishes you with his spear. Your adventuring days are over, unless you have a resurrection deal. If you do have a deal, when you come back to life, note that you have lost your ship and crew. As far as they are concerned, you never came back from the depths.

617

A desperate battle ensues.

Ghoul, COMBAT 3, Defence 7, Stamina 15

If you win, turn to **196**. If you lose, your adventures are over, unless you have a resurrection deal.

618

Becoming an initiate of Lacuna gives you the benefit of paying less for blessings and other services the temple can offer. It costs 30 Shards to become an initiate. You cannot do this if you are already an initiate of another temple. If you choose to become an initiate, write 'Lacuna' in the God box on your Adventure Sheet – and remember to cross off the 30 Shards.

Once you have finished here, turn back to **544**.

619 ☐

If there is a tick in the box, turn to **339** immediately. If not, put a tick there now, and read on.

You come across a blazing house in the poorer area of town. A crowd has gathered, watching the flames impassively. A young girl runs up to you, in tears. 'My mother is inside! Please, please help her!' she begs.

The fire is raging hard, and you are not sure whether anyone could be left alive inside.

Attempt a rescue	turn to **262**
Walk on	turn to **100**

620

Some local militiamen approach you with ill intent, presumably with a view to extorting a few Shards. They recognize you as a favourite of General Marlock, however, and leave you well alone, bowing and scraping to avoid your anger. Nothing else occurs tonight. Turn to **100**.

621

The coast road between Venefax and Yellowport is well-maintained and you make good time. You pass a few army patrols but they leave you alone.

Travel to Blessed Springs	turn to **510**
Head for Venefax	turn to **427**
Go north across country	turn to **548**
South to Yellowport	turn to **10**

622

The last time you were here, you had only a few minutes to grab some loot. Desperately, you search around for the **magic chest** that Oliphard the Wizardly wanted you to get for him. You find it (note the **magic chest** on your Adventure Sheet) but the sea dragon returns almost straight away, and you are forced to climb out of the hole in the roof without getting anything more, save for a pouch of 50 Shards.

You crawl out on to the island in the middle of lake and hitch a boat ride back to Cadmium. During the journey, you examine the magic chest, but it is guarded by great sorcery and is impossible to open.

Delete the codeword *Avenge* and turn to **135**.

You clamber down a ladder into a long low hall, the Venefax Market. Items with no purchase price listed are not available locally.

Armour	To buy	To sell
Leather (Defence +1)	50 Shards	45 Shards
Ring mail (Defence +2) –	90 Shards	

Weapons (sword, axe, etc)	To buy	To sell
Without COMBAT bonus	50 Shards	40 Shards
COMBAT bonus +1	–	200 Shards

Other items	To buy	To sell
Rope	50 Shards	45 Shards
Lantern	100 Shards	90 Shards
Climbing gear	100 Shards	90 Shards
Scorpion antidote	100 Shards	90 Shards

When you are finished, turn to **427**.

To renounce the worship of Alvir and Valmir, you must pay 30 Shards in compensation to the priesthood. The priest says nothing, he just points to a mural on the wall. It depicts the story of a woman who left the temple – a storm destroyed her ship and she drowned, to spend eternity as a lost soul, cleaning the barnacles off the thrones of Alvir and Valmir.

Do you want to change your mind? If you are determined to renounce your faith, pay the 30 Shards and delete 'Alvir and Valmir' from the God box on your Adventure Sheet.

When you have finished here, turn to **220**.

You realize that you have committed an act of sacrilege by stealing from the temple – you know in your heart that Tyrnai has cursed you.

You will never be a great fighter while you suffer the wrath of Tyrnai. Subtract 1 from your COMBAT score until you can find a way of lifting the curse. Perhaps the priests of Sig in Marlock City can help you. Note that you are under 'Tyrnai's Curse, -1 COMBAT.'

You sneak out of the temple. Turn to **400**.

626

You recite a devotional prayer to the gods, calling on your faith to aid you. The goblin folk are repelled by your piety, and purity of spirit. Even Gobrash finds the strength to get out from under you, and run off, such is your effect on them.

'Eeaurgh!' snarls the queen, recoiling, 'Please, your godliness is hurtful to us. Here, take this and leave!'

A jug of **faery mead** and an **enchanted spear (COMBAT +2)** are pushed towards you. Note them on your Adventure Sheet.

The wall behind you shimmers and disappears. You step through, back into the cold, night air of the Curstmoor. You leave the faery mound far behind, and camp for the night. The next day, you resume your travels.

Go north across country	turn to **560**
Head east to the road	turn to **558**
Go to Trefoille	turn to **250**
Go to Marlock City	turn to **100**
Head west towards the River Grimm	turn to **99**

627

A bard in the tavern recites an epic tale of ancient legend. He speaks of Xinoc the Priest King, the ruler of a mighty nation in the distant steppes, far to the north. A thousand years ago his empire flourished, and his wealth was enormous. He was buried in a great pyramid tomb, along with his riches. It is said the Pyramid of Xinoc lies beyond the Spine of Harkun, and beyond the Great Steppes, in the foothills of the Peaks at the Edge of the World. You question him further, but that is all he knows. You leave the tavern. Turn to **10**.

628

After a hard climb, you are half-way up the side of a mountain when you discover a thin, precarious path, leading up. The sun beats down, and you are sweating heavily. You take a swig of water from your canteen and proceed up the path.

After a while you have to stop to take more water. To your horror, your water supply has turned sour and undrinkable!

Make a MAGIC roll at Difficulty 10.

Successful MAGIC roll	turn to **374**
Failed MAGIC roll	turn to **643**

629

The soldier recognizes you and leads you to see the king. Nergan is pleased to see you. 'Have you succeeded in ridding us of Marloes?' he asks eagerly.

If you have the codeword *Assassin*, turn to **256** immediately. If not, read on.

You say that you have not completed your mission.

'What are you doing here, then? There is nothing I can do to help you. You will just have to use your own wits. Now go – fulfil my royal command!' says the king.

You are escorted to the foothills of the mountains. Turn to **474**.

630

You struggle deeper into the forest until you come to a thick wall of impenetrable thorn bushes. Circling it, you find there is a break in the hedge, but it is filled by a big tree.

To your surprise, a face forms in the trunk, and speaks in a woody voice, 'None can pass. Begone, human!'

If you have the codeword *Apple*, turn to **594**. If not, you can:

Return to the Trading Post	turn to **195**
Attack the tree	turn to **570**
Try to persuade it to let you pass	turn to **237**

631

The soldier nods. Suddenly, he shouts something and several archers pop up from behind rocks and start shooting at you.

An arrow embeds itself in your shoulder. Lose 3 Stamina points. If you still live, you realize you are a sitting duck, and you run for your life.

As you climb down, you are shot at again. Roll one die:

Score 1 or 2	Hit twice, lose 6 Stamina
Score 3 or 4	Hit once, lose 3 Stamina
Score 5 or 6	Missed completely, no wounds

After that, if you are still alive, you make it back to the foothills of the mountains. Turn to **474**.

632

Make a SANCTITY roll at Difficulty 12.

| Successful SANCTITY roll | turn to **392** |
| Failed SANCTITY roll | turn to **125** |

633

Your unerring sense of direction, even at sea, serves you well. It is not long before you find a familiar stretch of coast.

Roll one die.

Score 1 or 2	turn to **120**
Score 3 or 4	turn to **430**
Score 5 or 6	turn to **136**

634

The climb is slightly easier than the last time, and you heave yourself over the lip of the top of Devil's Peak. A gryphon – a creature that is half-lion, half-eagle, and at least the same size at you – has made its nest here. It immediately swoops in to the attack, intent on protecting its nest. You must fight.

Gryphon, COMBAT 4, Defence 5, Stamina 7

If you lose, you are birdfeed for gryphon chicks. Your adventures are over.

If you win, you find a **bag of pearls** and 10 Shards in the nest. There is nothing else up here, so you slog all the way down again. Turn to **658**.

635 □

If the box above is empty, put a tick in it now and turn to **80**. If it is already ticked, turn to **470**.

636

Becoming an initiate of Tyrnai gives you the benefit of paying less for blessings and other services the temple can offer. To qualify as an initiate you must have a COMBAT score of at least 6. Unlike other temples, there is no entry fee. You cannot become an initiate of Tyrnai if you are already an initiate of another temple. If you choose to become an initiate (and meet the qualification) write `Tyrnai' in the God box on your Adventure Sheet.

Once you have finished here, turn to **282**.

637

Somehow you manage to evade the creature's jaws, and swim back to shore. Hauling yourself up on to the beach, you are assaulted by an angry villager.

`Where's my boat?' he cries, `You've sunk it, haven't you? You city types don't know a thing! Well, you'll have to pay me back – fifty Shards at least!'

`Hah!' you reply, `The cost of hiring it was more than its worth in any case. As far as I'm concerned, that boat was mine to do with as I liked!'

The argument goes on all the way back to the village but eventually the fisherman gives up and storms off.

Turn to **135**.

638

You know from ancient texts of arcane lore that the repulsive ones cannot stand bright light. Using all your magical power, you cause the glowing moss to emit a a dazzling flash of yellow light. Blinded for a few seconds, the repulsive ones mill about helplessly, and you dart in and seize the **golden net** (note it on your Adventure Sheet).

You swim for the Shadar Tor as fast as you can. From here, you can:

Take the road to Trefoille	turn to **602**
Take the road to Marlock City	turn to **166**

639

Heavy black clouds race towards you across the sky, whipping the waves into a frenzy. The crew mutter among themselves fearfully. If you have the blessing of Alvir and Valmir, which confers Safety from Storms, you can ignore the storm. Cross off your blessing and turn to **507**. Otherwise the storm hits with full fury.

Roll one die if your ship is a barque, two dice if it is a brigantine, or three dice if it is a galleon. Add 1 to the roll if you have a good crew; add 2 if you have an excellent crew.

Score 1-3	Ship sinks	turn to **219**
Score 4-5	The mast splits	turn to **67**
Score 6-20	You weather the storm	turn to **507**

640

You are restored to life at the war god's temple in Caran Baru. Your Stamina is back to its normal score. The possessions and cash you were carrying at the time of your death are lost. Cross them off your Adventure Sheet. Also remember to delete the entry in the Resurrection box now it has been used.

The high priest, sweating from the effort of the ceremony of resurrection, says, 'Tyrnai has brought you back – honour him by the upholding the code of the warrior and by sending many the souls of those slain in battle to him.' Turn to **282**.

641

'Want to try your luck in the Gambler's Den?' asks a short, dark man, dressed as a mercenary bodyguard. 'Just 5 Shards entrance fee.'

He nods to a door at the top of some rickety stairs.

If you pay the money, cross it off and turn to **91**. If not, he shrugs, and hisses at another passerby. You wander off and pass an uneventful evening, turn to **100**.

642

You open the cage door. A wide grin suddenly appears at about head height within the dark shadows that wreath the trau. All you can see is a huge sliver of a grin, topped by two glowing red eyes.

`Free at last!' gushes the trau as it leaps out. `Now for home, and as much faery mead as I can drink!'

With that, it delves into the ground so fast that it has burrowed out of sight before you can do anything to stop it.

Shrugging your shoulders resignedly, you leave the market. Turn to **400**.

643

Gamely, you drive yourself on, but your thirst is becoming terrible, and soon you will be unable to continue. If you go on, you might die of thirst before finding a water supply.

Turn back	turn to **244**
Press on	turn to **78**

644

Using your sorcerous powers you breathe a cloud of greenish vapour over the ratmen. Coughing and gasping, they sink into an enchanted slumber. It is an easy matter to despatch them while they sleep. Turn to **554**.

645 ☐

If there is a tick in the box, turn to **248** immediately. If not, put a tick there now and read on.

You are brought before the druids' leader, the Oak Druid, a bearded fellow with earth and leaves all tangled up in his hair. He asks you to perform a service for them.

`Take this oak staff to the Willow Druid in the Forest of Larun. The sacred grove where he lives will be hard to find, but I'm sure you can do it. The Willow Druid will give you something to bring back to me. When you return with it, I will make you a better Wayfarer.'

Note the **oak staff** on your Adventure Sheet. You leave the City of Trees, turn to **678**.

646

Your mind is blasted into numbed confusion by the protective spells that guard the sacred grove. You wander off aimlessly into the forest, and get hopelessly lost for days. You don't even have the wit to eat and drink: lose 3 Stamina points. If you are still alive, you wander through the forest until you emerge, at last, at the Bronze Hills. Turn to **110**.

647

As you reach for the back of the golem's head, it turns and grabs your arm, yanking you to the ground. Then it swings its club at your head.

Run away	turn to **349**
Fight the golem	turn to **81**

648

You remain as quiet as a mouse, behind a pile of coins. After a long wait, the sea dragon slithers into the water, and swims out on some errand.

You have time to loot the hoard. You scrabble about for the chest that Oliphard the Wizardly wanted you to obtain for him. You find a rune-carved box which is positively glowing with magic. Note the **magic chest** on your Adventure Sheet. You can also choose up to three treasures from the following:

Enchanted sword (COMBAT +3)
Plate armour (Defence +5)
Ebony wand (MAGIC +2)
500 Shards
Magic mandolin (CHARISMA +2)
Gold compass (SCOUTING +2)
Magic lockpicks (THIEVERY +2)
Silver holy symbol (SANCTITY +2)

After you have taken the third treasure, you hear the sea dragon returning. You climb up through the hole in the roof, on to an island in the middle of the lake. From there, you manage to get a lift on a passing boat, and make it safely to Cadmium village.

During the journey, you examine the **magic chest**, but it is guarded by great sorcery and is impossible to open.

Delete the codeword *Avenge* and turn to **135**.

649 ☐

If there is a tick in the box, turn to **114** immediately. If not, put a tick there now, and read on.

The chief administrator is overjoyed to see you. The priests already know you have been successful in freeing Sul Veneris, the Lord of Thunder, because their crystal ball shows them that the storm demons have been driven away.

As a reward you receive the tuition of several high priests. You gain 1 Rank. Roll a single die. The result is the number of Stamina points you gain permanently.

`Visit me anytime,' says the chief administrator when you leave. Turn to **100**.

650

Cross the **moonstone** off your Adventure Sheet. There is a flash, and suddenly you find yourself in a warm, comfortable room, beside Elissia the Traveller, the sorceress you rescued from her burning house.

Elissia will heal you of all lost Stamina points, if you are wounded, and cure you of any diseases or poisons you may be suffering from.

`My debt to you is now paid,' she says. With that, she passes her hands through the air, and disappears in a cloud of smoke!

You find yourself in an inn at Marlock City. You venture out into town, slightly dazed. Turn to **100**.

651

The trau, realizing its fate, sinks into a dark, clouded silence. You haul it off to the mines where the overseer, a fat, cruel-looking man, gives you 150 Shards for the trau. You return to town. Turn to **400**.

652

You clamber up until you come to a mountain track. It rises up between a cleft in the rock, ahead of you.

A man steps out in front of you. He is clearly a soldier, but his clothes are rough and ready, as if he had been living in the wild for some time.

If you have the title King's Champion, turn to **2**. If not, but you have the codeword *Ambuscade*, turn to **629**. If you have neither of the above, but you do have the codeword *Ark*, turn to **353**. Otherwise read on.

The soldier looks you over critically. He signals that he wants to parley with you.

Talk to him	turn to **557**
Attack him straight away	turn to **49**

653

You are on a quest to take the oak staff to the Willow Druid who lives in a sacred grove somewhere in the forest. You wander around, looking for unusual tracks, strange creatures, anything that might lead you to a druid's den.

Make a SCOUTING roll at Difficulty 12.

Successful SCOUTING roll	turn to **217**
Failed SCOUTING roll	turn to **7**

654

You slip out of your chains, and hide inside an ore-laden mining car. When it is taken out of the mine, you creep out, and run off into the hills. Eventually you reach Caran Baru.

Turn to **400**.

655 □

If there is a tick in the box, turn to **574** immediately. If not, read on.

The general greets you with a smile and embraces you, saying, 'You have served me beyond my expectations, my friend!'

A servant drags over a heavy chest, and Grieve Marlock flips open the lid with his sword. Inside is 1000 Shards! 'Yours,' he says with a grin. Note the money on your Adventure Sheet.

He also gives you a title – in this case, whatever the title is of your next Rank. Gain 1 Rank, and roll a die. The result is the number of Stamina points you gain permanently.

As you leave, he says, 'Don't hesitate to ask, if you need anything.'

If you have a **coded missive**, turn to **677**. If not, turn to **100**.

656

You find a large, red pavilion which has been erected over a ruin. Oliphard the Wizardly is inside. He greets you warmly. If you have a **magic chest**, turn to **672**. If not, read on.

If you have a **verdigris key**, turn to **431**. If not, read on.

Oliphard can use his sorcery to teleport you instantly to certain places at a cost of 100 Shards a journey. If you want to be teleported, cross off the money and choose from the following destinations:

Marlock City	turn to **100**
Caran Baru	turn to **400**
Wishport	*Cities of Gold and Glory* **217**
Dweomer	*Over the Blood-DarkSea* **100**

Otherwise, you can travel more conventionally.

Take the road to the Shadar Tor	turn to **602**
Take the road to Marlock City	turn to **377**
Head into the Curstmoor	turn to **175**
Take the road north	turn to **558**
Take the road to Yellowport	turn to **233**

657

The creature falls dead. You can squeeze a little of its venom from its sting; if you do, note the **scorpion venom** on your Adventure Sheet.

If you were wounded in that fight, you have been poisoned by the scorpion man's venom. Subtract 1 from your COMBAT, THIEVERY and

SCOUTING scores, as you are severely weakened (although no ability can drop to zero). Note that you are poisoned; you can restore your ratings to normal if you get cured. If you have some **scorpion anti-dote**, it will cure the poison immediately – cross the **antidote** off your Adventure Sheet.

You wander on until you come to a ridge. Down below, in a shallow valley, is a great mound of earth. Many burrows have been dug through it, and scorpion men are crawling in and out. This is the mound of the scorpion men – their home.

If you have the codeword *Artefact*, turn to **406**. If not, you realize that it would simply be too dangerous to venture down there. You head back towards Venefax. Turn to **492**.

You are standing at the bottom of the Devil's Peak. It is a massive tower of black rock, like a stone tree-trunk, bare and branchless, climbing up into the sky. You cannot see the top, for it is shrouded in grey clouds. Thunder and lightning play about the clouded summit.

The sides of the peak are almost sheer, but there are many hand and footholds. It can be climbed, but only if you have **climbing gear**. If you have and you want to make the ascent, turn to **340**. Otherwise, turn to **560**.

You untie the little creature from its bonds. It gives a jubilant cry, and soars upwards.

'Thank you, large one!' it chatters, 'My name is Pikalik the Wing-warrior! We never forget. One day I will pay my debt.' With that, he flitters away into the clouds.

'That's 75 Shards you just let fly away,' comments the man in the palanquin wryly, 'Mannekyn People can't be trusted, believe me.'

You leave the slave market. Acquire the codeword *Altruist* and turn to **400**.

You are greeted warmly by the commander of the fort, whose daughter, Alissia, embraces you happily.

You can stay here, in comfortable lodgings, free of charge. You can restore any lost Stamina points, up to your maximum. When you are ready, you can leave.

East into Nerech	*The Plains of Howling Darkness* **225**
North west to Fort Mereth	turn to **299**
South east to Fort Brilon	turn to **259**
West into the Farmlands	turn to **548**

With a thrill of horror, you realize you have missed your footing, crossing the wrong line by millimetres. The lid of the sarcophagus explodes into the air with a deafening crash, and a pillar of black smoke erupts out of the stone coffin! The column of smoke hurtles towards you, like a miniature tornado.

If you have a weapon with a +1 COMBAT bonus or greater, turn to **43**. If you have only an ordinary weapon (or none at all) turn to **260**.

662

That night, after Lauria has picked the locks on your chains, you head off for the tunnel rendezvous. You find there has been a cave-in, but the overseer and a troop of guards are waiting for you!

Lauria steps out laughing. In return for her betraying you, the overseer has transferred her to work on the surface, from which she will be able to escape more easily. You have been stitched up again!

The overseer has you whipped for trying to escape and you are left with some nasty scars. Lose 1 point of CHARISMA permanently.

Gain the codeword *Anger*, and lose the codeword *Ashen*.

A few days later, you try another escape on your own. Turn to **565**.

663

They are too fast. You are caught and overwhelmed. You end up as food for scorpion larvae. Your adventuring days are over, unless you have a resurrection deal.

664

'That is fortunate – for you,' says the soldier. Several archers stand up from their hiding places behind the rocks overhead.

Another soldier, a captain, comes up to you and introduces himself as Captain Vorkung.

He is clearly one of the old aristocracy, the nobles loyal to the king and the old regime, before General Marlock and the army seized power, and executed the old king. Vorkung tells you to leave the mountains.

You have found a rebel base – men still loyal to Nergan Corin, the heir to the throne. Nergan went into hiding when General Marlock killed his father and took control of Sokara.

You can attempt to convince Captain Vorkung that you are on his side by making a CHARISMA roll at Difficulty 9. You can add 1 to your roll if you are a Warrior, Rogue or Wayfarer. If you succeed, turn to **25**. If you fail, turn to **179**. Otherwise, you can climb down the mountains, turn to **474**.

665

You enter the cave. It is large and dark. Unfortunately, it is the lair of a pack of wolves – a very big pack of wolves.

If you have a **wolf pelt**, turn to **516**. If not, turn to **280**.

666

A trader from the far north tells a story about a great wizard, Targdaz the Magnificent. who was tricked by a shaman of the Horde of the Thousand Winds on the Great Steppes.

'He imprisoned Targdaz inside a giant ruby, and proceeded to loot Targdaz's tower. But in his stupidity, he opened the great wizard's Casket of Imponderables, and unleashed a terrible storm that swept across the steppes, scattering many of the tribes far and wide. The shaman was killed, of course, but as far as anyone knows, Targdaz is still trapped in the ruby, waiting patiently for release... perhaps for another hundred years, who knows? One thing's for certain – it won't be me trying to get him out!' When you are ready, you can go:

South	turn to **558**
North	turn to **347**
West into the Forest of Larun	turn to **47**
East to the lake	turn to **135**

667 ☐

If there is a tick in the box, turn to **660** immediately. If not, put a tick there now, and read on.

You have rescued Alissia, the commander's daughter, from the manbeasts. They have a tearful, joyous reunion – all thanks to you!

The commander rewards you with combat training. Add one to your COMBAT score permanently. When you are ready, you can leave.

East into Nerech	*The Plains of Howling Darkness* **225**
North west to Fort Mereth	turn to **299**
South east to Fort Brilon	turn to **259**
West into the farmlands	turn to **548**

668

You are led to a rockface in the mine. You start digging. Roll two dice and consult the following table:

Score 2-4	Rockfall! You lose 2 Stamina
Score 5-8	No luck, and your hour is up
Score 9-12	A **silver nugget**!

When you are finished (if you are still alive), you leave the Bronze Hills.

To Caran Baru	turn to **400**
South into the Forest of Larun	turn to **47**
West to the River Grimm	turn to **333**
North into the Western Wilderness	turn to **276**

669

You are recognized by an official, and a few moments later, you are summoned to see the general himself! You are taken to the throne room, which has been converted to a military style headquarters. If you have the codeword *Assist*, turn to **102** immediately. If not, read on.

Grieve Marlock is a tall, hook-nosed man with cold, penetrating green eyes.

'You come highly recommended by my brother, the Governor of Yellowport. I was hoping you would turn up,' he says in a commanding voice. 'You did me a great service by getting rid of that pompous fool, Nergan.

'Now there is one more thing I need you for. The Citadel of Velis Corin, which sits astride the Pass of Eagles in the far north, is under imminent attack from an army of the steppes. The attackers are a rag-tag bunch of malcontents: nomads, Mannekyn People, some trau even, and of course, the usual traitorous dogs still loyal to the old king, may his soul burn in the hells, ha, ha, ha.

'I need you to go to the citadel, discuss the situation with Commandant Orin Telana, and do all you can to make sure that the citadel doesn't fall. I'm relying on you!'

Record the codeword *Assist*.

If you have a **coded missive**, turn to **677** immediately. If not, you are are escorted out. Turn to **100**.

670

You feel a wrenching moment of disorientation, and then you suddenly appear with a flash beside a ruined, burnt-out city. A passing builder stares at you in horror, unsure whether you are a human or a demon. Quickly, you hurry away. Turn to **250**.

671

Out of gratitude the villagers present you with 80 Shards. You do not wait around to see what fate befalls Old Megan and her accomplices. In theory they should be taken to the assizes in the nearest town, but feelings run so deep in this case that you suspect there will be some rough justice meted out.

You resume your journey.

Follow the river north	turn to **576**
Follow the river south	turn to **82**
Head east into the countryside	turn to **278**
Go west to the main road	turn to **558**

672

'My chest!' yells Oliphard joyfully as you hand it over. Cross the **magic chest** off your Adventure Sheet.

Oliphard thanks you, and teaches you how be a better Mage. Gain 1 Rank and roll a die. The result is the number of Stamina points you gain permanently.

When you are ready, turn to **656**.

673

You are trekking across the aptly named Curstmoor. A great rolling expanse of blasted heath stretches before you. Grey clouds hang over a mournful, dirty-water coloured plain, studded with rocky outcrops and low hills.

Roll one die.

Score 1 or 2	You are attacked by a wolf.
	Wolf, COMBAT 3, Defence 5, Stamina 7
	If you win, you get a **wolf pelt**
Score 3 or 4	Nothing happens
Score 5 or 6	You find 10 Shards on an old skeleton

When you are ready, you can go:

North across the country	turn to **560**
East to the road	turn to **558**
To Trefoille	turn to **250**
To Marlock City	turn to **100**
West towards the River Grimm	turn to **99**

674

You realize from your magical studies that there is a safe path through the pentacle. If you step off the correct symbols, drawn on the ground, there is no telling what sorcerous trap you will set off.

If you decide the whole thing is too dangerous, and leave, turn to **47**.

If you want to try the path to the sarcophagus, make a THIEVERY roll at Difficulty 9.

Successful THIEVERY roll	turn to **606**
Failed THIEVERY roll	turn to **661**

675

You fall into the yawning blackness with a despairing cry. You plummet like a stone through the air for what seems like an age. You are engulfed in absolute darkness, and all you can hear is the whistling of the wind past your ears.

Suddenly you shoot into bright sunlight, and land with an almighty splash into the sea! Coughing and spluttering, you rise to the surface. You are not far from a forested island, and you swim for shore. A small settlement crowds the shore – it looks like you have arrived at the

Trading Post on the Isle of Druids.

Turn to **195**.

676

You were given the message to take to the king by some spies in Golnir. The king takes the **coded missive**. Cross it off your Adventure Sheet. He hands it to one of his counsellors to read.

`You have done well in bringing this to me. It is important,' says the king.

You are rewarded with 200 Shards.

If you have the codeword *Deliver*, turn to **98** immediately. If not, read on.

The king goes on, `However, I was hoping you had spoken with General Beladai of the allied army by now. We need that citadel. Now go. That is a Royal command!'

You leave, climbing down to the foothills of the mountains. Turn to **474**.

677

You were given the missive to take to the general by spies in Golnir. He takes the **coded missive** and reads it. Cross it off your Adventure Sheet.

`Interesting. You have done well in bringing this to me,' he says. `I thank you, once more!'

He rewards you with 150 Shards.

When you are ready, you leave the palace. Turn to **100**.

678

If you have the codeword *Aspen*, turn to **195**. Otherwise, read on.

The journey through the trees proves as difficult as when you first ventured into the forest. Make a SCOUTING roll at a Difficulty of 10.

Successful SCOUTING roll   turn to **679**
Failed SCOUTING roll   turn to **36**

679

The scent of the sea proves strongest in one direction. Following your nose, you eventually break free of the trees and find yourself on the coast. Turn to **128**.

Adventure Sheet

NAME

PROFESSION

GOD

RANK

DEFENCE

ABILITY   SCORE

CHARISMA	
COMBAT	
MAGIC	
SANCTITY	
SCOUNTING	
THIEVERY	

POSSESSIONS (maximum of 12)

STAMINA

| When unwounded | |
| Current: | |

RESURRECTION ARRANGEMENTS

MONEY

TITLES and HONOURS

BLESSINGS

Codewords

- ☐ Acid
- ☐ Afraid
- ☐ Ague
- ☐ Aid
- ☐ Aklar
- ☐ Alissia
- ☐ Almanac
- ☐ Aloft
- ☐ Altitude
- ☐ Altruist
- ☐ Ambuscade
- ☐ Amcha
- ☐ Amends
- ☐ Anchor
- ☐ Anger
- ☐ Animal
- ☐ Anthem
- ☐ Anvil
- ☐ Apache
- ☐ Appease
- ☐ Apple
- ☐ Ark
- ☐ Armour
- ☐ Artefact
- ☐ Artery
- ☐ Ashen
- ☐ Aspen
- ☐ Assassin
- ☐ Assault
- ☐ Assist
- ☐ Attar
- ☐ Auric
- ☐ Avenge
- ☐ Avert
- ☐ Axe
- ☐ Azure

Ship's Manifest

SHIP TYPE	NAME	CREW QUALITY	CARGO CAPACITY	CURRENT CARGO	WHERE DOCKED

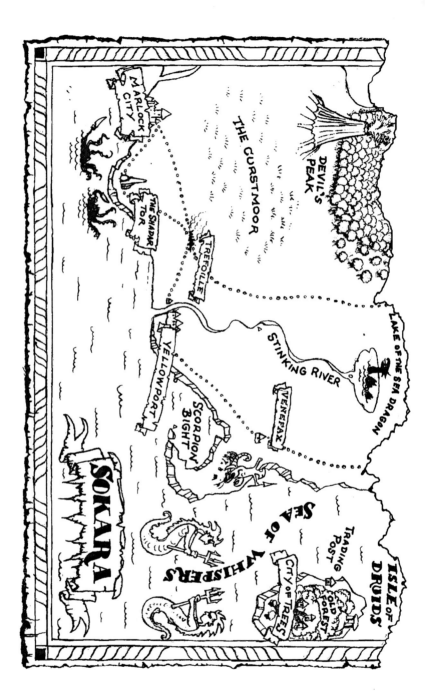

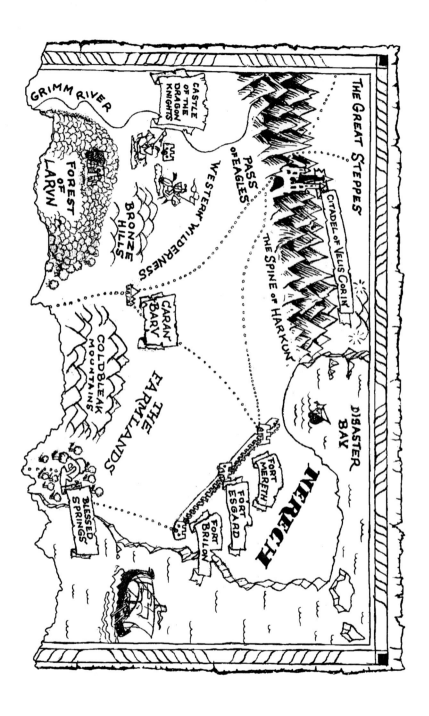

CPSIA information can be obtained at www.ICGtesting.com
Printed in the USA
BVOW081051250911

272078BV00006B/4/P